THE KING OF KRESKIN AVENUE

THE
KING OF
KRESKIN
AVENUE

A.K. VITBERG

For my wife and best friend, Janice, who was supportive when I needed it, critical when I deserved it, and enthusiastic when I finally finished it.

And thanks for the hankies.

TABLE OF CONTENTS

Robbie Shumstein ended the call and, teary-eyed, sank into his overstuffed chair.

The King of Kreskin Avenue dead?

His mother had not intended to upset him. Their twice-weekly conversations were snatched from a treasure trove of her evergreen gossip, full of minutiae and banter, most of which would be unintelligible to outsiders. Somewhere between disclosure of another ailment of her elderly friends, a request for updates about the grandkids, curiosity about what was happening with the latest book, the tale of her doctor's appointment, and the new recipe for kugel she got from Helen Shapiro, she casually mentioned that The King had died, sitting in his lawn chair in the middle of his driveway.

She was aware that Robbie had a close relationship with Mario Colucci, The King of Kreskin Avenue, but not why. Even her treasure trove yielded no clues. Robbie and the Coluccis had accomplished a masterful job of protecting their secrets, now for over fifty years.

To Esther Shumstein, even though she lived less than five houses down the block from him for all her married and widowed life, The King was just an odd-ball neighbor who at best merited a wave hello or goodbye, but to Robbie Shumstein The King was and would forever be a hero of the highest order.

Her disclosure took Robbie back to a time and place of unwelcome deaths, now grown distant and hazy.

Tearful, he made a few phone calls: to Mario's wife, Mattie Colucci; to his cousin Ben, the first beneficiary of Mario's compassion; and to Donald MacIntyre, an old friend and an original collaborator. He made a request that Don spread the news of Mario's death. Don knew what to do.

The news was shared and passed and parsed across the United States and Canada. Thousands of people in extended families that had become the beneficiaries of Mario's selflessness learned that a hero had passed on.

Robbie quickly made travel arrangements, and in less than eight hours, together with his wife, Susan, he worked his way through one massive parking lot, two connecting flights, three magazines, and a surly car rental agent at the Greater Buffalo International Airport.

Robbie was only fifteen in 1968, when he, Mario, Don, and Ben broke the law and committed treason. A few years later, it was off to college for Robbie, then law school and a stint in corporate law, then owner-ship of a small but respectable publishing company in Roanoke, Virginia. Although he returned to Buffalo and his childhood home with less and less frequency, his trips home always included a stop at the Colucci house at 77 Kreskin Avenue.

No matter how hard she pressed for an explanation or for the reasons he seemed so much more upbeat and less stressed after seeing the Coluccis, Robbie's mother had to be content with his typical response: "because I like seeing them."

The last time he had seen Mario was earlier in the year, when Robbie and Susan, who was one of the very few people who knew the entire story, brought their one-year-old granddaughter for her first visit to Buffalo. Robbie strollered over to Mario's house, where he and his wife, Mattie, cooed and cuddled with her. Mario sat in the decrepit lawn chair in the drive-way where Robbie usually saw him, wearing the same battered checkered porkpie hat that he had parked—tipped slightly back—on his balding pate every day of his life for the last jillion or so years.

As old neighbors moved away and new ones moved in, Mario Colucci was always called The King of Kreskin Avenue, sometimes behind his back and sometimes to his face. Through the years he handled the insult with the same indifference and nonchalance—although you might call it grace—he had exhibited since the 1950s. He never challenged or saw a reason to correct the neighborhood's superficial perceptions, and over time he became the oddity that every neighborhood needs when conversations run dry or it's time to have a mass speculation.

Kreskin Avenue residents were smug in their self-assurance that the Mario they saw was exactly and precisely an oddball, a caricature, a kind-of-king who used a lawn chair as a throne and a dirty hat as a crown.

They were wrong.

Robbie turned the rental car left onto Kreskin from Delaware Avenue and parked it in front of his mother's flat. After an hour or so with his mother, he left, walked down the familiar street, and knocked on the door of number 77.

A tall, thin woman with silvery white hair and a pinched, wrinkled face answered his knock. Robbie gathered her into his arms.

"Hello, Robbie," whispered Mattie. "Welcome home."

PART I
Mario Colucci

CHAPTER 1

The Littlest Pickle

The Coluccis emigrated to the United States shortly after Mario's father completed his service in the Italian Army, where he had risen to the rank of corporal in World War I. With his young wife in tow, Antonio Colucci landed on Ellis Island in 1921, then eventually made his way to Buffalo, where he immediately resumed his trade as a cobbler.

By the time the Japanese bombed Pearl Harbor, the Coluccis had been in America for nearly twenty years, yet they still struggled with English. Throughout her life, Mama Colucci never came anywhere close to mastering her adopted country's tongue, managing only a few hundred fractured words. Antonio had a somewhat better—albeit vastly incomplete—command of the language, preferring to mix Italian and English and slang in a cacophony of syntax that was a constant source of amusement to the customers of his little shoe shop in City Hall.

The Coluccis lived in a small, shanty-like house on Busti Avenue on the west side of the city, in a neighborhood where hundreds of closely packed two-story dwellings on narrow, unpaved streets were home to thousands of poor immigrants, mostly Italians. Mario, two years older than his sister Connie, shared a tiny bedroom with his younger brothers, Giuseppe and Carl. Baby Angelina slept with her parents. The scroungy mutt the children rescued from the streets after intense pleadings and negotiations with Mama and Papa slept wherever it pleased.

At home Mama and Papa would always speak Italian, whether discussing the news of the day or ordering the brothers to wash behind their ears before sitting down to dinner.

"Aw, Mama," the kids would plead, "can't you talk even a little English for once?"

Every once in a while, under his breath, Mario would add, "fer Chrissake!"

Of course, Mama had the type of hearing possessed by mamas all over the world. "Hey!!!! What did you say, you little hardhead?!" she would reply to Mario, her eyes blazing. "*Mio Dio*! Did you take the name of the Lord in vain?"

The Colucci boys would speak only English, except when they squabbled. But as tempers rose, *Italiano* somehow seemed to be the only natural way to force a point. Pretty soon Mario and Mama would be yapping back and forth in Italian, their voices rising higher and higher and more forcefully with each exchange. After a while, with Papa looking on in amusement, Mama would make Mario come over and give her a hug, and like a summer storm, their argument would quickly blow over, leaving the air crisp and clean.

Growing up tough and scrappy, Mario learned to fend for himself on the harsh streets of the west side of the city. From the time he was six years old, he worked at any odd job he could get his hands on, keeping a few pennies or a nickel or two for himself and turning the rest over to Mama for the *bambinos*. His brothers and sisters adored him, knowing that he usually had a cheery word or a joke for them and, from time to time, a special treat in his pocket.

Mario had to be tough, for no matter the situation, he was always the runt. "The smallest pickle in the barrel," his father would joke. "I don't know where God put the rest of him, especially considering the big pickle he came from!"

That would make Mama giggle and blush and titter, but it didn't stop her from scolding him about his language in front of the children, and it didn't stop Papa from retelling the joke when the occasion demanded it.

Throughout grade school Mario was always the boy at the very end of the line when his class was required to line up by height. With his wide, gap-toothed grin, he knew the girls thought he was cute and elf-like. But the boys treated him as though he was weak and made solely to be their target for bullying.

In the winter he would come home wet and cold after being pushed into and held down in snowbanks; occasionally, if the neighborhood toughs were feeling especially cruel, he would get the "glacier express"—a hard snowball jammed down his pants. In the fall and spring, he would come home from school with torn clothing or abrasions on his knees from being shoved around or otherwise hazed.

"Mario, *mio Dio*, not again!" Mama would cry out in frustration. "Torn pants! Do you think I got solid gold dripping from my poor, overworked fingertips for another trip to Woolworths?"

"Sorry," Mario would mumble, "but I fell offa my bike. But I sure would like t' see that gold-makin'-outta-yer-fingertips trick, if ya don't mind!"

Whatever his bullies dished out Mario could take. He never cried or ran home to tell Mama or Papa—preferring their harsh words or punishments for being clumsy or not caring about his clothes to letting them fight his battles. Instead, he bit his lip and internalized his torment, never letting his family, teachers, or tormentors see the depths of his building, burning anger.

And so it went until the sixth grade, when Mario turned eleven.

Until that grade, boys and girls took physical education together. In sixth grade, however, they were separated, as it was deemed necessary that after gym the boys shower before returning to their regular class. Unfortunately for Mario, he was undersized in every possible dimension, adding fuel to what seemed to be an eternal flame of harassment.

"Hey! Wazzat, Mario?" they would tease and point as he struggled to cover his nakedness with the flimsy towel supplied by the school. "What do ya do when ya gotta take a piss…use tweezers or somethin' to find it?" Then they would have a conspiratorial communal laugh until the humor of the moment had passed. Mario never said anything or responded in any way, but his eyes became hard and his jaw firm.

Chief among his tormentors was Sal "Pally" Consiglione, one of the biggest boys in sixth grade. He was a bully who had tormented Mario for years and who was fond of terrorizing all the smaller and younger boys and girls in the neighborhood. Pally was often joined in misdeeds by Tommy Tedesco and Luigi LaFalce, two sheep-like morons who were more afraid of what Pally might do to them if they didn't accede to his demands for accomplices than they were of any consequent punishment.

Mario had taken to showering late to avoid being teased, hoping that by the time he came out of the shower, his fellow classmates would be dressed and on their way to class. One day, however, he came out of the shower to find himself alone with Pally, Tommy, and Luigi, who were huddled together in a corner of the locker room whispering to one another. He kept a wary eye out while he put on his socks, and he was tugging up his boxer shorts when the boys suddenly rushed him. Tommy and Luigi pinned Mario's arms to his sides while Pally grabbed his legs, and together they hoisted and hung him up by the back of his shorts on a metal clothing hook.

Laughing hysterically, they left Mario there kicking and flailing his arms and legs, desperately trying to free himself, but he did not cry out for the gym teacher. Instead, he waited a few moments until he was calm. Then he slowly and methodically exploited a rip in his shorts until it was big enough to give all the way, and he tumbled to the floor. He finished dressing, put his ripped shorts into his pocket, and made his way to class, where all the boys and girls snickered, several laughing out loud, as he walked red-faced to his desk.

That afternoon, after the school bell had chimed to release the captives for the day, Mario waited until

Pally, Tommy, and Luigi left the building and then followed about ten steps behind. As quietly as he could, he eased up behind Pally and tapped him on the shoulder.

Pally turned around.

"I gotta little present for ya," said Mario calmly and without emotion. Then with all the strength he could muster, he unleashed a roundhouse from the depths of his soul. It landed smack on Pally's nose.

Even before the blood began to pour out in prodigious quantity, Mario loaded up his left hand. "And here's another."

He connected squarely with Pally's right eye.

The crowd of children that had gathered to see the commotion, drawn to a fight like moths to a flame, witnessed years of pent-up frustration and anger finally released. Mario aimed to knee the now-doubled-over Pally in his stomach, but because of his short stature instead connected solidly with a lower-placed, infinitely more sensitive region. Pally finally crashed to the ground, writhing in pain, as blood gushed from his nose and an award-winning shiner began to sprout under his eye.

"I ain't finished just yet."

Mario straddled Pally's chest, pulled his own torn shorts from his pocket, and used them to mop his antagonist's blood all over his face, then finished his assault by jamming the now-bloody undergarment into Pally's mouth.

When Mario got off his chest, Pally turned over and scrambled away on his hands and knees. As soon as he judged himself to be a safe distance away, he got up and ran away, humiliated and sobbing. During the melee, Tommy and Luigi had stood by in stunned silence, paralyzed and unable to help as their *capo di tutti capi* got the stuffing beat out of him.

Mario cinched up his pants, looked at the two of them, and said simply, "You're next."

That was enough to send them running away at top speed, to the jeers and cheers of the assembled crowd.

Mario kept true to his promise.

Two days later, Tommy showed up at school with two shiners of immense proportions, and a week after that, Luigi appeared with a grossly swollen nose, massively split lip, and, for good measure, a tremendous red lump on his forehead. From that day forward, Mario never, ever had troubles with any kid in the neighborhood. He had earned both respect and a deserved reputation for toughness.

Pally and his family moved out of the neighborhood about a month after the incident, and oddly enough, Mario, Tommy, and Luigi became the very best of friends, managing to finish grade school with reputations that grew over time. Once in a rare while, like the head male in a pride of lions, Mario had to defend his reputation when challenged by a new tough guy. Quickly the challenger was made aware that his assumptions about the relationship between size and toughness, as far as Mario was concerned, were completely incorrect.

Perhaps it was the teasing and harassment about his size that made him particularly sensitive to the feelings and circumstances of others, or perhaps he unconsciously modeled himself after his mama, who was known throughout the neighborhood for her kindness to strangers and those less fortunate. But Mario was generally the first to offer a helping hand to anyone who appeared to be in need of help.

He did favors and odd chores for the grandmothers in the neighborhood without seeking reward, though he would take a handful of freshly baked pizzelle if offered.

He never joined in the cruel games of experimentation upon helpless insects or other animals, though the neighborhood kids seemed to enjoy torturing them. He was protective of smaller or weaker children in the rough-and-tumble games of the neighborhood.

And he never forgot the lesson of what it was like to be bullied.

It turns out that even a little pickle could be tough pickle, a pickle with a big heart.

CHAPTER 2

Porkpie Hat, Jauntily Worn

By the time he reached his thirteenth birthday, Mario had achieved his five-foot-four height and would grow no more. As the years passed, his two brothers and two sisters shot by him in stature, but it wasn't the size of his body that mattered to them; it was the size of his heart. When Mario finished eighth grade, he decided that he had had enough schooling and simply told his parents, who readily concurred in his decision, that he was ready to find a real job.

That was in 1944, and Mario, like every other patriotic, red-blooded fifteen-year-old American boy, was captivated by the progress of The War. Starting at the War's beginning, the walls of his bedroom became a gallery for photographs clipped from *The Buffalo News*, *Life*, and *The Saturday Evening Post*. He made rough hand-drawn maps so he could follow the triumphs and failures of the brave American boys who were sacrificing their lives for love of God and country in faraway places with strange-sounding names. At night the family would gather around the radio to listen to that day's news of the war, cheering with each victory and grieving for each loss.

Mario would supplement his papa's *Italian Weekly Courier* by reading and translating stories for his parents about what was going on in the Old Country. Together they learned of *Il Duce*'s cowardly entry into the war after France had fallen, and soon after, the abject failures of the Italian armies in Greece and Africa. They cheered upon hearing of the Allied invasion of Sicily, and Mario's father was ecstatic when he learned of Mussolini's arrest, the failure of the Fascist government, and the announcement in September of 1943 that the new Italian government had surrendered.

But Mario's hopes for an American victory were dealt a severe blow by Mussolini's dramatic rescue and establishment of a new puppet Fascist government, and Mario was angered reading about the German occupation of Rome. From January of 1944 when the Allies landed at Anzio through June when they entered Rome, he could not seem to get enough information, and he shared his parents' concerns about the fate of their native countrymen and the brave soldiers fighting fiercely to liberate them.

As they learned of each attack, the Coluccis were infused with hope, but each German counterattack was met with pessimism and gloom. Almost one anxiety-ridden year later, the entire Colucci family rejoiced when the Allies took Venice. When Mussolini was captured, then summarily tried and hanged with his mistress Clara Petacci, Mario's father uncorked a vintage bottle of homemade wine. He gave each member of the family a glass and in a silent toast saluted, with tears in his eyes, the American flag that hung over their mantel.

A few short weeks after Mario finished his formal education, he excitedly ran into the house, nearly bowling over his mother, who was carrying baby Angelina in her arms.

"Mario, you galoot!" she cried. "What's the big deal? Why are you makin' with alla dis foolishness? Tell me now, what's wrong? *Che succede?* What's going on? It's Papa, right? Oh my God, did something happen to Papa?"

"No! No! No, Mama!" His eyes brimming with excitement, Mario panted and struggled to catch his breath. "There's nothin' wrong with Papa! I got a job...a really good job where I'm gonna make a lotta dough an' be famous an' you an' Papa are gonna be real proud of me! I ain't gonna tell ya until Papa comes home, 'cause I want the whole family t'know at one time!"

Even though his brothers and sisters pestered him throughout the afternoon, Mario refused to reveal his secret and teased everybody unmercifully. "Giuseppe, how about a brand-new bike, eh? Carlo, all you gotta do is think 'bout that catcher's mitt ya got yer eye on. Mama? Would it be nice t'have one of those 'lectric 'frigerators instead a the icebox?"

By the time Papa came home, Mario had whipped the entire family into a frenzy. The younger boys rushed out the door, jumping all over their father as he struggled to make his way into the house. "Papa! Papa! Guess what! Mario's gotta job anna secret an' I'm gonna get a new bike an' Carlo's gonna get a mitt and Mama's gonna get a 'frigerator!"

Papa looked skeptically at the boys and glanced at his wife, whose shrugged shoulders, arched eyebrows, and wide eyes told him that she, too, was clueless about the surprise. Mario waited until the family sat down to dinner, his brothers squirming in their chairs in antici-pation, before he started his story.

"Hmm. Lemme see now…I know I was gonna tell youse somethin', but fer the love of Mary, I can't seem t'remember what it is."

"Aww, c'mon, Mario! Quit yer kiddin'! Tell Papa 'bout the bike an' stuff!"

"Yeah, Mario, tell him "bout how yer gonna be fa-mous an' all that!"

"Well…if I gotta, I gotta, so here goes. Me 'n' Tommy were hangin' out at Sammy the Barber's when Luigi was gettin' a haircut, and suddenly this big black car pulls up—I think it was a Packard—and out gets two guys. One of 'em is a great big guy in a bee-you-tee-ful suit with a bran' new fedora, an' the other one is a little guy, about my size but bigger, if ya know what I mean. Now dis little guy is dressed pretty sharp, too, only you could see that he was tough 'n' wiry, kinda like me.

"Well, the little guy sits down an' starts readin' a magazine, an' Sammy brushes off a chair, an' the big guy takes off his suit jacket an' sits down. Sammy's latherin' the guy up fer a shave, an' he asks him how's it goin' and such, an' the guy starts talkin' 'bout how he can't find any good jockeys 'cause the war has taken 'em all inta the service an' so forth an' so on. 'That so,' says Sammy, as if he knows what he's talkin' 'bout, an' then he asks the guy fer a tip on which pony to bet on fer t'night's races over the border at Fort Erie."

"So I gets curious an' I ask the big guy if he's lookin' fer jockeys, an'—"

Mario's mother stopped the conversation dead in its tracks. "NO! NO! NO! NO, Mario! A jockey that sits and races on horses? What do you know about horses and racing? I'll tell you what you know: nothing! *Mio Dio*…you'll get killed."

Mario's father sat silent.

"Wait a minute, Mama," Mario said. "I ain't finished with the story.

"Well, the big guy raises up an' gives me a good lookin' over and says ta me, 'Whadda ya know about ponies an' ridin'?' an' I says back to him, 'Nothin',' but I tol' him that I was really strong an' could learn real good, an' that I would work real hard an' that I really needed a job, and so forth and so on. So he says ta me, 'Just how old are you, son?' an' I tell him that I just turned sixteen an'—"

"Mario! You lied to a stranger?!"

"Hold on, Mama, I ain't finished yet.

"Now, where was I? Oh yeah. So I says t' him that I'm sixteen an' could he use a dependable fella t'ride his horses. He gits this big ol' grin on his face and says, 'Son, it's not as easy as that. You have to come up slowly in order to become a jockey, starting with being a stable hand, shoveling horse shit all around. Then, if me and my trainers see that you can handle a horse, especially after you see what they can do to a man, then we can start to train you to become a jockey.'

"So I says, 'Well, yes sir, I b'lieve that I can handle shovelin' horse shit' if he's willin' ta give me a chance. Then he sez to the little guy, 'Hey, George, c'mere an' check this kid out.' An' George comes over an' starts t'poke me all over an' asks me t'do stuff like touch my toes an' do ten push-ups and 'See if you can beat me in arm wrasslin' '—which I almost did—an' then he sez to the big guy, 'I think he'll do.'

"The big guy says that he'll start me off at fifteen bucks a week an' raise it ta thirty if I last more 'n a month. I promise I'll give you my pay every week, an' that'll sure be better 'n a poke in a eye with a sharp stick, huh? But here's the best part: if I can make it up ta being a jockey, they pay me a hunnert bucks a week, an' if I win a race, they give me ten percent of the purse! Think about it, Mama—from what the big guy said t'me, some of those races got prizes of ten thousan' dollars. I could bring home a grand for about two minutes' worth a work!"

For a moment the family sat in stunned silence, and then as if somebody had pushed an On button— except for Papa—they began to speak at once, raising voices higher and higher to be heard over the cacophonous riot.

"*SILENZIO!*" demanded Papa, and the family quieted immediately.

"Mario, is this what you want to do?" Papa asked. "Don't let this kinda dough make you blind, 'cause this ting is a lot harder 'n you think! Ah, Mario, it's dangerous, *molto pericoloso*. Didn't I tell you a story 'bout when I wuz a boy, I hadda friend killed racin' horses?"

"But Papa, that wasn't real racin'—that was racin' plow horses in a field!"

"*Minga!* Mario, racin' is racin' an' it don't make a difference if it's on a fancy track or in a field. It's still dangerous, but I ain't gonna say no, if it's all right with Mama."

Mario looked pleadingly at his mother.

"I'll be extra careful, Mama! Promise! Look at the card the big fella gave me." The card read M. Frank Bouchard, Owner, Hamilton Stables, Fort Erie, Ontario, Canada. "I gotta be at the stable t'morrow mornin' at four thirty t' start."

Mario saw a barely perceptible nod of her head, and her scowl was gone. He knew that all that was necessary was a little nudge.

"I gotta show you one other thing that the little guy give me," Mario added. "Hang on a second—I got it in my room—an' I'll be right back."

When he returned, Mario was wearing a brand-new, checkered porkpie hat that looked as if it had been fitted by the city's finest hat maker. The family oohed and ahhed, remarking how well it fit and how handsome Mario looked in it.

Mama folded her arms across her chest and surrendered to the inevitable.

The next morning, new hat perched saucily upon his head, Mario got up at three, washed and dressed, and hopped on his bike for the thirty-minute ride over the Peace Bridge into Canada and over to the Fort Erie racetrack.

While Mario wished and believed that after paying his dues he was destined to climb the ranks of horse-racing legend and travel the international racing circuit, it was just not meant to be.

Night after night he would come home filthy, tired, and perpetually smelling of manure. His hands blistered, then callused, from shovel and pitchfork. In the six months he lasted, Mario shoveled enough manure and pitched enough hay to sink a battleship.

The horses seemed to have a natural dislike for Mario, nipping him when they could, several times hard enough to draw blood. In their stalls they took perverse delight in using their large bodies to pin him against the walls, and on several occasions, despite Mario's valiant efforts, he had to call out to anyone who might have been passing by to help move a horse off him.

When Mario was leading the horses to their daily exercise, they would trot up and use their large heads to butt him in the back of his head. One horse, Gallante, would inevitably mess his stall immediately after Mario had cleaned it, as if the combination of Mario's efforts and the sight and smell of fresh straw was a sign from God to release his mighty bowels yet again.

The final straw, so to speak, came late one afternoon when Gallante was tied outside his stall. Mario temporarily forgot Mr. Bouchard's warnings about turning his back to the horses and was behind Gallante and bending over to pick up a piece of scrap paper. The target was all too inviting and in exactly the right range, and Gallante kicked Mario directly in the center of the bull's-eye, lifting and propelling him through the air so he landed facedown in the day's collection of piled manure.

Mario got up, wiped the sticky, smelly goo from his eyes and face, rubbed his buttocks vigorously, marched over to Mr. Bouchard, and quit.

So ended a fling in the equestrian world. Mario left a little richer, much stronger, and with a lifelong distaste for horses. He also left with an almost-new but now slightly beat-up checkered porkpie hat.

CHAPTER 3

The Lion's Tail

Though Mario's interest in the war in Europe generally and in Italy specifically was strong, it paled in significance to his interest in the marines and what was happening in the Pacific. From Pearl Harbor to Hiroshima, Mario was enraptured—disheartened by the seemingly easy Japanese victories early in the war on Wake Island and Bataan and emboldened and reinvigorated by later naval victories in the Coral Sea and at Midway.

His patriotism and pride in America were second to none, and his hatred for the enemy was virtually immeasurable. If German or (especially) Japanese troops had conquered Canada and were about to launch a massive invasion of America by crossing the Niagara River, he would have been the first to take a position on the front lines of defense. In fact, he would have gladly made whatever sacrifice his country demanded of him to resist dastardly foes trying to reach America's shores.

Mario had a voracious appetite for the patriotic propaganda of radio, newspapers, magazines, and the latest newsreels down at the Rialto Theater, and although the news was everywhere, he could never get enough. He would go out of his way to stop by and see Papa at his little shoe shop, because City Hall was also the site of the major recruiting depot for the entire county.

There, stopping and staring for hours at the various recruiting posters, Mario felt his love of his country and its moral righteousness grow by leaps and bounds. The hardened grimaces, steely eyes, and frozen-in-time shouts of whiskered, helmeted soldiers carrying a rifle in one hand and waving their fellow warriors on toward battle with the other chilled and thrilled him to no end. More than anything else, what moved Mario and stirred his soul was the look of grim determination on the faces of the young men lined up at the recruiting office, ready to do whatever their country demanded of them, no matter how unpleasant the task.

The way that some unknown artist had captured the sacrosanct look of uniformed men and women standing shoulder behind shoulder, gazing upward as a spot of hallowed light illuminated their reverential faces, was more than enough to convince Mario that, indeed, his country needed him, too.

For Mario, posters reminding him that "loose lips sink ships" or urging families to "do with less so they'll have enough" were more than just pleas —they were a call to action. Consequently, he was very serious in his self-appointed role as Neighborhood Watcher, marching up and down and though his neighborhood, keeping a keen eye out for spies and traitors and even the most minute of infractions.

The favorite game of the kids in the neighborhood, War, was played on an almost-daily basis and always resulted in yet another triumph for the invincible Allies. Mario and his pals would watch the kids play, albeit with a small pang of jealousy as they thought of themselves as too sophisticated to be diving behind cars or dodging imaginary bullets and artillery shells.

Instead, they observed the neighborhood's pint-sized warriors swiftly and unmercifully dispatching foes to the nether regions of hell with a *pow* or *BOOM*, or—for those kids lucky enough to have an imaginary Thompson submachine gun—an *ack-ack-ack-ack*.

Nobody wanted to be a Nazi or a Japanese, so the enemy's ranks were always depleted. The enemies, as intractable as they were, were also invisible. This made War all that much more challenging. It was impossible to see exactly where the enemy was, but on the other hand, as Mario observed, Allied casualties were always surprisingly light.

From time to time Mario or Tommy or Luigi was called upon to make a difficult judgment that so-and-so was wounded or that so-and-so died valiantly and heroically on the battlefields of Busti Avenue after killing thousands of Japanese or Germans.

Patriotism, pride, propaganda, the glorious exploits of cinematic combat, and a continuing supply of good news of Allied victories had woven a spell over Mario, culminating in a single-minded focus on the goal that when he was old enough to enlist, he was going to serve his country in uniform. As the war moved toward its conclusion—while Mario's dream of crossing the finish line mounted upon a lathered steed to the cheers of thousands came to its post-manured end—he knew, beyond any doubt whatsoever, that his destiny was to become a United States Marine.

While brimming with pride at the efforts and successes of the navy, army, and air force, Mario's heart belonged to the marines. From the heroic yet ill-fated defense of Wake Island to the 1st Marine Division's successful invasions of Tulagi and Guadalcanal in the Solomon Islands, Mario's respect and admiration grew. He envisioned himself on the beaches and in the forests of Guadalcanal or in bunkers representing the Americans' tenuous hold on Henderson Field, repulsing fierce Japanese ground attacks.

The marines' successful efforts at Bougainville, Cape Gloucester, Saipan, Guam, and Tinian were all fought and won with a powerful psychic assist from Mario, miraculously broadcast back through the precious Philco radio in the family's living room, over the airwaves, and into the hearts and minds of marines thousands of miles from home. Listening to the newscasts, he fantasized about the opportunity to prove his manly bravado, leadership capabilities, and love of country and fellow man. In his mind he was right there, charging ashore with each beach landing, dispatching the enemy with a level of ferocity and intensity unmatched by any marine in the entire Pacific theater.

The blackened sands of Iwo Jima, however, became the crowning glory. When he first saw Joe Rosenthal's later-famous picture of the raising of the flag on Mount Suribachi, his destiny was forecast.

He generally got along with his brothers and sisters, except for his sister Connie. Her complaint voiced often and loudly in the Colucci home was that Mario tended to intimidate her potential boyfriends.

"You gotta make him stop, Mama!" she would implore, "Whenever a boy even looks in my direction, he and those dumb-lookin' goombahs of his give him one hard look and off he runs! How am I ever gonna get married if every time a boy is interested in me, Mario scares him away?"

Mario respected his parents, believed in God, and attended Mass on a regular basis. The Church was a cornerstone of Mario's existence, and his faith was boundless and without conflict—he never questioned the teachings delivered in moral imperatives of black and white. His childish confusion over reconciling Jesus's teachings of love for fellow man with the all-pervasive calls to kill Germans and Japanese was assuaged by the priests and nuns who assured him that God was on the side of the Allies, and that it was God's intention, expressed through the free will of man, that these things be done in his name.

Mario's spirituality came wrapped in a blanket of patriotism, reinforced by the Church. "Thou shall not kill" was not an absolute but merely the beginning of a means of reaching God that concluded with an understood "except for America's enemies, the Church's enemies, and for love of God and country."

Although he was street savvy, Mario was not particularly smart in the ways of business. He sought to get rich quick, hoping that one of his schemes would put him on Easy Street, where he could sip cocktails on the veranda of the most prestigious country club in Buffalo with the other entrepreneurs and capitalists of the day. While they wore tails and top hats, he would wear his porkpie hat and chinos, for, after all, being the richest of the rich provides wide latitude for certain eccentricities and invulnerability to scorn.

Mario often managed to convince Tommy and Luigi to join him in his harebrained schemes, making all of them just a little poorer and not that much wiser. Usually the cash and sweat equity they poured into a venture netted only chagrin, but the tales of their attempts at entrepreneurship often provided the neighborhood a measure of comic relief from otherwise ordinary days. From lacquered cow-hoof ashtrays to pre-hooked fishing worms to the very earliest attempts known to mankind to create powdered spaghetti sauce, they just couldn't get it right.

Their grandest scheme, the one that has survived time and taken its place in the continuing lore of Buffalo's west side, came simply to be known as the Lion's Tail. It took place in August of 1946, a year after the war ended, when the boys were fifteen.

Early that summer, Mario spent a considerable number of hours racking his brain to come up with a way to celebrate the one-year anniversary of the victory over Japan and in the process to make some serious money. He revealed his desire to his friends, who were somewhat skeptical and a little gun-shy so soon after the Red, White & Blue Shoelace debacle, particularly as all their hands were still tinted a fading color of blue from one unfortunate dye mix.

"I dunno, fellas," said Mario. "We just gotta come up with somethin', 'cause this is a once-in-a-lifetime opportunity. There ain't never gonna be another one-year anniversary of V-J Day!"

"But, Mario," they pleaded, "let's give it a rest fer a while. We still got about two hunnert pairs of shoelaces rottin' away in Luigi's basement."

Their pleas were to no avail, and one day in late June, Mario interrupted Tommy and Luigi's game of catch, bubbling over with enthusiasm and flashing that wide, gap-toothed grin they found so hard to say no to.

"I got it! I got it! I got it!" gushed Mario. "It's perfect! Everybody's gonna want at least one—if not two or three or even four of 'em! There ain't nobody in th' whole universe who's gonna come up with a better way t'make this a real celebration. And boys, get this, for this is the best part of all… it's gonna make us rich!"

Mario's enthusiasm was infectious, and the boys quickly forgot about their blue hands. "C'mon, Mario, spill the beans! Whatcha got cookin'?"

Mario had a devilish gleam in his eye. He took his porkpie hat off, wiped his forearm across his brow, replaced his hat, and squatted down. Tommy and Luigi were soon squatting down beside him as Mario outlined his plan. "Here it is, boys: we're gonna make us some firecrackers, and then sell 'em all over the neighborhood. But these ain't gonna be just any ol' kinda firecrackers—they're gonna be special, once-in-a-lifetime

V-J firecrackers that'll explode in all kinda colors, and we're gonna make 'em in all kinda sizes.

"See, here's what I figger—we kin go down t'Chinatown an' get alla stuff we need t'make the boom an' the colors. We'll get ahold of a whole buncha toilet paper tubes, an' pack 'em fulla the stuff, put a wick in, and presto whammo—V-J firecrackers, brought ta ya exclusively by Colucci, Tedesco & LaFalce, Incorporated!

"We'll get it so's that when they boom, they'll make different colors like red 'n' blue 'n' orange 'n' stuff. Everybody's gonna want more 'n' one color, right? An' here's what we'll tell 'em—ya can't light' em off until precisely seven o' clock on the night of August fourteenth. Otherwise, the whole effect'll be lost. That way, we'll get 'em to buy even more, so's they don't feel like they're bein' left outta the celebration!"

Tommy and Luigi looked at him as if Saint Secundus of Asti, the patron saint of all shopkeepers, had descended and was sitting on top of Mario's shoulders, smiling and nodding in agreement with his brilliant plan. Slowly, both broke into impossibly wide grins and slapped Mario on his back for the most ingenious idea ever conceived. Once again, Colucci, Tedesco & LaFalce, Inc. was in business.

This turn at capitalism began with a foray into Chinatown, where, pooling their meager funds together, they bought a quantity of wicks and black powder and various chemicals in funny-looking bottles—the shop owner guaranteed they would produce spectacular colors. "Now you boys listen an' listen real good to Unca Cholly, 'cause if you don't do tings right, then you gonna get big time hurt.

"First, you go get buncha bowls like this," he continued, using his hands to indicate a container about eight inches across by twelve inches deep. "Then you filla bowls 'bout halfway wi' powder 'n' a pinch—justa pinch—from little bottles. Each bowl, pinch from different little bottle, 'kay? Different bottle, different color. More'n pinch—gonna be too much an' you gonna make smelly smoke instead of boom, 'kay?"

The boys nodded in agreement.

"Now, you stirr'em up bowls with wooden spoon. Do not use anyting else, or maybe you gonna get a smackin' great big boom and you boys gonna become little pieces!" he cackled.

The boys looked at each other warily.

"Now, you take tube an' plug up end," he said, demonstrating with an invisible model. "Stick wick inna middle, push powder down tight—'cause mo' tight powder, bigger boom—plug up other end with somet'in' so's wick sticks out. Then, light 'em up 'n' run away 'cause you not gonna know if you gonna get a smackin' big boom or little *phfffft. Heeeheeeheeeheee*!"

That night in Tommy's garage, they conducted their first experiment under the glow of a single naked light bulb. They melted wax ("Aw, fer Chrissake, Luigi, melt that crap outside an' away from the powder next time, will ya!") onto a small flat piece of cardboard, and before it set, jammed a two-inch piece of toilet paper roll into it along with a four-inch piece of wick. When that had dried, they carefully put powder into the tube and tamped it down, adding and tamping until they had reached a quarter inch from the top. Using more melted wax, they sealed the tube and huddled like mad scientists around their latest unspeakable creation, laughing and cackling at what they had wrought.

Gently, they took their creation outside and laid it carefully on the ground. Tommy produced a match. They looked at each other one last time—each nodding his head that they should proceed—and Tommy lit the wick. Then they ran like Jesse Owens in the 1936 Olympics to seek shelter behind a hastily constructed barricade of metal garbage cans. Colucci, Tedesco & LaFalce, Inc. waited anxiously for the little flame to sputter its way down the wick and into the tube.

Like the engineers and physicists huddled on the flats near Los Alamos, New Mexico, on July 16, 1945, they were unsure whether they were going to witness complete failure or the destruction of Earth and mankind.

For a few precious seconds nothing happened, and Mario looked at Tommy and Luigi, disappointed and somewhat embarrassed. Just as they were starting to rise from their shelter, their homemade firecracker exploded, sending a satisfying hail of cardboard debris and red, white, and blue smoke into the air. Mad with the excitement of their success, they locked arms and executed an improvised tarantella, twirling and hopping around Tommy's backyard until one of his neighbors shouted at them to shut up.

Over the next several days, Colucci, Tedesco & LaFalce, Inc. repeated the experiment, trying different lengths of toilet-paper tubing and minuscule pinches of the chemicals from the small, evil-looking bottles. Each experiment was a resounding success, producing explosions both small and large in a variety of fantastic colors.

Luigi, however, was not entirely pleased. "I dunno, fellas—somethin's missin' but I can't figger it out. It's like this: who's gonna buy just a plain ol' toilet-paper-tube firecracker? Sure, we got it t'explode 'n' so forth 'n' so on, but they're kinda plain lookin', ain't they? What if we painted the tubes or somethin'?"

Mario and Tommy looked at Luigi in amazement, knowing instantly that he was right and that they had a packaging problem. Of equal amazement was the fact that he was able to come up with an insightful observation. "Maybe we could even paint 'em red, white, 'n' blue," offered Luigi. "After all, we're celebratin' an American victory, ain't we?"

Given the time left for production and marketing, and their last unsuccessful venture with a red-white-and-blue-themed product, that idea was abandoned, and they were momentarily stumped. That was, until Tommy, looking at a finished but unfilled tube they had rejected because the wick was cut too long, happened to remark that with the wick sticking out like that, it kind of reminded him of a tail.

"Tommy!" shouted Mario, "yer a freakin' genius! Those bastids learnt a pretty good lesson that ya don't pull onna lion's tail, right? So, here's what we do: we paint those tubes an' the stand a kinda sandy brown, an' then draw somethin' that looks like a lion roarin'. Then we'll fray the very end of the wick that's stickin' out and make it a dark brown."

"Then"—continued Tommy, picking up where Mario left off—"we call the whole ting a 'Lion's Tail', and—"

Luigi continued, "We tell everybody the whole story 'bout how those assholes learnt that lesson 'bout not tuggin' on a lion's tail, an' here's what happens to ya if ya forgits that lesson…*BOOM*!"

That moment represented perhaps the finest moment of marketing genius that had ever occurred in the entire history of the west side of Buffalo. They had fabricated a product that created its own demand, in different varieties of color and size. They knew that there was an abundance of raw materials available that could be had for next to nothing, as just about everybody threw away toilet-paper tubes, and with the proper incentives and cheap labor (their brothers and sisters), it was a product that could be produced easily and inexpensively.

Best of all, they knew that with the right sales pitch, multiple orders were virtually guaranteed.

The reinvigorated company quickly made up about twenty samples of the Lion's Tail and agreed that Mario would oversee sales, while Tommy and Luigi were to oversee production and quality control. They paid the neighborhood kids a penny for every ten toilet-paper tubes they brought to Tommy's garage, and the boys' brothers and sisters got a dollar a day for constructing, wicking, painting, and drawing up to the point where the tubes were ready for assembly.

By August 4 they had nearly two thousand tubes ready to be filled and sealed. It was agreed that for safety's sake the brothers and sisters were not going to be allowed to participate in the filling and sealing part of the production process. This was to be handled by Mario, Tommy, and Luigi starting on the morning of August 10, in preparation for delivery of the product just four short days later.

Considering that he had only twenty samples to work with, Mario did a masterful job of salesmanship. He waited for the right opportunities to gather just the right type of crowd before he dramatically told his story, leading up to the awe-inspiring conclusion that seemed to magically open change purses and wallets at blistering speeds.

He talked of God and country and patriotism.

He extolled the glories and bravery of America's fighting men.

He talked of the significance and importance of August 14, leaving some in the crowd teary-eyed and others coming away with the belief that the day should rank right up there as a holiday, second only to Christmas and Easter in importance.

Then it was time to close the sale.

"—An' this is what happened to dem creeps, and this is what's gonna happen t' anybody else who thinks they can pull on our country's tail ever again!" His pitch reached its crescendo with the lighting of a Lion's Tail that would invariably explode with a loud bang and a rush of colors. Then he would wait for the gasps and oohs and ahhs to die down before telling the assembled crowd that he would now take their orders and cash.

It was twenty-five cents for a small Lion's Tail, half a buck for the medium size, and a whopping one dollar for the giant, whole-toilet-roll-tube model, guaranteed to make a bang that would rattle windows a block away.

Mario couldn't take orders fast enough.

At Sammy the Barber's alone he took in nearly $300, and at the grocery it was closer to $400. Strangers would stop him on the street to give him an order, and even the priest and the nuns at Saint Andrews ponied up ten bucks. By the time Mario closed sales on August 9, Colucci, Tedesco & LaFalce, Inc. had taken in orders totaling $2,842.25. With each sale came a simple request: that no Lion's Tail be lit before seven on the night of the 14, and that at that time, they be lit simultaneously to produce a large, colorful, loud dramatic show of support for V-J Day.

Each purchaser had to give Mario his solemn vow to this condition before he would take their order.

Colucci, Tedesco & LaFalce, Inc.'s troubles began the afternoon of August 10, when they suddenly realized, after filling about 10 percent of the orders, that they were far, far short of the black powder they were going to need to fill the rest. Their troubles multiplied when they found out their supplier had closed his doors for a week's vacation, and that he was the only source in Chinatown for black powder. Rather than panic, they reasoned that it might be possible to use some kind of filler for the black powder and substantially more than a pinch of chemicals to make up for whatever effects might be lost by the absence of the powder.

But what could they use that was abundant, cost little or nothing, and was easy to obtain? They tried experiments with dirt and sand, but the Lion's Tail failed to explode. They tried small pebbles and abandoned the idea after the very first attempt peppered their garbage-can fortress with realistic "bullet holes."

With their vision of riches starting to fade, they became depressed until Mario, in a flash of insight motivated by panic, hit on the idea of using sawdust as filler material. It was cheap, they could get plenty of it because Luigi's papa was a carpenter with a shop in his garage, and, unlike the mineral-based substances they had tried, it would burn.

It worked.

A mixture that was about 75 percent black powder, 25 percent sawdust, and three pinches of chemicals produced a highly colorful result that was perhaps a bit smoky and with perhaps a bit less of a bang, but nevertheless, it worked. They swung back into production after securing all the sawdust they could collect from Luigi's garage but soon realized that as brilliant as they were in coming up with the idea, they were still going to run short of black powder.

Using finely honed reasoning, they figured that they could put more sawdust in the mix if they increased the amounts of color-producing chemicals, and back to work they went.

Soon they were making a 50:50-and-three-pinch mixture.

Then it went to 40:60 and four pinches.

Then, finally, to 30 percent black powder, 70 percent sawdust, and five pinches of chemicals.

By the time production ended, about six out of every ten Lion's Tails they produced were of the 30:70-and-five-pinch mixture.

By the morning of August 14, they were exhausted, having filled orders for over three thousand Lion's Tails of various sizes and colors. That did not stop them from making delivery rounds and collecting their money, and by 6:30 that evening, they were on the verge of collapse but ecstatic, figuring that each of them had cleared about $800.

As a special bonus, Mario was bursting with pride that they had also performed a patriotic service, and he could hardly wait while the next thirty minutes passed, until the neighborhood would erupt in a riot of sound and color. His inspired visionary tribute to Doug MacArthur accepting the Japanese surrender on the decks of the battleship USS *Missouri* was now only moments away.

Then, like a well-oiled machine, precisely at seven o'clock, the sounds of mini-explosions ripped through the neighborhood—that is, for the 30 percent or so of the Lion's Tails that actually detonated as promised.

The proud purchasers of the other two thousand devices soon came to discover that their mostly-saw-dust-with-other-chemicals-thrown-in   contraptions were, in fact, highly effective smoke bombs. Without even an explosion to mark their destruction, nearly two thousand smoke bombs went off in the neighborhood at approximately the same time.

They threw bilious, choking clouds of red, yellow, purple, black, orange, blue, and white smoke into the air, reducing visibility to near zero and producing a riotous confusion of biblical proportions. Mothers clutched their children. Daughters screamed. Babies cried. Grown men swore curses at the top of their lungs. Even Father Bernadetti let forth a few blasts that made his nuns blush and, eventually, left his confessor aghast. Everybody was rubbing their eyes and waving their hands frantically in the air to chase the smoke away. The sound of an entire neighborhood coughing harshly at the same time was bizarre.

Police, fearing that a tragedy of monumental proportions had occurred, rushed into the neighborhood, their red flashing lights trying to penetrate the multi-color fog that swirled around and stuck to their cars like iron filings to magnets. They called for the fire department, who rushed engines and companies from all over the city, each looking for the epicenter of doom and destruction, each fearing that they would be facing a disaster on a scale they had never seen before. The mayor, the deputy mayor, and most of the city council rushed to the scene, looking as much for press opportunities as they were for opportunities to render assistance or take charge.

After what seemed like an eternity, amidst sirens and flashing lights and confused officials, policemen and firemen running around and into one another, the great fog of smoke that covered nearly twenty square city blocks began to rise in a curtain-like fashion. Up and up it crept, first revealing shoes, then people, and then the lower flats of the two-story houses in the neighborhood. Wispy tendrils crawled over the tops of the houses and through the boughs and limbs of the Dutch elms that lined the streets. Then away the smoke went, pushed as if by an invisible hand up from the city and over the lake, where it continued to dissipate, leaving stunned and angry neighbors, politicians, and various officials in its wake.

After everything had been sorted out and the culprits identified (and arrested and released) and after the story had lost its appeal to the newspapers, Colucci, Tedesco & LaFalce, Inc. returned nearly every cent of every dollar back to the people who had purchased Lion's Tails. A sincere apology, a handshake, and a promise that they would never, ever do something like that again accompanied each return.

As a consequence, Mario and his friends went from being "fools" to being "respectful young gentlemen," but as far as the neighborhood was concerned, it was pretty much a certainty that any of their future schemes would be dead even before they got off the ground.

Throughout Mario's ill-fated brushes with capitalism, he never lost sight of his desire to be a marine. He couldn't wait until he turned eighteen, and he told everyone he knew of his desires and plans. Not even for a moment did he waver in his convictions, and with his parents' blessings, on the very day he turned eighteen, Mario marched into the marine recruiting office in City Hall and enlisted.

It was 1949. Less than ten months later, America would find itself at war once again.

CHAPTER 4

American Hero

I t was cold, bitterly cold.

Nearly a quarter of the two-hundred-man company had already been evacuated, all suffering debilitating cases of frostbite, some so severe that amputation was inevitable. Seventy had been wounded, and another twenty-seven were dead, secured in their sleeping bags, waiting for graves registration.

Of the fifty men left in Captain William Henderson's C Company, Fifth Marines, less than a dozen remained completely unscathed; most suffered from wounds ranging from insignificant to major, but not severe enough that they could not still stand and fight like United States Marines.

Private Mario Colucci was one of the lucky ones. Over three successive nights of fierce attacks by the Chinese, each preceded by a cacophony of bugles, cymbals, whistles, and finally illuminating flares, C Company had held its ground, inflicting massive casualties in the process. The company's bravery had allowed other elements of the Fifth and Seventh Marines to slip out of the noose created by three Chinese Communist divisions around the now-battered and unrecognizable village of Yudam-ni, just west of the Chosin Reservoir. Next, the Fifth and Seventh faced the difficult task of fighting their way through the Toktong Pass and on to Hagaru-ri.

At the top of Hill 1498, fewer than fifty marines now remained—the very end of the tail responsible for closing the back door and stopping nearly fifteen hundred Chinese troops from rolling over and through the retreating forces. To the marines it wasn't a retreat. It was, as one of their generals said, "just an attack from a different direction."

On Hill 1502, to the southeast of C Company, was a company of ill-prepared, ill-equipped, and ill-trained U.S. Army soldiers from the Third Battalion, Forty-second Regiment, whose mission was to protect C Company's flank. Several hours before the last and final devastating Chinese attack on the night of December 1, in a move that was later to be soundly criticized, the commander of the Forty-second issued orders to the battalion to withdraw and join the Fifth and Seventh in their breakout down the narrow and treacherous road to Hagaru-ri.

That the battalion's commander would be fired only a few days later and then court martialed for what was to be characterized as an act of betrayal and cowardice proved to be of no consolation to the men on top of Hill 1498. In fact, Captain Henderson was completely unaware of the Third Battalion's withdrawal.

He and forty-eight other marines would not live to learn they'd been abandoned.

Chinese bugles and whistles marked the start of their fourth major attack at 2:34 a.m. on the bitterly cold and dark night of December 1. C Company was alone and surrounded on three sides, facing over fifteen hundred advancing enemy troops.

In a trench on the rocky hilltop, clutching his obstinate M1 rifle in mittened hands, Mario trembled almost uncontrollably, more from the unbearable cold than from fear. He was proud, damned proud, to be a marine, and although he was affected by the death and misery surrounding him, he was neither fearful of death nor hesitant to do his duty.

Awaiting the enemy's inevitable charge up the steep hill, he remembered waving goodbye to his family at Buffalo's Union Station, the long train ride to California, and the miseries of boot camp—where he once again made a reputation for himself by standing up to even the largest and brawniest of antagonists picking on him because of his size.

Mario looked around the hilltop at familiar faces awaiting their destiny—Dale Lapsmayer, a farm boy from Arkansas; Johnny "Poker" Osborne, a card sharp from New Orleans; Seamus "Hairy" O'Clary, a rambunctious Irishman from the South Side of Chicago. He reflected upon the special bonds he had formed with all of them, the living and the dead, bonds that went beyond mere friendship.

By a little outcropping a few yards from Mario crouched twenty-eight-year-old Gunny Lowenstein, manning a .50 caliber machine gun. Gunny was a tough Jew from Hell's Kitchen in New York, and he was a father/brother/advisor/confessor to all the nineteen- and twenty-year-old members of the company. In the middle of their position stood Captain Henderson, who could be understanding when needed or a demanding bastard when necessary. A dependable, honest-to-God marine's marine who had seen action at Tarawa, Saipan, and a host of other battles, Henderson was now shouting orders setting positions and fields of fire.

"Here they come!" shouted Gunny Lowenstein in response to the repulsively familiar sounds of the bugles and whistles. The first tracers flew from Gunny's machine gun, briefly outlining the advancing hordes. It wasn't until rounds of illuminating flares had been fired that the remainder of C Company knew that they were most likely not going to survive the night.

He was squatting in the frozen mud at bottom of the slit trench, virtually paralyzed, surrounded by smoke and noise. The allegro of Chinese battle bugles and cymbals with shrieking whistles was coming from the slope below, a foreshadowing of impending death. It was cold, so very, very cold—colder than he had ever known in his life.

Mario's feet felt dead and useless, his breath froze in midair, and he had almost no feeling in his fingers. But he smelled the acrid odor of cordite and heard the explosions from mortars and grenades. Bullets smacked into the earth—and into the bodies of his friends—with ghastly, sickening plops. The sound was inescapable.

He ran from firing position to firing position in response to shouted orders, slipping and sliding on the ground covered in still-warm blood, feces, urine, and grayish brain matter and littered with pink entrails and body parts.

Jefferson stood up to fire his M1, and the next moment he was headless, still holding his rifle up to his shoulder in a firing position, bright blood spouting in gouts from his neck where his head used to be. Mario tripped and fell to his knees on top of Freddie Walpole, whose vacant and lifeless eyes penetrated to the depths of Mario's soul, asking a question that could not and would not ever be answered: "Why me?"

Then came the screaming—screams of rage, screams of anguish and agony, screams of desperation, screams of triumph, joined in dissonant chorus by his own screams, at first from the white-hot burning pain coursing through his shoulder from the bullet he had caught. Then he screamed in defiance at the shock of being hit.

Next came screams of revenge as he grabbed the .50 caliber machine gun from the lifeless hands of Gunny Lowenstein and unmercifully fired round after round after round directly into the faces of the Chinese troops less than ten yards away. Death was approaching as quickly as his ammunition was exhausting, until a surreal moment of calm hovered over the battlefield.

Mario realized that the Chinese attack had broken off and that he was alive.

Slinging a shrieking Captain Henderson over his uninjured shoulder, Mario ran toward safety through a confusion of smoke and a crescendo of new, close explosions. Every running step made the captain howl in pain. They slipped and fell several times as he navigated down the rocky slope, each tumble and rise bringing him closer and closer to the brink of collapse.

A wet, coppery-smelling mix of his own blood and the captain's splashed and soaked through the front of his jacket. Henderson was pleading and shouting, "For God's sake, please be gentle!"

A violent bright white light suddenly appeared out of nowhere, and Mario was flying, flying, flying through the air like a bird or an angel.

Then came nothingness.

At first, the voices were indistinguishable and indiscernible, but they grew louder and clearer as Mario crept slowly and inexorably toward consciousness. His vision was fogged and blurry, as if someone were holding both hands over his eyes, and he felt heavy, very heavy, as if someone were sitting on his chest and legs. His thirst was overwhelming, and his tongue felt huge and grotesque. He struggled to rise but found he could not, and as his awareness grew, so too did waves of monstrous pain which racked his body in ever-increasing peaks.

"Wh—wh—where am I? Hurts. Hurts bad," he mumbled, again trying to rise, with no success.

A quiet, feminine voice and a small but firm hand on his shoulder easily restrained him. "*Shh. Shh. Shh*. Be easy now. You're at the U.S. Naval Hospital in Yokosuka, Japan. You were wounded very badly, and you've been asleep for seventeen days. We're glad to see that you're back with us. Would you like a sip of water?"

Mario nodded, spiking his pain and exhausting the little reservoir of strength he had. The nurse took a damp cloth and wiped his parched and cracked lips, then held his head so he could take small sips from the glass she was holding. "Easy, easy there! Not too much at one time, we don't want you to sick up on us now, do we?"

"Wh-wha-wha——happen' t'me?" Mario croaked. "Why can't I see anythin'? Wh-wh-why can't I move? Fer Chrissake, why's everthin' hurt so bad? Am I in heaven?"

"No, Private Colucci, you're definitely not in heaven." The nurse chuckled, offering another sip of water. She continued in a soothing voice, "Oh, and by the way, I'm Nurse Tureen, Lieutenant Tureen, but all my friends call me Mattie."

After a few moments, she continued, matter-of-factly but soothingly: "You were severely wounded at Chosin, and for a while there, we weren't sure you were even going to make it…but with a little time and a lot of effort on your part, we think you're going to be just fine—now that you've woken up. You've got bandages around your head and eyes; that's why you can't see anything. And as for why you can't move, well, let's wait until the doctor comes, and let's let him explain things, OK?"

Mario collapsed back against the pillow, groaning at the effort, fighting against the rush of demons tearing him apart.

A few days later, a still heavily bandaged Mario heard the rumors about the Forty-second's sneaky and uncommunicated withdrawal from Hill 1502. One bedmate in the ward had scuttlebutt that the army refused to maintain the flank of the outmanned and outgunned marine company. He got the word from a buddy—who got word from a buddy, who got word from another buddy, who typed up the After Action Report—that the Forty-second's commander considered that staying in the flanking position would be a waste of men and material and "inconvenient."

Hard on the heels of this revelation came an intense, enveloping sense of being betrayed—betrayed by the weather and the night; betrayed by his conscience that wholeheartedly acceded to the savage within him; betrayed by his close friends, marines, who were never supposed to leave their buddies but who left in death, anyway; betrayed by officers who said they would take care of him. Finally, perhaps worst of all, Mario felt betrayed by the chilling contrast between reality and his boyhood visions of honor and glory.

Terrified he thrashed violently from side to side in his bed, bellowing and threatening to rip apart the handiwork of the surgeons who had put him back together.

Before Nurse Tureen could get help from another nurse she called for, Mario stiffened and collapsed, mercifully sinking back into unconsciousness—where he could take shelter from his ravaging memories.

It would be three days before he once again came back.

CHAPTER 5

Mattie Tureen

Second Lieutenant Mattie Tureen thrust her hands toward the sputtering fire in the oil can to capture the small measure of comfort it afforded. Shivering, she pulled her long green coat tight around her, tucked wisps of unwashed black hair back under her woolen hat, and instinctively jammed her helmet on when the shelling began again.

It was another cold, gray, and snowy day in Bastogne, and even though it was Christmas Eve, 1944, two divisions of the German XLVII Panzer Corps and six heavy assault amphibian battalions were preparing to use their five to one manpower advantage to annihilate the American 101. The American forces lacked cold-weather gear, ammunition, food, medical supplies, and senior leadership—it was an impending catastrophe for those who, just two weeks earlier, had been brimming with confidence that the war would end before the end of the year.

A combat nurse in the Sixty-fourth Medical Group, VII Corps, First U.S. Army, Nurse Tureen had experienced more than her fair share of horrors since landing in France in July of 1944. But in the small, charming town now in its second week of being besieged, the smell of blood and feces, the frenetic pace of surgeons trying to stitch wounded soldiers together in the primitive field hospitals, and the screams of dying boys crying out for their mothers had reached an intensity that could be handled only by the very strongest of wills.

Mattie Tureen was one of the strong willed.

Mattie was the only child of a dour, lifeless mother and an abusive, alcoholic father who in Mattie's early childhood worked in a strip mine located about halfway between Herrin and Marion, Illinois. Rumor had it that in 1922, when Mattie was just two years old, John Tureen was one of the United Mine Workers strikers behind the long rifles that killed the mine superintendent and twenty-two laborers brought in to break the strike.

He barely eked out a living, and they would be destitute if his wife, Bettys, didn't earn pin money selling the fruits and vegetables she canned. As it was, he spent most of his paycheck at the bar, coming home reeking of coal dust and cheap whisky. On good days he would be just verbally abusive, but on bad days he used his fists or brought out the strap to "make sure my girls know who's the boss of the family."

Mattie learned how to run and hide on the bad days, but her mother was submissive and not as nimble. "C'mere, you sow!" her father would bellow, fists bunched and ready to strike. "Gimme some money! I'm headed back to Danny's!"

"We'll make do somehow," Betty would tell Mattie in a whisper after being punched or belt-whipped. "I've just gotta do better!"

It wasn't unusual to see the Tureen girls with a black eye or abrasions, and it got worse when the Depression caused the mine to shut down in 1930. As the household's poverty worsened, the intensity of the abuse reached new levels. Mattie became better at escaping slaps and swipes of his belt as she got older and as her father's alcoholism grew out of control. But while John Tureen didn't use his fists as often, his verbal abuse grew in timbre and intensity.

"You must be the most god-awful ugliest girl on the face of the earth!" he would shout at her in a slurred voice while Mattie's mother cowered in a corner. "And yer stupid, too! Ugly and stupid. Stupid and ugly. What kinda man is gonna wanna be with you?"

Mattie was aware that she was not a beauty by any stretch of the imagination. Taller by a head than her classmates, thin black hair always pinned up in a severe bun, and a wardrobe consisting of a few well-worn and patched dresses—she was a target of scorn. Her teen-age years came with an unwelcome case of severe acne and the worse pain of cruel and unmerciful taunting. She matured later than the other girls, so she got little to no attention from boys.

Mattie had no real girlfriends and—other than going to church—no social interactions. She did not chat with other girls in class or after school, and she was never seen laughing or even smiling. Her silent re-sponse was taken as an indication of stupidity or back-wardness, but in fact it was a sign of total, self-con-fident indifference. Mattie preferred the company of books or—when she could scrape up a quarter—an afternoon spent at the movies.

"Mattie, what exactly is wrong with you?" asked her favorite teacher one day. "You're a whiz in math and science, a brilliant writer with a keen mind, and a big reader. Why aren't you talking in class or sharing your ideas? I haven't heard nary a peep out of you this semester!

"Gosh sakes, girl," she continued, "you're de-vouring everything from Isaac Newton to Ernest Hemingway. Did you know that you're on the way to a perfect A average? Why, it's been over ten years since anyone at Herrin Senior High hit that mark!"

Mattie was the smartest and most gifted student at the school, and her intensely private inner confidence was a perfect Zen-like foil to the ego of accomplishment.

Other than her teachers, no one knew, and Mattie was not inclined to share her academic achievements with anyone, especially not her mother and father.

In early 1938, John Tureen was killed when he drunkenly stumbled out of Danny's into the street and the path of a truck that neither slowed nor stopped after hitting him. Later that evening at the county coroner's office, when asked if the mangled body she was shown was her father, Mattie replied with a one-word answer: "Yes."

Then she turned and walked out.

Several days after the funeral, a letter from the Cook County School of Nursing was delivered to Mattie's house, informing her that they were delighted to offer her a slot in the Fall 1939 semester and that she was to be awarded a full scholarship and small stipend.

Two months later she left home, carrying all her belongings in a well-worn cardboard suitcase held together by a piece of brown twine. She said goodbye to her sobbing mother and marched to the bus station. Mattie returned to Herrin only one more time in her life, two years later, to bury Betty, who had died of a heart attack at age thirty-nine, worn and wispy and submissive.

In 1942 Mattie earned her nursing degree and by the beginning of the next year, volunteered to serve in the twelve-thousand-strong Army Nurse Corps. She completed her basic training at Camp McCoy in Wisconsin and earned her commission as a second lieutenant.

By 1944 Mattie was one of more than fifty-seven thousand nurses serving in the Army Nurse Corps. They were assigned to hospital ships and trains, flying ambulances, and field, evacuation, station, and general hospitals at home and overseas. By the end of the war, they had touched the lives of hundreds of thousands of American boys, those who would later be part of what came to be known as the Greatest Generation.

At the war's end—even after combat nursing in make shift aid stations just after D-Day, across the Rhine in the breakthrough into Germany, and then as part of the first medical team to enter Dachau—Mattie wanted to stay and make her career in the army. With glowing recommendations from superior officers who reported her bravery under fire and described her calm bedside demeanor that gave patients hope even in dire circumstances, Mattie was granted her re-enlistment request.

"So where is it going to be?" asked her command. "Off to teach, or for more medical training? Have you thought about becoming a physician?"

Mattie had done a lot of thinking about her future in the army, and she looked forward to serving in a hospital stateside during a time of peace.

"No, sir," she replied, "I'm applying to be part of the team stationed at Halloran General Hospital to come up with a way to deal with battle fatigue. I think there are better ways, better treatments, and even new drugs that can help the severely psychologically wounded find a path to recovery."

"Ah, yes," he replied, "I believe I've heard about that work. Very challenging, but most of that battle fatigue nonsense can be cured with rest, so I hope you're not just wasting your time and wasting a valuable resource for the army!"

Within five minutes the commander had approved her duty station request.

But her time at Halloran was unexpectedly cut short.

By 1950 she was back in combat boots, masked and gowned, standing on a bloody operating room floor at the 503 MASH in some godforsaken and unpronounceable place in Korea. Mattie had quickly and efficiently stepped back into the world of patching up kids who were young and scared, gently stroking their hands as if she could conjure a spell to shield them from the inevitable, approaching tsunami in a mind besieged, traumatized, and ill prepared to deal with memories of battle and its aftereffects.

Her time at Halloran was not wasted. She brought to the latest assignment her new ideas about field-treating battle-shocked and wounded soldiers, even if it meant butting heads against army brass and even army surgeons who believed psychological scars were myths at best and treatable with aspirin and a few days' rest.

But Mattie wouldn't stop advocating for what she knew was right, and after two years in Korea, she got what she wanted.

In 1952 she was ordered to report for nursing duties at the U.S. Naval Hospital in Yokosuka, Japan, where she met Mario Colucci and fell hopelessly in love.

CHAPTER 6

First Steps of a King

A hand gently shook Mario's shoulder, and from what seemed to be an infinite distance away, he heard someone calling his name softly.

"Mario? Mario? It's time to wake up. C'mon sleepyhead, up and at 'em!"

"Mama? Is that you, Mama? I don' wanna get up. Sleepy," mumbled Mario. "Lemme sleep s'more, will ya?"

The hand on his shoulder shook him a little harder. "No, Mario, it's time to get up now. You've slept long enough."

His eyes fluttered open, and at first Mario thought he was still dreaming and looking at the face of an angel. As awareness slowly returned, triggered by powerful itches in his shoulders and all up and down his legs, he remembered where he was and why he was there.

"Hello, Private, remember me? Nurse Tureen. Mattie to my friends, which I hope we'll become."

Mario was prevented from descending into the terror of his memories by Nurse Tureen's calming countenance, entrancing deep-blue eyes, and a thin-lipped smile which Mario thought was the single most beautiful smile he had ever seen in his entire life. Her face was thin and oval, and even though her hair was hidden by a nursing cap, he knew that it was long and dark and when let loose would frame her face in a way that would make her all that much more angelic. His involuntary gasp was the first sign that he was destined to fall in love.

Assisted by an orderly, Nurse Tureen cranked up the bed to put Mario into a semi-upright position. He winced in pain at the movement and found that he couldn't move his arms, torso, or legs. He immediately concluded that he had lost one or several limbs—and perhaps even his manhood—on Hill 1498.

Mattie could see his eyes begin to cloud over with fear and immediately reached out to touch and stroke Mario's face, calming him instantaneously. "There, there now. That's better, isn't it? We took the bandages off your eyes while you were asleep, and if you give me your promise that you're not going to try to hurt yourself, I'll have the corpsman remove your restraints. How about it?"

Mario nodded his head in agreement, and the corpsman undid the leather straps that had been tightly cinched around Mario's torso and legs. Almost immediately Mario could feel sensations returning to his limbs and was able to peer down the length of his body, emitting an audible *whoosh* of relief, accompanied by tears of joy, to discover that everything that was supposed to be there was still there.

His right leg was encased in bandages, his left leg was in a cast from hip to toe, and from chest to fingertips his right arm was in yet another cast, raised and suspended over the bed by a bizarre contraption of metal rings and bars. He was connected to an IV.

The corpsman had hastened to another part of the ward, so Mattie and Mario were alone.

"Now, that's better than before, isn't it?" asked Nurse Tureen, again smiling that thin-lipped smile Mario found increasingly appealing. "I bet you're hungry."

Mario nodded. He was hungry, ravenously hungry, and felt that he could eat an entire cow by himself. Instead, Mattie started to feed him a pabulum-like mixture that Mario immediately spat out, turning his head to avoid being assaulted again by the vile-tasting concoction.

"Hmm. I guess that probably does taste bad to a tough guy like you who hasn't eaten anything solid in a while. I'm really not supposed to do this, but…"

From a pocket on her apron she produced a small packet of sugar, which she sprinkled on the pabulum and then stirred in. She offered a spoonful to Mario. He was hesitant at first, but after taking a small taste and finding it somewhat to his liking, he eagerly accepted, with open mouth, the succeeding spoonfuls.

"You see, Private, we've got to break you back into eating solid foods. If we don't, you'll just get sick. Don't worry—in just a few days, you'll be getting those dee-lish-us hospital meals," she said, wrinkling and pinching her nose, which made Mario smile. "After you've eaten, I'm going to shave and clean you up, then Doc Battaglia is going to come in and tell you what's going on."

Mario wanted the shave to never end. While she talked, Mattie's small, cool hands lathered his face in a way that Sammy the Barber had never done, and she efficiently scraped his whiskers away. Mario forgot where he was. Collecting the various trays and bowls and other remnants of their encounter, she turned on her heel and walked away with a "See ya later." As she left the room, Mario caught a glimpse of one thin, stockinged leg between her ankle and mid-calf-length nurse's uniform.

His reaction brought another *whoosh* of relief as he discovered, somewhat to his embarrassment, that he was indeed completely functional and had not left a most precious part of himself on the battlefield.

A few minutes later, a short, balding man wearing a lab coat, with a stethoscope around his neck, entered the ward carrying a clipboard. "Hello, *paisan*," he said in a booming voice as he approached Mario's bed, "I am Major Battaglia, Doc Battaglia if you wish, and I'm the guy who helped put you back together again. Let's see what we've got here." The doctor proceeded to check Mario's heart and pulse, eered into his eyes and lifted various bandages covering a multitude of wounds, making notes on his clipboard as he went.

"You gave us quite a scare there, Private. For a while it was touch and go, but you gotta be one tough little bastard to take what you did and still come out alive."

Mario looked at the doctor with a combination of question and concern. "I know I was hit inna shoulder," whispered Mario, "but that's all I remember 'cept for carrying the captain. Did he make it? Did the captain make it?"

Doc Battaglia sat on the edge of the bed and looked directly into Mario's eyes. "No, I'm afraid not, Mario. As a matter of fact, you're the only one of the entire company on that hill that night who made it out alive."

Mario gasped in horror.

Doc scanned through the clipboard he was carrying.

"Ah, here it is right in the After Action Report." He pointed and continued, "When you were carrying the captain down the hill, a mortar round went off about ten feet in front of you. The shrapnel killed the captain, and if it weren't for the fact that he was over your shoulder and covering most of your body, you would be dead too. From what I'm reading here, you were soaked from head to toe in blood and so bloody they thought for sure that you were dead.

"If you hadn't groaned, a corpsman would never have picked you up, and if those fine docs at the MASH unit hadn't done such a wonderful job at patching you up—they saved your leg, by the way—your mama and papa would be displaying a gold star on a black field in their window.

"As it was, in addition to the bullet you took, you suffered a severe concussion, which the doc at the MASH thought was going to blind you for the rest of your life.

"You still took a pretty good load of China's best all up and down your leg—it barely missed your femoral artery. The explosion also lifted you up, apparently, and when you came down you landed funny on your left leg and broke it in two places. I had to put a metal pin in your thigh, as a matter of fact."

Mario began crying softly at first, and as the doctor continued, Mario sobbed, then bawled loudly and without embarrassment, each sob racking his body. A swelling, confusing symphony of memory added an unwelcome soundtrack to his misery.

After he slowly calmed, Mario sank back into his pillow, closed his eyes, and retreated.

It was time to finish the conversation he had started with God as he was running down the hill with the wounded captain over his shoulder, just before the mortar round hit.

Hey God, Lowenstein, dead? Walpole dead? Both the lieutenant an' the captain gone? What about Lapsmayer and the Skitcher and poker-mad Johnny Osborne? What about Newport and O'Clary? We wuz supposed t'get together after the war so we could swap stories like th' one 'bout the trip we took to Tijuana before we shipped. We got all rip-roarin' drunk an' Newport and O'Clary both lost their cherries!

Quiet Marty Teacher who wore dose funny lookin' glasses and used his leave t'teach English to th' whores in Seoul? Gone?!

Hey, God…what about their wives an' their children an' their mamas an' papas an' brothers an' sisters who aren't ever gonna see them again?

Why?

Hey, God…didja really care about some shitty little hill in some meaningless country ten thousan' miles away?

Hey, God….why didn't they die like they did in the movies, quiet, like heroes, instead of screamin' and

cryin' for their mamas, covered with blood an' shit an'
piss, trying t'jam their guts back inta their bodies?

Witnessing a horrible change come over Mario, and before the terror could escalate any further, Doc Battaglia quickly jumped up from the edge of the bed, reached into his pocket, withdrew a syringe, and forcefully administered a powerful sedative into his patient's IV tubing. With profound sadness and shaking his head from side to side as Mario slipped back into unconsciousness, the physician witnessed something more than just the light fading from Mario's eyes. He knew it was something beyond his ability to fix.

Later that evening in the still of the night when the ward was quiet save for the moans and cacophony of his fellow patients' night music, Mario slowly came back to awareness.

Hey, God…it's me again. Did I do what I wuz expected t'do in your eyes?

I gotta know.

Wuz it your will that made me pull that trigger or wuz it my duty? How many did I kill, God? Five? Ten? Dozens? Hundreds? Didja see if I wuz happy or sad when my bullets tore inta their bodies? When their blood mixed with ours, was it like th' blood of your Son?

Hey, God….do ya forgive me? I didn't know what I wuz doing.

Mumbling under his breath, Mario slipped back into a troubled sleep.

What occurred that day was nothing less than Mario's very first steps toward becoming The King of Kreskin Avenue.

Mattie Colucci and the Return of the Porkpie Hat

A few days later, Mario was dozing quietly when he was awakened by Mattie gently shaking his shoulder. "You're getting visitors," she said, helping him to sit up. Her pursed lips showed her concern about the vacant stare in his eyes that went beyond the painkillers. "Let's get you cleaned up and presentable, shall we?" She went about her business quickly and efficiently, and soon Mario was shaved and groomed and sitting up in his bed, propped up by a battalion of pillows. He was there, but not there, uninterested in the extraordinary hustle and bustle happening in the wardroom.

A tall, balding man clenching a familiar corncob pipe and wearing simple yet impeccably tailored battle fatigues approached his bed. A corps of high-ranking officers, doctors, and nurses hurried at his heels like a pack of puppies following their master. After conferring briefly with Doctor Battaglia, who pointed at Mario and nodded, he strode to the foot of Mario's bed.

"Private, do you know who I am?"

Mario turned his head away.

"*Harrumph. Harrumph.* Well now, that's OK, son, I know how you feel. I'm General Douglas MacArthur, and I came to give you something. Major, if you will."

A ramrod-straight marine major took a sheet of paper out of his breast pocket and began to read from a carefully prepared text which recounted Mario's actions that horrible night of December first on Hill 1498 above the small village of Yudam-ni: "Single-handedly, and without concern for his personal safety, Private Colucci did…"

Mario refused to look at the growing audience surrounding his bed. Doc Battaglia noticed Mario's eyes beginning to cloud over once again and reached into his pocket to make sure that he had a syringe ready.

"…stopped a horde of the advancing enemy with a .50 caliber machine gun, and when his ammunition ran out, Private Colucci…"

Mario finally turned and looked at the general, tears silently coursing down his cheeks.

"…and great personal valor in the face of tremendous odds, he contributed immeasurably to the repulse of a hostile force. His inspiring actions were in keeping with the highest traditions of the United Sates Naval Service, and it is with the thanks of a grateful nation that we proudly present him with the Navy Cross."

MacArthur took a slim black-velvet-covered box from the major, opened it, lifted a thick gold cross suspended from a simple ribbon from the box's silvery white lining, and hung it around Mario's neck. He snapped to attention at the side of the bed and saluted Mario and was quickly joined in the salute by the assembled crowd.

"Congratulations, son," he said, speaking more to the crowd than to the wounded marine. "This medal ranks second only to the Congressional Medal of Honor in the Navy's Pyramid of Honor. It's my privilege to be able to be here to put this on one of our brave boys. We need more men like you in Korea, and I'm proud of what you've done. You're a shining example for the rest of us."

Mario looked up at MacArthur, and in a barely audible voice, said, "General, can I ask a question?"

MacArthur smiled. "Of course, son."

"Why?"

"Why what, son?"

"Why did they all hafta die like that? What was it for?"

MacArthur's eyes turned steely, and he fidgeted for a moment before replying. "Why, son, you stopped a whole goddam Chinese army from breaking through our lines. If it wasn't for what you did, the entire Fifth and Seventh would have been routed, with hundreds and hundreds more casualties, and if that captain you were carrying had lived, you would have gotten the Medal of Honor."

"I know, sir. But it weren't like it was supposed t'be. I just don't unnerstan', an' I don' feel real good 'bout what I did."

MacArthur did not reply. Instead, he turned sharply on his heels and walked away, muttering to his adjutant. The assembled crowd quickly followed him as he continued to make his way down the ward, saying words of encouragement or stopping to offer some small measures of comfort to the wounded men.

Later that afternoon when Mario was once again dozing, Mattie passed by and noticed that the Navy Cross was lying on the floor next to his bed. She put it back in its box and slipped it into her pocket, then she continued her rounds.

The next nine months were a mixture of bliss and horror for Mario. His body completed the long, difficult, and often unpleasant process of healing, but his mind continued a downward spiral that his doctors found impossible to slow. As the days passed, his sense of betrayal grew, and each time he relived that night in his nightmares, another little piece of Mario got lost.

Except when he was near Mattie, Mario never laughed or even smiled, and he refused the entreaties of his ward mates for the simplest of conversations, dismissing them with a back-of-the-hand wave and a curse. The psychiatrists and other physicians who tended him received only grunts or monosyllabic responses to their queries, and he often isolated himself, even avoiding letters or phone calls from his family.

Pride and spirit were replaced by emotional numbness, and if it were not for the growing relationship with his nurse, Mario's depression would have driven him into the realms of insanity.

The only bright spot in Mario's existence was Mattie. Gangly and considered to be on the downhill side of plain, she formed a special bond with Mario. Around the hospital she was considered practical, efficient, and somewhat dour, but with Mario she was tender when he needed consolation, calming when he became suspicious or frightened, and cheerful when she saw him moody or irritable.

As the months passed, their relationship evolved from patient/nurse to friends and then to lovers. Their relationship was not one-sided, as Mario was the missing piece Mattie needed to complete the puzzle of her own life.

"I've seen a lot of pain and suffering, but I'm not a worldly person," Mattie confided to Mario. "I have a feeling that if I stay in the service or return home, I'm going to just fade away.

"There weren't very many happy spots in my younger days," she explained, "and I wasn't what you would call a popular gal. I can't put my finger on it, but for some reason, I can talk to you about anything, and I know that you're listening. I love hearing your stories."

"Well, I love t'hear ya laugh, 'cause it makes me feel all warm and good inside," he told her with a wink and a gleam in his eyes. "And all dose stories are 100 percent guar-un-teed t'be the honest truth, 'cause if I'm lyin', I'm dyin'!"

As Mario healed and became ambulatory, the two of them could often be seen walking around the hospital grounds after her shift ended, oblivious to stares and behind-the-back whispers. "Hey, look! It's Mutt and Jeff holdin' hands!" was one of the favorites of both patients and staff.

It didn't really matter, because they were falling in love and entering that self-protected and self-contained universe to which all lovers transcend.

Mattie became Mario's lifeline to reality, giving him a forum in which to release his guilt and express the betrayals that were tearing him apart. Her hand on his cheek could instantly check his anger;

her hugs were a panacea for his fears and sensations of doom.

By the time the cherry trees on the hospital grounds had bloomed that spring, Mattie know that Mario was a kind and caring man who would always remain faithful and true.

"Mario, you've melted my heart," she confessed to him as they walked under a canopy of pink and white cherry blossoms. "Every time you smile at me, I get lost in those brown eyes."

He grabbed her hand and got down on a knee.

"So, how's about you 'n' me getting hitched?"

Upon Mario's release from the hospital, coincidental with his honorable discharge, Mattie resigned her commission, and in a simple ceremony attended only by Doc Battaglia and a few nurses, they married.

While he was recovering, both Mario's letters home and the irregular phone calls he made or received were terse, saying only that he was getting better and that he had met someone special. In the last letter he sent before he was discharged to return home, he told them about his marriage.

Mario and Mattie returned to Buffalo, both in uniform, where his concerned family were overjoyed to see him after nearly a two-year absence. His parents, siblings, and friends threw the couple a big, Italian combination welcome-home and wedding party that first day home. They pointed and in a good-natured way laughed and made jokes about the little paunch Mario was growing and ribbed Mattie about her height, asking her how the weather was up there.

"I haven't told my family or friends hardly anything," Mario confessed to Mattie the night before their homecoming and the party. "They know I was hurt bad, and they read about the battle, but not the details. I ain't shared anything about the medal 'cause it ain't all that important t' me."

"What about what's going on in your head?" asked Mattie. "Don't you think they should know about that battle going on every day?"

"Nope," he replied, "that just ain't my way."

Everyone wanted to know about Mario's wounds and his war experiences, particularly Tommy and Luigi. Although they were older and now married, they were still gung-ho and gushing with pride and patriotism. They were unrelenting in their curiosity to know what it was like, and their questions tumbled on, one after another.

"Hey, Mario, how many Commies did ya kill?"

"Mario, what happened t'yer buddies?"

"Hey, Mario, did those Chinks scream out funny like when ya shot 'em, like in the movies?"

His brothers and sisters, who were glued to Mattie and Mario at the party, clamored for war souvenirs, and even Father Bernadetti, although upset that Mario had married outside the faith, could not contain his curiosity, firing question after question about what it was like on the frozen hilltop.

Seeing Mario's eyes beginning to glaze and his body beginning to tremble, Mattie squeezed Mario's hand and quickly reached out to stroke his cheek as she had done so many times over the last nine months. Calmed, Mario looked around at the family and friends encircling them.

In a low and measured voice, Mattie at his side, he spoke: "Youse wanna know what it was like, huh? Well, I'll tell ya what it was like.… It was worse 'n' hell. I saw things and did things that no human being should ever have t'see or do. I didn't think 'bout God and country or bein' a marine or even about any of youse—all I thought about was how and when I was gonna get it an' whether it was gonna be quick or slow.

"What was it like?" he continued. "I ain't never, ever, never gonna tell ya what it was like, so don't ever ask me ever again. Ya don' wanna really know what it was like, an' no matter what I might tell ya, y'ain't never, ever, never gonna know what it was really like.

"An' that's all I'm ever gonna say 'bout this stuff ever again," he said with a tone of finality, "so don't ask me 'bout it ever again!"

The assembled crowd slowly drifted away, stung by Mario's words, mumbling to one another about how much Mario had changed. Gone was the sensitive, spirited, fun-loving boy they knew. The stranger who replaced him appeared numb and lifeless. He made no attempts to circulate, to work the crowd as he had done in his days of being an entrepreneur, or to toss a jibe or two at his friends as he used to do. While he acknowledged the congratulations and good wishes, he did so vacantly and without enthusiasm, obviously forcing smiles that made his well-wishers uncomfortable.

When the party broke up, Mario took Mattie into his old bedroom, where he removed his uniform and tossed it in a crumpled heap in a corner. As Mattie sat on the edge of his bed, Mario rummaged in his closet and found an old pair of chinos and a T-shirt that he quickly donned. Then he reached up for something on a shelf in the closet, but Mattie couldn't quite make out what it was.

When Mario turned around, he was smiling the smile that had made Mattie fall in love with him. Perched on his head was a somewhat beat-up checkered porkpie hat.

By the time another year had passed, Mattie was pregnant, and they had bought and moved into a home at 77 Kreskin Avenue, on the north side of the city. In 1954, Mattie gave birth to a son they called A.J., and the family tried to settle into a quiet and unobtrusive life.

Mario began work at a truck depot on Busti Avenue, a few blocks from his parents' home, and by the early 1960s he was earning a paycheck as an independent "international" truck driver.

Daily, at least twice and sometimes three times or more, depending upon the size of the load, weather conditions, or the traffic on the Peace Bridge, he would pick up a load of boxes at the truck depot, transport the boxes across the border into Canada, and unload them at the depot in Fort Erie. Then the trip reversed with Mario carrying goods from Canada back to the Busti Avenue Depot, where his truck was quickly unloaded and made ready for the next day and a rehash of the same routine.

He never varied the routine, always stopping at the same inspection booth on the American side and at the same inspection booth on the Canadian side. Ninety-nine out of a hundred times, his familiarity with both countries' inspectors got him waved through customs with little more than a cursory glance.

But the passage of time did not bring relief to Mario.

There were days of anxiety and depression and nights of darkness when moments of terror were relived in sweat-soaked bad dreams time and time again. A close thunderstorm could trigger hallucinations and flashbacks, or a scene from a movie could prompt memories that led to uncontrollable bursts of anger.

"I just can't bring myself back t'where I used to be," he complained to Mattie after a particularly bad incident.

"I'm always thinkin' *Why me?* and wonderin' if I'm going crazy or if I just gotta man up."

At those times she would gently take his hands into hers, look deeply and lovingly into his eyes, and soothe him into sharing his thoughts and feelings. Often this was enough to bring him a measure of serenity and stability, and the moment would pass.

Then there were the times that were particularly bad and violent, and unbeknownst to family, friends, and neighbors, Mattie would need to take Mario to the Buffalo VA hospital.

Psychiatrists first used insulin shock therapy to try to cure Mario of what they were calling a psychoneurotic disorder, putting him into insulin overload that triggered mini comas, in the hope of jolting him out of his mental illness. During each barbaric treatment Mattie was at his side, offering comfort and encouragement..

Any relief Mario got from the treatment was temporary at best. When the next major rage took place a few months later, they used electric shock therapy over Mattie's protestations. She sat by his bedside, holding his hand, and watched and wept as they restrained her husband, placed electrodes on both sides of his head, then waved her away before sending 120 volts of electricity through his brain.

The next incident was a tipping point. Mattie had just returned home from a visit to a specialist to discuss why A.J. didn't seem quite normal. Her thoughts were interrupted by the jarring ring of the telephone.

"Mrs. Colucci?" called out a panicked voice on the other end of the line, "ahh, we had some trouble down at the depot. Mario went loony and collapsed. They took him in a ambulance over to the VA."

She slipped back into her combat nurse persona.

"Just the facts, please," she said.

A forklift operator had accidently pushed over a stack of vacuum-sealed cathode ray television tubes bound for Canada.

As the cartons hit the ground they exploded, each sounding like a mortar shell. The impact sent thousands of shards of glass and metal components flying throughout the facility, wounding five workers, who screamed in pained with shrieks that could be heard above the shouts of supervisors barking orders. It was a chaotic dance of disaster.

"Mario wasn't hurt or nuthin'," the voice on the phone continued, "but somethin' snapped, and he started t'yell about 'watchin' out for them yellow bastards. There was blood everywhere, and when we went over t'help him, he grabbed a crowbar and start swingin', all the while yellin' for some guy named Henderson. He was howlin' and cussin' and callin' out to people we don't know…maybe marine buddies?

"We managed to grab ahold of him, and he just passed out right there on the floor. That's when we called for an ambulance, and they just picked him up."

At the VA hospital, Mattie arrived as a group of doctors were discussing what to do. The head of psychiatry approached her.

"Mrs. Colucci?" he began tentatively, "we've patched up Mario's cuts, but his mental condition is not getting better despite all the initial measures—and after all the other treatments we've tried. In fact, we all agree that he's getting worse. I think our best bet is to try psychosurgery, and—"

Mattie exploded.

"You want to lobotomize him?!" she cried out in disbelief.

"Yes, I'm afraid that's the only course of action left."

"It's not," she replied. "Have you done any work with chlorpromazine?"

"No," the doctor replied, unaware of Mattie's background and credentials. "It's rather new, and for Mario's safety and for the safety of those around him, we think that our recommendation is the right one. As a matter of fact, we're prepping the OR right now.

"If you don't agree, you can always go to a private facility, but I must warn you that if you don't let us proceed, the VA will not be an option for you in the future for treating his psych trauma."

"Well, we disagree, Doctor," she said without spite or rancor. "Are you aware of the work that was done at Halloran a few years back?" At his nod she said, "I was the lead nurse on that team. What is the most recent data on success with surgery as a cure for this battle-related psychosis?

"I've kept up with the literature, and it's not very promising," he admitted.

"As a matter of fact," Mattie pressed, "what you're suggesting is nothing more than the easy way out, and I don't know if you're looking hard enough at options. Besides that, I'm pretty sure that our senator would not be particularly pleased at how you're treating me or how you're taking the low road for a vet who has received the Navy's Distinguished Service Cross."

Mattie stood her ground and refused to authorize surgery for Mario. Destroying a part of her husband's brain was the easy choice for the doctors, not the cure he needed or deserved. Except for one young psychiatrist on the staff, Mattie was alone in her fight, using her postwar training—and years of nursing hundreds of terrified, combat-fatigued soldiers on the battle-field—to stand her ground.

She knew in her heart that surgery was not the answer, but without any available studies, she was uncertain about using drugs to manage her husband's illness. Every time she saw Mario slipping away, it was her talk therapy that brought him back. By deciding to put Mario on a drug-and-talk-therapy regimen, she was charting new territory with uncertain outcomes.

The decision was finalized after much discussion with Mario at the hospital, when after a few days, he appeared to have regained his mental balance. With Mattie at his side, Mario implored the young psychiatrist to help him prevent any surgeries and to try the new pills instead.

"You know I'm putting my career at risk," the psychiatrist said. "I'm not sure that this is going to work, but I agree that there's got to be a better way to treat you, and I'm willing to go out on a limb."

"Thank you, Doctor," Mattie said. "If we're right about combining drugs with talk therapy, you'll be recognized as a pioneer."

So even at great personal risk, the young psychiatrist agreed to oversee Mario's care, much to the chagrin, yet callous indifference, of his traditionalist superiors. He wrote a prescription for chlorpromazine, then gave it to Mario as soon as it was available. The effect of the drug was quickly apparent as Mario became calmer.

"I don't wantcha t'say anything to the family or the neighbors, 'cept to tell them I was hurt at work," Mario implored Mattie, "Dis is a private thing that ain't nobody else needs t'know about!"

Within a week the combination of Mattie's tender care and Mario's twice-a-day chlorpromazine dose was enough to earn him a discharge from the hospital. Mattie picked up A.J. from Nonna Colucci's house where he had been staying while Mattie tended Mario in the hospital. Honoring Mario's wishes, Mattie told the family and inquisitive neighbors nothing about his psychological trauma and battles, instead letting them know that the docs at the VA had patched up the lacerations from the exploding television tubes and that he was recovering.

He returned to work, mumbled apologies to his coworkers, and told them that the docs gave him some medicine to make him better. One or two remarked to one another that Mario seemed duller than usual. The workers chalked up the incident to Mario being caught off guard, and over time it was forgotten. However, as time passed, Mario retreated more and more into a shell, isolated and interacting only when absolutely necessary for a very few minutes at the beginning and end of each workday.

The chlorpromazine was not a magic cure, as it made Mario less responsive, disconnected. It took several years to find the right balance and dosage.. During that time, Mario's temper flared on several occasions, though the outbursts were made more manageable by the chlorpromazine, Mattie's calm and gentle loving touches, and hours of frank and sometimes disturbing conversations in which he vividly recalled the sights, sounds, and smells of experiences best forgotten.

On Kreskin Avenue, the neighbors left them alone. They knew nothing of the fiercely proud and self-reliant boy, the sensitive jokester, the hapless entrepreneur, the tormented Korean War hero. They did not know of Mattie's struggles to save his soul. The neighbors were completely unequipped to understand his mind's working and the spirit that gave Mario the gift of self-preservation.

The unknown life of the Coluccis was of sufficient mystery to spawn speculation that spiced up the neighborhood conversations. But they knew little of the Mario Colucci they observed, and their beliefs about who and what he was were wrong, even though it took almost fifty years to discover the truth.

PART II

Kreskin Avenue

All Hail The King of Kreskin Avenue

In 1967 Martin Luther King and Bobby Kennedy were still alive. The Beatles, Jimi Hendrix, and Cream released albums now regarded as some of the greatest rock-and-roll music ever written. Military involvement in Vietnam was growing by leaps and bounds, brought into living rooms on a daily basis, yet the horrors of Tet and Khe Sanh were still a year away.

Gas was twenty-three cents a gallon, smokes were thirty cents a pack. Twelve cents bought you the latest Superman comic, and with thirteen empty small pop bottles or five large ones turned in at Joe's Corner Deli, you had enough cash for a giant collector's edition of *Batman* or *Green Lantern*. A dime's worth of penny candy was enough to ruin appetites and make dentists smile.

In 1967, Dutch elm trees stood tall, long-boughed and rough-barked, on narrow strips of land between the sidewalk and the street in front of each two-story upper-and lower-flat house on Kreskin Avenue.

The trees' full and sturdy trunks relinquished their power to massive limbs, then smaller limbs, then finally to green-leafed branches and twigs. Each tree met and touched its sibling on the other side of the street, and together the tall trees wove a graceful and protective canopy stretching the entire block of eighty houses, forty on a side, each separated by little more than the width of a driveway that ended at a detached garage in the rear.

In the summer of 1967 these majestic Dutch elms were dying, but nobody yet knew. Just four years later, Buffalo city workers tasked by weary bureaucrats on the losing end of a war with a microscopic enemy were given the order to take down every Dutch elm tree in the city.

The factories of Lackawanna Steel, General Motors, and scores of other noisy, fire-belching industries in full-tilt, three-shift production dotted the landscape down by the Niagara River and along Lake Erie. Men returned home to Kreskin Avenue grimy after an eight-hour shift, with dirty fingernails, smelling of sour sweat and the nickel beers they tossed down at any one of dozens of local bars that sprouted like weeds throughout the north side of Buffalo.

Angry white and black smokestack plumes created by behemoth factories painted the sky with polluted clouds of majestic proportions and cast the city in dull and dingy tones of gray and brown. It would be less than ten years later that hardened factory workers were told that they had killed Lake Erie and the Niagara River with the toxic byproducts of the cars and girders and thousands of other goods they produced.

Twenty years later these proud men would be brought low by the sting of unemployment and its associated social and economic baggage as they struggled to reconcile what had been with what would never be again. Befuddled by the helplessness of union and government leaders to turn back the hands of time, torn between rage and surrender, they stood paralyzed as the factories that were once at the center of their universe became silent and decaying hulks.

But in 1967 they didn't care, for they couldn't possibly see the future. The decent steady paycheck that produced a manageable lower-middle-class life was a more-than-adequate buttress against the unforeseen and unknown.

Kreskin Avenue was home to a mix of conservative European Jews and faithful Italian Catholics, with a smattering of Ireland's finest—and, thrown in for good measure, one of the three black families in the entire north side of Buffalo. Ethnic lines were visible and impenetrable within the homes but fairly invisible on the street.

Fifteen-year-old Robbie Shumstein's neighbors to the left of his house at 54 Kreskin Avenue, the Kleins, bore the tattoos of Dachau. He was thankful that they rented their lower and rear flats to female college students, who sunbathed in the backyard wearing skimpier and skimpier swimwear as time marched on. To the right of the Shumsteins were the Partonis, whose twin sons, Larry and Guiseppe ("Call me Jesse, goddammit!"), were Robbie's off-and-on best friends.

Directly across the street were the Johnsons. Their daughter, Aurora, was a genius who smashed though color barriers to later become one of the country's foremost oncologists. Their son George, a key member of the Kreskin Krushers, was the second on the block to be killed in Vietnam. They lived below Ralph and Martha Sullivan, a childless middle-aged couple, perhaps the sweetest and gentlest people on the block, but scorned for breaching the color barrier by renting to the Johnsons.

Next to the Johnsons was Rabbi Menachim Grossberg, a widower with an older daughter, Emma, in college, and a son, Moishe, who was Robbie's age. The rabbi was the principal at one of the Hebrew schools where, twice a week after school and on Sunday mornings, Robbie learned the guttural and phonetic vagaries of Hebrew and the fundamentals of Torah.

Fathers came home from work and from the bars tired and hungry. Dinner was always on the table by six o'clock. A stranger walking down Kreskin Avenue exactly at that time could smell an eclectic mix of mouth-watering homemade meals, from roast chicken with potatoes to lasagna made with sauce from tomatoes picked out of the plots of small backyard gardens.

After dinner, fathers living in upper flats retired to their second-story front porches and lower-flatters to concrete stoops that jutted gracelessly from each house. Smoking cigarettes in silent enjoyment in the shade of the Dutch elms, they would watch the neighborhood kids play touch football or kick-the-can or one of dozens of other games on the narrow black asphalt playground that was Kreskin Avenue. Sometimes they would shout a word or two of encouragement for a particularly good play, but they remained outwardly silent and inwardly prideful if their kid happened to be the star of the moment.

Then the fathers would vacate their porches and stoops and gather on the sidewalk in a ritualistic huddle where, with no kids allowed, they would talk of the day's triumphs and disappointments, the latest sports news, and other manly subjects of discourse. They called that "shootin' the bull," and except for the fact that every fourth or fifth word was a curse word, like the all-time favorite, "fuckin' A!," it was nothing more than man gossip, and for eavesdropping neighborhood kids instruction for a lifetime of patois.

Wives would usually flock to the Partonis's backyard where the talk was of shopping, discounts, recipes, and the latest scoops on who was doing what to whom and why and when.

In the summer, at nine o'clock when the streetlights went on, they would bid each other goodbye and return home, the ritual again completed.

Mario Colucci, nicknamed "The King of Kreskin Avenue" by the neighbors, would typically not join the gatherings. Instead he perched low upon his lawn-chair throne, turned his head from side to side, and followed the comings and goings of the neighborhood.

In 1967, the face of The King of Kreskin Avenue— the one that the teenage Robbie and the rest of the neighborhood saw day in and day out—was vapid and uninspiring. Drooping as if in complete surrender to the forces of gravity, his face broadcast a message of dullness, punctuated by his lackluster brown eyes and what appeared to be a permanently etched scowl.

To say that Mario was plain would not do justice to the word *plain*. He occupied a position on the looks scale somewhere between odd and ugly, standing about five-foot-four upon spindly, knobby-kneed legs, and weighing in about 180. Most of his weight cascaded gracelessly in a massive two-fold beer gut hanging over the belt of his drab work pants, usually escaping from beneath the tight, white T-shirts he favored.

His red hair was perpetually greasy, and as if someone had tilted the bowl incorrectly, cut short in the back and straight and long over his forehead and ears. He was rarely seen without his crown—a dirty and battered checkered porkpie hat, now over twenty years old.

He was expressionless, emotionless, and statue-like except for occasional shuffling walks up and down the street. It was easy to understand why neighbors filled their screenplay of his story with innuendo and conjecture. That made it easier to match their sense of superiority to a rationale for their cruel observations and barbs.

"Wonder what the ol' king is up to," neighbors would say within earshot of the kids when they saw him sitting in his lawn chair, unmoving, silent, and watchful.

"Probably thinking up new ways to get rockets to the moon," some would snigger.

"Nah," others would reply in what was the standing joke of the neighborhood, "he's just working up to his next b.m.!"

Then everyone would laugh even though they had heard the same line hundreds of times before.

Robbie never saw Mrs. Colucci participate in any of the nightly neighborhood gabfests. She didn't seem to have any girlfriends, and except for an occasional walk down the street beside The King, was rarely seen at all. Side by side they looked like an exclamation point gone awry as she towered over Mario, stretching skyward, while he looked as if a giant invisible hand was squashing him down.

The sum total of the neighborhood's insights and knowledge of the Coluccis' relationship and marriage was that he met her in the hospital while recovering from severe wounds suffered in Korea and that she was a coal miner's daughter from somewhere in the Midwest who became a combat nurse. What went on behind the closed doors of their flat, the common denominators that hold husbands and wives together, was unknown.

CHAPTER 9

The Shumsteins of Kreskin Avenue

Robbie's parents were second-generation Americans and children of the Depression. His mom, Esther, was the bolder and more vocal parent, quick to criticize at worst and a soft touch at best. A dutiful housewife who kept a kosher kitchen, she was also the keeper of things that needed to be remembered, like when to light the Shabbos candles or the name of her cousin-in-twice-removed on her mother's side. She tended to be overprotective, a fierce defender of the family's health, welfare, and security.

Robbie's father, Abe, a salesman of restaurant supplies, was generally timid but could occasionally be a source of strength and wisdom. He was a champion of education and gave his children a love of reading and a thirst for knowledge, often remarking upon the fact that one of his biggest regrets in life was his lack of formal education.

By the 1960s Abe Shumstein had reached his mid-fifties. His life was ruled by fiscal conservatism born in the Depression, which made it tough for Robbie to cage spare change for a trip to Joe's Corner Grocery.

The Shumsteins' rented upper flat at 54 Kreskin Avenue was modestly appointed and always immaculate. Three bedrooms, a bath, a kitchen, and a living room was the standard layout for every upper and lower flat of the houses on Kreskin avenue. What made the upper flat of 54 Kreskin Avenue special was a front porch covered by a green and gray canvas awning protecting a collection of five orphan pieces of porch furniture. In late fall the awning was rolled up and the furniture was taken to the attic; late the following spring, the awning was unrolled and each piece of furniture was returned to its usual place.

Robbie often heard his mother asking his father why they had to rent instead of buying a place and why they never seemed to have the money to buy, but Robbie was far too young to understand either the intricacies of the family's finances or his father's timidity when it came to spending large sums of money. It was only after Abe died that Esther finally bought the house.

Abe was more than just a little to the right of center in '60s politics as a result of service in World War II, where he saw combat action in Africa and Italy before being wounded and sent home. There was rarely a night he viewed Walter or Chet or David on the evening news and didn't launch a diatribe about "those goddam Commies!"

On rare occasions after a little too much to drink, Robbie's father would sink into his chair, mumbling and cursing in menacing, ugly tones under his breath. "Those fuckin' fascists and fuckin' Nazis and fuckin' murderous bastards need to die painful deaths a thousand times over," he would say to no one in particular.

Abe's indelible experiences in the "Good War," his perceptions of good and evil and of the morality of using of strength to right a wrong, the seeming invincibility of America, and the value of honor and sacrifice were the bedrocks of his fatherhood. But what began as solid foundation turned into quicksand, and what seemed to be impregnable was fissured by cracks where the seeds of his clashes with Robbie's brother, David, began to take root.

The bane of Robbie's life was his little sister, Adrienne, Addie for short. Three years younger, she was a constant source of aggravation, from her pestering, endless questions to a penchant for tattling about the slightest of transgressions. Addie hoped, she told him, that Robbie might be forever banished to some nether region where he would have to face and, of course, be utterly vanquished by the combined forces of all that was evil and unholy.

Robbie bore no remorse whatsoever for satisfying her chocolate addiction with Ex-Lax cupcakes when she was ten nor for his revenge when she was twelve for ratting him out to his parents for stealing a smoke in the backyard. Hanging her two-for-a-buck Woolworth lime-green panties from a hastily constructed flagpole lashed to the middle of the front porch quickly made its way into the lore and legend of Kreskin Avenue.

Robbie's grandmother, Bubbe, and grandfather, Zeydeh, lived just around the corner on Rigby Avenue, in a house that was virtually a carbon copy of the Shumsteins'. They lived in the first-story flat, and above them lived Robbie's cousin Ben, who was a senior at the University of Buffalo, and his father, Uncle Sol Shumstein—two men alone after Aunt Sarah was killed in a traffic accident in 1955. The Shumsteins were a very close-knit extended family, celebrating Jewish holidays and going on vacations together, and it was rare to see a day go by that someone from the family did not end up in the house of the other.

When David was in New York and Chicago in the early and midsixties, Robbie missed him terribly, but Ben was a pretty good substitute, taking Robbie to the movies, or out for a game of catch or roughhousing with him in David's absence.

Zeydeh was a wonderful character with a wealth of stories that Robbie found both horrible and inspirational. He was a pious man who fled Russia as a teen in the winter of 1900 when, according to a story told only occasionally, he beheaded a Cossack officer with his own sword after the Cossack's troops carried out a pogrom that killed Zeydeh's mother, father, and sister and destroyed the little village they lived in.

Zeydeh walked with a limp, the result of a broken hip that had never quite healed properly. "I got dis little gem back in 1933 from being clubbed by strike-breaking thugs when I gots the girls at the pants factory on Broadway to walk out," he told Robbie, David, Ben, and Addie.

Uncle Sol told the kids that in the 1920s Zeydeh was a firebrand, a union organizer attempting to bring his own unique brand of socialism to the fledgling garment industry that had sprung up in the seedy streets and alleys on the city's south side. In a rough voice, harsh from too many years of smoking unfiltered cigarettes, he would always start the broken-hip story the same way:

"You should have seen those *mamzers*, those ass kissers," he would say, sprinkling Yiddish into his heavily accented English. "There was twenty of 'em, but me and the boys gave out as good as we got!"

Even though his thick Yiddish-laced Russian accent was sometimes difficult to understand, the morals of most of his stories were not. On the Sabbath and at every Jewish holiday, he told his family that there was good and evil in the world, that it was harder to take a stand and fight for good than to comply with evil, and that good sometimes demanded sacrifices that did not always lead to fairy-tale endings.

Robbie's brother David was nine years older and his idol, even though David was not above delivering an occasional noogie or wedgie when warranted by time, circumstance, or level of pestering

David was off to New York University in 1961 when Robbie turned nine. David gave him an NYU sweatshirt for his birthday, and Robbie wore it until their mother threw it away, declaring that its odor had reached a level of existence that could only be terminated by residency in the Erie County Landfill.

Once he left for college, David returned home less frequently than anyone in the family wanted. For his siblings, each visit home was accompanied by a great buildup of impatient anticipation, days of joy and laughter while he was there, and a period of grief-like silence when he left.

Just after Robbie turned twelve, David called and asked him to think about a special treat for just the two of them when he came home from New York during winter break of David's senior year.

A few days later, after getting permission to make a long-distance phone call, Robbie called back.

I know just the thing for the two of us," Robbie said excitedly. "Saturday, 7 p.m. War Memorial Auditorium. It's the one and only Bruno Sammartino against Hans 'The Teuton Terror' Schmidt for the WWE World Heavyweight Championship!

How cool is that?"

David was momentarily speechless.

"A wrestling match?" he asked in disbelief. "Hmm. I was thinking more about something like a trip to the science museum followed by a fifteen-cent burger and twelve-cent french fries at some place I heard about called McDonald's."

"Aww, c'mon, David! B-O-R-I-N-G! Don't be a wiener…it's gonna be great, and you're gonna love it!"

One could say that it was the power of brotherly love that overshadowed the power of intelligentsia that day.

"Hmm. Well, if that's what you got your heart set on, far be it from me to crush your dreams. I'll get tickets. And by the way, you're the wiener, not me!"

And what tickets they were! Two rows back from ringside where every body collision, every grunt, every slam on the mat made the hair on the backs of the boys' necks rise and, from time to time, involuntarily shutter their eyes. Even the taunts and insults hurled back and forth between the combatants were as clear as day. All of Robbie's favorites—Bobo Brazil, The Sheik, Gorilla Monsoon, Haystacks Calhoun—heroes that heretofore he saw only once a week on the small rabbit-eared black-and-white television in the Shumstein's living room—were now mashing and smashing one another a mere few feet away.

David watched with an air of nonchalance and detachment, as if the experience were an experiment concocted for an NYU sociology class. Robbie yelled, screamed, and enthusiastically leaped to his feet with every takedown. Punching David's shoulder, he'd ask, "Didja see that? Didja see that?" when a wrestler executed his signature move.

But the championship event saved the best for last when, before Schmidt lost the bout in a spectacularly dramatic fashion, the dastardly Nazi-wannabe Teutonic villain bloodied the champ with an obvious cheap shot. Bruno staggered around the ring and gushed what seemed to be a gallon of blood from a cut on his forehead that thoroughly splashed the fans sitting in ringside seats, including Robbie and David.

They were covered in a sticky, red, gooey concoction that looked exactly like blood but tasted suspiciously like chocolate syrup. They conspiratorially agreed to not wash the mess off at the arena so they could wear their masks of gore like badges of honor—a bond of brotherhood worth double the price of the admission ticket.

When they got home and nonchalantly said hello to their mother, she nearly fainted.

"Oy. Oy. Oy vey!! What's with the blood?" she cried, her voice rising toward hysteria. "Are you hurt? Do we need to get to the hospital?

"Abe! Abe!" she called. "Hurry up and get your jacket on and start up the car!"

They just laughed.

David wiped his finger on Robbie's face, licked, and smacked his lips, making a yum-yum sound. They left their mother in dazed disbelief, the brothers in a state of collaborative silence that was never broken.

By the time Robbie turned fifteen, Dr. David, as he made Robbie call him, ("Almost a Doc-tuh, but not yet," Robbie would taunt back) was a graduate of the master's program in philosophy at the University of Chicago and nearing completion of his PhD. Wiry, bearded, and gifted, he possessed an awesome ability to craft ideas into words he could wield like a weapon as sharp as any spear or as palliative and calming as any sedative.

By 1967 their relationship had grown from one of conspirators-in-wrestling to one of admirer/admiree. David treated Robbie like an adult, sharing—or at least attempting to share—some of the things he had been learning and observing. That didn't mean he was not above giving Robbie a noogie or wedgie when warranted.

The Shumstein family, like others on Kreskin avenue, existed within its own universe, replete with its share of competition between the good and the bad, the light and the dark, and the positive and the negative, co-existing side by side yet separated by sharp boundaries.

None of these boundaries was sharper or more divisive than that between David and his father about a war in small, strange country more than eighty-seven hundred miles away from Kreskin Avenue on the other side of the world, where, by 1967, tens of thousands of combatants and civilians had been killed or wounded.

By the end of 1967, however, Robbie and the entire Shumstein family were all of one mind about the Vietnam War.

CHAPTER 10

The Kreskin Avenue Krushers

The tale of how the Kreskin Avenue boys became the Krushers is lost in the fog of time.

It wasn't a name passed down through generations of neighborhood kids. It wasn't the result of manly dispositions or imposing physiques. It certainly wasn't a product of testosterone-powered prowess withstanding the test of time and legends about conquests with the girls in the neighborhood. Truth be told, the teenage temptresses of Kreskin Avenue tended to either ignore or taunt the boys with insults.

So the Krushers becoming the Krushers just happened, but that didn't make it any less a rally point for the dozen or so teenage boys on the block. It was no secret, especially to them, that the Kreskin Avenue Krushers were invincible. The Vietnam War did not concern them. The onrushing tide of social change was of little concern. They were too young to understand the impact on their lives of the assassinations of John F. Kennedy and Malcolm X.

They were infinitely more concerned about what the Yankees were doing or whether the Bills were going to bring home another AFL championship. But the latest overseas casualty statistics and creeping social and economic forces were silently and inevitably changing their lives.

Robbie's best friend, Bruce Lucas, was the acknowledged genius of the Krushers. Bruce was the only kid on Kreskin Avenue, and maybe even in the whole north side of Buffalo, who owned the awe-inspiring Lionel Porter Chemcraft Chemistry Lab This behemoth had a working blowtorch, scales, small glass containers of chemicals including sodium ferrocyanide and calcium hypochlorite, and—just in case those and the other dozen or so toxic chemicals weren't enough—you could get poisoned from exposure to samples of radioactive uranium ore included with every kit.

In the Kreskin Avenue neighborhood, the concept of a working mother was foreign, although some moms picked up extra cash working part time at the A&P or selling cosmetics door to door. Tony Baratino's mom was one of these, and Tony doubled as shortstop and as his mom's delivery and pickup schlepper. His pals delighted in teasing him whenever they saw him on his bike, delivery basket piled high with bag after bag of perfumes, lipsticks, eye shadows, and other assorted goo, making his way to yet another cosmetics-deprived housewife.

"Hey, Avon boy," they would chime in unison from the stoop, "I got stinky pits. Got anything in them bags to make stinky pits go away?"

Tony's revenge on the Krushers for insulting his integrity and manhood was enviable. One of his regular deliveries was to Mrs. Konstakous—tall, long-legged, short-tight-skirted, big-breasted, curly-blond-haired, sparkling-blue-eyed, thirty-something Mrs. Konstakous, whose husband never seemed to be home and who exuded an aura of sexuality somewhere north of Annette Funicello and south of Raquel Welch.

While a normal delivery should have taken Tony three to five minutes, tops, a delivery to Mrs. Konstakous took him thirty minutes. No matter how hard they pressed or how cleverly the Krushers posed their queries, Tony never, ever revealed the secrets of the lost twenty-seven minutes or the reason for his be-atific, post-delivery countenance.

Catholic brethren suffered for their religion by attending Sunday Mass and twice-weekly religious instruction. Back in the day, that meant that Young Commanders for Christ and Little Flowers of Christ disappeared from school about 2:30 p.m., hurrying into massive structures of stone and stained glass with imposing names like Saint Mary's of the Immaculate Divine or scary names like Holy Blood Kingdom of Christ. God's words began promptly at three, and woe to those not seated and ready for another step on their spiritual journey.

So on Mondays and Wednesdays, teachers had to come up with ways to engage half the school, survivors of the mass exodus, until the 3:30 bell announced the end of another day of eager minds soaking up the *veritas* of 1967.

Sundays included an hour or so of Mass, complete with Sunday-best clothing, and an early family dinner with relatives aplenty. Things got back to normal on Kreskin Avenue about four in the afternoon, when polished leather shoes vanished and dirty, scuffed sneakers reappeared.

As goes the balance of justice, the Princes (and Princesses) of Judea were not exempt from religious instruction; they attended Hebrew school on Tuesdays and Thursdays from four to six. There, at synagogues sprinkled throughout the neighborhood, they learned Torah, Jewish history, rituals, and dogma, and reasons for the dozens of Jewish holidays that took them out of public school for a day or more, much to their joy and to the jealousy of their *goyish* friends, even though it meant what seemed to be an eternity of hours trying to sit still during services.

On Friday nights, Robbie's mother would welcome the Sabbath in traditional ways with food, blessings, and Shabbos candles nestled in silver candlesticks that were her mother's mother's. Occasionally she would grab Robbie and Addie and hustle off to Friday night services.

On Saturday mornings Robbie would put on suit and tie, grab his *tallis* bag, and peek inside to make sure his favorite yarmulke was there. Then he would get Zeydeh, and arm in arm for support, escort him to the synagogue.

Robbie could always get a story or two along the way and never interrupted even if he had heard the same story dozens of times before. Zeydeh often told the one about how, in the small *shtetl* where he lived before coming to America, Zeydeh trained a cat to ride on top of a goat trained to ride on top of a mule, which he did just to impress Bubbe's father so he could begin courting her.

Every once in a while, the story would change a little bit. Perhaps instead of a cat, it was a mouse, or instead of a mule, it was a zebra. Robbie believed that every change made the stories better.

It is safe to say that for Princes, Princesses, Commanders, and Little Flowers combined, it was a toss-up, at best, whether the total amount of time spent in pews or receiving religious instruction was successful in moving them to a deeper spirituality or closer to an understanding of God's mysteries.

The Kreskin Krushers were a socioeconomic and demographic mirror of their neighborhood. They accepted the fact that differences of faith existed, and since each Krusher could at best bring only a modicum of faith to the table, the differences were rooted in dogma.

The unity or tripartite nature of God. Rosaries and crucifixes or mezuzahs and tallises. Old Testament or New Testament. Priests or Rabbis. Matzo-ball soup or pasta fagioli. Friday's fish fry or gefilte fish from a jar.

At ages fourteen and fifteen the Krushers could trade barbs and insults and belittle one another's religion without harsh words or fisticuffs. Nobody was afraid of getting beaten up, not only because the Krushers were a fifty-fifty mix of Catholics and Jews and evenly matched in size and strength, but because they were friends.

That was going to change in an unexpected way in the late spring.

CHAPTER 11

"WHOOP WHOOP"

The King and Mattie had one child, a son named Andrew James, whom they called A.J. He had the great misfortune of embodying the worst aspects of his parent's genetic contributions to his being. By the time he turned sixteen in 1967, A.J. was bulky, standing six-foot-four and going close to two hundred eighty pounds.

The deck was stacked against A.J. because he suffered from a severe case of Tourette's syndrome, expressed as a motor tic that caused him to involuntarily shrug his shoulder and contort his face and a vocal tic that made him helplessly whoop and shout a wide variety of obscenities.

Tourette's made A.J.'s life a living hell. His outbursts at school were not handled well by teachers ill-equipped to deal with his disruptions. His classmates considered him to be slow and were not kind in making their feelings known. His imposing size frightened people at first until he abruptly ticced or whooped or let fly with a string of obscenities.

Then they laughed.

At him, not with him.

A.J. was an average student and, despite his appearance, he was sensitive, gentle, and altogether much too trusting. He wasn't cut out for college, and he was not any more dim-witted than the average kid.

He knew he wasn't quite normal but didn't know how he got his "condition," as his mother would say. He didn't know when an outburst was about to happen, he didn't know how to control it, and he didn't know how to stop it, but he did learn to not show that he cared when he saw pointed fingers, looks of disapproval, and small titters that led to barely controlled laughter.

It was different on his insides.

"Hey, Ma, WHOOPWHOOP SHIT," he would complain to his mother from time to time with visibly hurt feelings, "how come those kids are always HEEP HEEP HOOP makin' fun of me? I just wanna play with 'em fer a bit."

A.J. accepted the stares and hostile remarks with subdued grace. He was desperate for the acceptance he hardly ever got.

When A.J. was eleven, his fifth-grade teacher's complaints about A.J. reached a crescendo, and Mattie was called to the school for a talk with the principal.

"Mrs. Colucci, we had another incident in class today with A.J.," he began nervously. "His...ahh...condition got out of control, and there was a near riot in the classroom. It required several teachers to restore order.

"For everybody concerned," he continued, "and I've made this point to you several times over the years, I think it's best that we move A.J. to the Thomas Johnson School for Special Students where his needs can better be served."

"Is he behind in his work?" Mattie asked.

"Well, no."

"Has he failed any tests?"

"Umm. Not that I'm aware of."

"Got into any fights or altercations that he started?"

"Uh...I don't believe so."

"Then, Mr. Principal, here's my take," she said, steely-eyed and firm of voice. "The problem here is not A.J. The problem here is you, your staff, and your inability to understand and deal with him. The problem here is that you're failing A.J. Part of that failure is not educating his teachers and classmates on Tourette's. They need to understand, not fear or ridicule. The problem here is that you've turned an opportunity into a battle.

"We will not move A.J. to Thomas Johnson unless forced by law," she continued, "and should that happen, get ready for the fight of your life. I'll be protecting my son like a mother bear protects her cub."

Because his teachers seemed unwilling or unable to give A.J. the extra attention he needed with his schoolwork and since Mattie and Mario wanted to help him build friendships, Mario came up with the idea of a tutor.

It was Mattie's particular idea to hire Robbie Shumstein, who was a few months shy of this sixteenth birthday. She didn't know him very well, but from time to time, she saw him sitting on his porch reading by himself or to his younger sister. And on those rare occasions when A.J. was included in the games of the neighborhood, Mattie never saw Robbie make fun of him.

Mattie walked to the Shumsteins' house to ask Robbie's parents about giving him a job as A.J.'s tutor.

"A.J. needs help with his homework," she began, "and I'm hopeful that Robbie may be the right boy for the job."

Robbie's mother spoke up. "Robbie's a smart boy, always getting good grades, and always doing his homework! But isn't your son, ah, a little bit slow? Doesn't he need special help?"

"I'm not sure Robbie is equipped for that," his father chimed in.

"You need to understand that A.J. is not slow or retarded, even though it may seem so," Mattie responded. "He's got a problem called Tourette's syndrome that makes him act the way he does, but once you look past that, you'll see that he's just as smart and just as willing to learn as any kid in the neighborhood."

She went on to explain more about A.J.'s affliction and her desire to see him happier on his inside than what others saw on his outside.

"Why don't we give it a try?" she asked, smiling. "And if it doesn't work out, no hard feelings."

Mattie got the Shumsteins' blessing but no guarantee that Robbie would take the job. In fact, upon hearing about it from his parents, Robbie only hesitantly agreed to meet with the Coluccis.

Mattie welcomed him into their house for the very first of what were to be many visits. A.J.'s impossibly wide gap-toothed smile and the smell of freshly baked cookies softened Robbie's defenses.

"WHOOP WHOOP! BIGASSBIGASBIGASS!" A.J. shouted when he saw Robbie. "I heard you're gonna make me smarter, right? HAHOOP? Are ya gonna do it? WHOOP WHOOP!"

"That's the plan," Robbie answered warily.

"YEAH! WHOOP WHOOP," A.J. added. "But you gotta watch out that ya don't get too fat from eatin' all of Ma's cookies when ya come over!"

After learning more about A.J. and the truth of his condition, intellect, and capabilities, Robbie reluctantly agreed to take the job of tutoring A.J. in math and reading for fifty cents an hour. He told Mattie and Mario that the couple of extra dollars a week meant he might realize his dream of becoming a rock star as each weekly paycheck would bring him that much closer to marching into Sears on Main Street and slapping down $169.95 plus tax for the Sears Silverstone electric guitar with a built-in case amplifier, cord, pick, chord charts, and *How to Play Guitar* 45 rpm record.

The job lasted through the end of high school, and Robbie was a big reason why A.J. never failed a test or was held back a grade on his way to a high school diploma. Over time, Mattie beamed at the special relationship Robbie had with A.J. and then with her and Mario.

The parents would sit in the kitchen drinking coffee, listening in while A.J. and Robbie sat at the dining room table, books piled high, next to a plate of cookies that never failed to disappear by the end of a tutoring session. Sometimes Mario and Mattie laughed, as quietly as possible, when Robbie got flustered trying to explain to A.J. why problems in algebra always used X and Y instead other values like P or C. Sometimes they smiled pridefully when A.J. managed to flawlessly read through a difficult passage without a physical or vocal tic or was able to articulate why a historical event was important. And sometimes after the session, Robbie would sit with Mario and Mattie, talking about their son's efforts or an upcoming test, or to make sure they got A.J. to finish all his homework.

"Yer doin' a helluva job with my boy," Mario told him one day, with Mattie nodding in agreement. "And me and Mattie 'preciate everything.

"But if you was expectin' a raise," he grinned, "forgeddaboutit! I ain't takin' on annuder job so's I can pay you more so's you and my kid can laugh yer Tom Sawyer reading asses off!"

A.J. was not a member of the Krushers, but it was easy to see that he desperately wanted to be. If they were an odd man out or needed another body to play a game, they called on A.J. At best, he served as a large protective obstruction or an imposing blocking force. His funny gap-toothed smile quickly flashed whenever he was asked to join.

The neighbors seldom saw Mattie out of the house except for those rare occasions when the Krushers had a need for A.J. and asked him to join in a game. Standing at The King's side, a hand resting lightly on his shoulder, she would watch for a few silent minutes before disappearing back into their downstairs flat, leaving her husband alone on his lawn-chair throne.

So, when the Krushers called on A.J. to play touch football in the street, he was enthusiastic about the opportunity but seemingly oblivious to his real role as both an unmovable object and a source of entertainment.

"Haaaa WHOOOOOP WHOOP WHOOP WHOOP! SHITSHIT! TIT TIT! WHOOP WHOOP! Sure, I'll play!"

Then, ticcing and shrugging and dipping his shoulder, he would join the Krushers on the street. Being young teens, they did not quite have the sensitivity of Dear Abby and at times could not help but break into muffled snickers, then a few chuckles, and finally full-scale riotous laughter as A.J. would stand in the middle of the street, shrugging, whooping, and urging, "WHOOPOOP! MAWF! MAWF! C'mon, fellas, let's play us some ball!"

And they would play ball, and just about every time A.J. ticced physically or vocally, they would laugh. For some like Robbie, it wasn't a laughter of cruelty, it was a laughter of exuberance at A.J.'s sheer enthusiasm and excitement that made him shrug and whoop even more, making the Krushers laugh harder.

But for some Krushers it was a laugh of cruelty and derision. Their laughter reflected how superior they felt, and truth be told, it was an echo of their parents' perceptions of A.J. To them he was dim-witted and an oddity to be observed, instead of a young boy with a devastating disorder whose brain was ruled by tiny neurological hiccups. A.J. reveled in the limelight. At these moments he believed his affliction was an asset, not a liability, and he had no qualms about capitalizing upon it.

Maybe best of all, his antics and the Krushers' laughter made his father smile, briefly. In those moments The King turned into Mario.

PART III
Directions of a Moral Compass

CHAPTER 12

Virgil Virgins 54, Kreskin Krushers 21

The Krushers had arranged to play a game of tackle football against a team from Virgil Street that they called the Virgil Virgins—which they were to the last man—a full eleven-on-eleven game, with all the equipment that could be mustered. Nobody had or could afford real uniforms, yet the ragtag collection of helmets and shoulder pads the Krushers wore made even the puniest look massive and impressive. Proud of a team that featured George Johnson at running back, Jesse Partini at quarterback, and Robbie at tight end, the Krushers hadn't lost a game in close to two years.

This wasn't organized, official, sanitized league tackle football; this was pure and unadulterated sandlot football. Coaches or refs or rules or scheduled practices and games were unnecessary. Parents didn't need to take off work to schlep their precious cargo all over the place, and they never organized a demanding schedule of responsibility for halftime snacks or after-game treats. No lawyers postured behind waivers of release, nor did insurance agents hope to make a buck or two on liability policies. Nope, it was generally a word-of-mouth thing where a guy on one block challenged a guy on another block and agreed on a time and place for combat.

The Krushers' home turf was the practice field at the Sherman A. Foster School for Boys, a prestigious academy for the male scions of Buffalo's upper-crust families. Not only did the school have a stadium, it also had a full-length practice field, which the faculty was kind enough to let the neighborhood kids use when it was unoccupied by the powerful high school team.

There were two options for getting to the field. The first was a fifteen-minute walk or five-minute bike ride up Linthen Avenue, and then just past the overpass on Kelvin Street, a hop onto a trash strewn path through the woods to the practice field. The second option meant running like hell though the backyard of one of the houses on Linthen, hopping a fence, climbing up and over a railroad embankment and down the other side. With that option a Krusher could be at the field in about forty seconds. Although the embankment held three of the most active tracks in the city, it was the preferred route of the Krushers and a continuing topic of discussion in each Krusher household.

With her infamous evil eye just waiting to be unleashed, Robbie's mother would sweetly ask, "So my little Robbela…you aren't hopping the tracks to get to the field, are you?"

"No, Mama, that's dangerous."

Then, in a slightly harder voice, she'd say, "You know about that poor boy that got run over by a train and lost both of his legs?"

"Yes, Mama. You've told me about a million times."

And with a thunderous conclusion, she would order, "So look me in the eye"—*Auughh*! said the little voice in Robbie's head—"and tell me you're a good boy and you're riding around to the field, right?"

"Yes, Mama, that's right."

Then, carrying his equipment, Robbie would kiss his mama goodbye and join up with a couple of other Krushers. With a quick glance to make sure that no one was watching, they'd run like hell through the backyard of one of the houses on Linthen and up and over the embankment and be at the field in forty seconds. Robbie was, however, somewhat respectful to his mama in that he looked both ways before scrambling across the railroad tracks.

But that one Saturday in May of 1967, courtesy of his younger sister, Robbie was laid up in the house with a case of chicken pox. The Krushers were going to have to do battle without him. Short one man, with the pride of Kreskin Avenue and their winning streak on the line, they had no recourse other than to forfeit or to ask A.J. if he wanted to play.

"Are ya sure ya want me t'play ?" he asked when Joe and Bruce came knocking at the door. "WHOOP WHOOP!"

"Sure. Robbie got ahold of a case of chicken pox and can't make it, so we're short a man. How 'bout it, Mario, can A.J. play with us?" they pleaded.

The King looked at the two boys suspiciously and told A.J. to go back into his room to get the equipment he had never really used before.

"Lemme talk with youse fer a minute before I let A.J. go," Mario said, using a voice of parental concern. "You boys lookin' fer some entertainment, or are ya gonna take care of my boy?" The King stood blocking the doorway, his hand rubbing the stubble on his chin.

"No sir! We'll take care a him real good. Honest!"

"Now you boys know that he ain't never played this kinda football before, don'cha?"

They nodded in agreement.

"And you ain't gonna let him get hurt, are ya?"

They shook their heads. "No."

"Are ya gonna hop the tracks or go the long way?" Mario asked, wavering on the doorstep of permission. "I ain't gonna let him go if yer gonna hop the tracks."

They looked at each other, then at The King, and slowly shook their heads in agreement. "Aw, c'mon, Mario, we ain't gonna hop the tracks with A.J.! Honest!"

From the back of the house, they could hear whooping, sounds of clothing and shoes being thrown around, and boxes crashing to the floor. A minute or two later A.J. appeared, holding a pair of shiny new shoulder pads and a cracked, well-worn, and old-style leather helmet that had gone out of favor back in the early 1950s.

"Found it! HOOPHOOP. PISSNPOOP. PISSNPOOP. PISSNPOOP!" A.J. shouted enthusiastically. "Lookit this, guys. It ain't hardly ever been used!"

True to their promise to The King, they took the long way around to the field where the other Krushers were assembled and in the process of putting on their equipment. They greeted A.J. enthusiastically, and Bruce and Joe helped him put on and lace up his shoulder pads. Then a couple of other Krushers helped in a monumental struggle to pull A.J.'s sweatshirt over his head and down over his pads. When they were done and after A.J. jammed the old leather helmet down on his head, he became an awesome, hulking man-child-beast. He towered over everybody on the field, looking like a Visigoth ready for battle and pillage.

If he hadn't started shrugging and whooping and saying things like "FARTY. FART. FART. FART. WHOOP WHOOP," the entire Virgil Street team would have turned tail and run.

But exposed to A.J. and his utterances for the first time, the Virgil Street team was not kind.

"Hey, who's the monster?"

"What gives with those noises an' stuff he's makin'?"

"Hey, is he some kinda retard or somethin'? He's not gonna hurt us, is he?"

It wasn't more than ten seconds into the game before the Virgil team discovered that A.J. was, well, A.J. Slow, oafish, and confused, he was clearly out of his place among the twenty or so other boys, all of whom had visions of a future in the National Football League. The Krushers kicked off, and the ball sailed down the field and into the arms of the Virgil team's star player, Vinny Turangelo, who, incidentally, would go on to become the Mayor of Buffalo some twenty-five years later.

As the two teams ran head-on toward each other for the first monumental clash of the game, A.J. was left some twenty yards behind, huffing and puffing and struggling to catch up. When he finally reached the point of contact, a player a foot shorter and 150 pounds lighter immediately leveled him with a solid, legal block, unceremoniously dumping him on his behind, where he landed with a whoosh and ground-shaking thump. The block was enough to spring Vinny, who ran unmolested the rest of the way down the field, for the first score of the game.

To the accompaniment of cheers and congratulatory back slaps, the comparatively tiny Virgil Street player jumped up and down with unbridled glee. "Hey! Lookit that! I killed the Hulk!"

For the Krushers and A.J., the rest of the game went downhill. The Virgil team exploited every possible opportunity after quickly perceiving that A.J. was significantly more liability than asset. On offense, they ran their running plays directly at A.J.; on defense, they aimed their backfield charges through him. Instead of the solid dam they expected from the Krushers' reputation, they found a sieve.

As bad as the day was for the Krushers, A.J. seemed singularly unconcerned. No matter how hard he was dumped or how vicious and intense the opposing team's insults became, his enthusiasm never wavered. He seemed totally oblivious to the dejected and disappointed looks of his teammates and their slow but steady decline of spirit as the game marched on.

His affectations quickly led to embarrassment for the team. With each tic they became increasingly unsympathetic and hostile. Even with valiant efforts by George Johnson and the Partoni twins, the Krushers were doomed. They lost the game 54 to 21, the most lopsided defeat they had ever experienced. The Virgil Street team, by virtue of their well-earned victory, tossed a barrage of insults and taunts at the dejected Krushers as they left the field in high spirits.

"Nice game, fellas," scoffed Vinny before hopping on his bike with the rest of his gang. Laughing, he aimed one final slur at the dejected team: "Let's do it again real soon and don't forget t'bring the Hulk with ya so's we can give ya another real good ass-whuppin'!"

Sweaty, dirt-streaked, bruised, and covered with a score of cuts and abrasions, the Krushers left the field to sit under the shade of the trees lining the railroad embankment. They removed their helmets, disheartened, slamming them on the ground. They pushed the sweaty, matted hair out of their eyes and began pulling off their grimy, torn shirts and reeking shoulder pads.

A.J. sat by himself to the side, quite pleased that "the fellas" had asked him to play and proud of the fact that he had played the whole game. Whether the Krushers won or lost was of no concern, for scores or records held little meaning. The fact that his performance was one of the key reasons for the loss was of no importance. He was proud of himself. He felt a part of the gang and could not see the darkening storm clouds.

"Waa HOOP HOOP!" he gleefully shrieked, "we sure showed FUCKYOUFUCKYOU those guys, din't we! That'll teach'm t'mess with the Krushers!"

The Partoni brothers looked at each other with disgust. Bruce and Joe were muttering angrily beneath their breath. George Johnson, incensed by the Virgil team's racial epithets, was enraged. Johnny Tabone, Joe Vitelli, and Stan Hershowitz looked at A.J. with abject contempt.

While they didn't have a specific plan in mind, their separate dark thoughts seemed to coalesce into one consciousness and one collective thought of revenge. Combined thoughts turned into even darker action when an opportunity suddenly presented itself.

A.J. struggled to lift his sweatshirt over his head, a task made difficult by his bulk, the tight fabric stretched to the tearing point by the dimensions of his shoulder pads, and the fact that he had forgotten to remove his helmet. He managed to get only as far as pulling the bottom of the sweatshirt up and over his head, where it got stuck, and he fell to the ground wrestling with the entrapping garment. This made him struggle even more, exacerbating his dilemma.

Helpless, he cried out, "Hey, fellas! Help me, wouldja? WHOOPWHOOP. I'm stuck in here!"

As the Krushers surrounded A.J., they weren't laughing at what ordinarily would have been a scene that would have had them in stitches. Instead, Stan and Bruce jumped on the chest of the helpless and headless A.J., while Bruce and George pinned his arms over his head and to the ground. The Partonis then proceeded to remove A.J.'s sneakers and socks, while Stan unbuttoned his jeans and began to pull down his zipper.

"Hey! Hey! WHOOOP HOOP HOOP. What're you guys FUCKYOUFUCKYOUFUCKYOU doin'? HELP! HELP! HOOP HOOP!" A.J.'s voice rose in timbre and pitch until he was screaming in a high, girlish voice, "Lemme alone! HELP HELP HELP! Aw c'mon. HOOP HOOP. DAMMITSHITSHIT. Please don't do this. Somebody HELLLLPPPPMEEEEEEEE! HELLLLPPPPMEEEEEEEE!"

The gang ignored A.J. even when he started to cry—softly at first and then in great uncontrollable sobs. They tugged at the cuffs of his pants, slowly jerking them over his hips, then past his knees, and finally off his legs. A.J. was left in only his underpants, trapped beneath his sweatshirt and a T-shirt that had traveled up to reveal a soft tire of baby fat surrounding his middle.

There they left him, dropping his sneakers, socks, and pants on the railroad tracks as they made their way up and over, then down the embankment on their way back home.

One of the school's ground crew found A.J. that way about an hour later, still trapped in his sweatshirt. He was sobbing and screaming for help and shrugging and whooping away with unparalleled intensity. The groundskeeper cut the shirt off A.J. to release him and was both revolted and immensely saddened by the sight of the helmeted, dirty, tear-streaked face of the man-child he freed. Calming the boy down as best as he could, he borrowed a car from a fellow groundskeeper and took A.J. home.

A.J., still crying, scrambled out of the car carrying his shoulder pads and wearing only his dirty T-shirt and underpants, yet he remembered to thank the groundskeeper for helping him. He ran past The King sitting on his throne and into the house, slamming the door behind him. The King's initial befuddlement at seeing his filthy, crying, almost-naked son streak past him was replaced with a burning, seething anger, and he quickly jumped up and ran after A.J. into the house.

The Krushers hadn't yet returned home. Instead, they made their way to Joe the Grocer's where they combined the change they had to buy a few bottles of pop. Leaning or sitting against the wall of the grocery store, at first they laughed when they thought about what they had just done to A.J. As they reflected a bit more, a few of them started to feel bad, and several Krushers had tears beginning to well up.

A few of the hard cases—the Partonis and Stan Hershowitz—rationalized that A.J. deserved what he got for losing the game and blemishing their record. One or two others nodded, more in acknowledgment of the statement than in agreement; others said nothing, staring at the top of their sneakers. By ones and twos they slowly peeled off and made their way back home, hoping against all hope that they could return unseen, especially by The King.

As is the way of teenage boys, the incident would soon have been forgotten, or at least relegated to the memory pile where stories always begin with, "Do you remember when…"

But that night, after suppers had been eaten and cigarettes smoked on porches, and after all the neighborhood parents had assembled in front of the Baritino house to look at their new aluminum siding, they noticed that The King's throne sat silent and vacant.

One pundit remarked that The King must be inside his house polishing his crown. Another said that it must be time for the monthly royal bath. Yet another remarked that a regal b.m. must be in the process, and because it completed the time-worn joke, everybody laughed.

Then The King appeared with Mattie at his side. But he was somehow different from The King they knew or thought they knew.

His stride was direct and purposeful, his eyes were flashing and hard, and his face a mask of chiseled stone. He was still wearing the familiar porkpie hat, but his

T-shirt and well-worn work pants were clean and crisp. He appeared tall and manly, and at that moment, in that place, he wasn't The King and he wasn't Mario—he was something greater than the neighborhood had seen before.

Even Robbie's mother gasped when she saw him break into the middle of the crowd, triggering a response that pinballed from husband to wife and then from person to person until the last snatches of conversation and laughter died away. He stood in the center of the crowd, Mattie standing slightly behind and to the left of him, silently weeping.

For a few long, agonizing moments he didn't say anything. He just turned slowly around, looking into the eyes and souls of those assembled. Nobody offered a greeting. The envelope of silence intensified as birds and insects abruptly terminated their evening song.

"I want t'tell youse a story," he began in a strong and unwavering, yet subdued voice.

It was a love story. It began with the birth of his son and was a tale of joy, disappointment, acceptance, and grace. When he talked of protecting a child from all dangers both physical and mental, the assembled parents nodded their heads in agreement, although they still had no explanation for The King's sudden and dramatic appearance. As he described pride—the pride a parent gets from the accomplishments of his children—a murmur went through the crowd as each acknowledged and then began to offer a tale of their own, which The King swiftly silenced with a hard, directed gaze. He talked to the still-confused assembly of A.J.'s affliction and of the Colucci family's heartaches, and briefly they all shared a moment of collective empathy.

But when he talked about what their children had done to A.J. that afternoon, they shouted back at him in disappointment and anger. "NO! NO!" they cried, voices rising, all bidding to make themselves heard. "Not our kid, not our son…that's barbaric…he'd never do a thing like that!" And what began as a normal evening of friendly conversation turned into a night of embarrassment and anguish, as the unwritten axiom that the child was a reflection of the parents assaulted carefully maintained family reputations.

In the middle of the maelstrom, The King and Mattie, hand in hand, simply turned and walked away without saying anything further.

That evening, Robbie's parents came home from the confrontation angry and upset. Robbie's dad slapped his forehead and lapsed into Yiddish:

"*Oy g'vald*! These little pisspot bastards you call your friends, Robbie? They're *meshugeh* crazy, and you shouldn't play with them anymore! They're dung! The goyim maybe I can understand, but the Jewish boys? It's a shame and a disgrace!"

"'Zactly what are you talking about?" Robbie asked, dumbfounded.

He didn't like their answer, or what he gleaned over the next several days from the half dozen or so opinionated stories offered by his Krusher friends

"You should have seen The King, Robbela," added his mother. "I never saw him like that before. He was different, powerful, not like the *shmendrik* we see on his throne. I'm still upset—that poor family, that poor young scatterbrain. That family gets joy from that child. *Oy*, what those boys did! They should all go to hell!"

What would I have done if I had been there? he thought. *Would I have participated? Would I have tried to stop them? Would I have just watched and been silent?*

While Robbie had a hope that perhaps the whole incident would be forgotten, fading into just an embarrassing memory, he knew what had been done was wrong. He had an overwhelming premonition that the proverbial poop was going to hit the fan.

Hell would be too nice a word to describe the next week in the households of the Krushers who lost to the Virgil Virgins on that Saturday. In several flats more than just words were exchanged as this was in the days before child psychologists and other certified experts had discarded the old parenting guidance of "spare the rod, spoil the child."

Tony went to church on Sunday with a handprint etched quite visibly on his face. It was a week before George Johnson could sit down without pain, and Stan Hershowitz had to wear long pants for nearly a month before the welts on the backs of his legs disappeared. The Partoni brothers had a cherished week at Crystal Beach taken away, and Johnny Tabone, sporting an ugly black-and-blue bruise under his right eye, spent every single spare minute of the next month painting fences and his parents' garage.

For the most part the Krushers were good boys— not quite angels but certainly not mean-spirited juvenile delinquents. It is an inevitable fact of nature that teenage boys will get in trouble, often of the spur-of-the-moment variety. A mental fog descends, temporarily extinguishing the mores of church and home, and at those moments they believe and act as if they exist under a magic shield protecting them from discovery and sanction. Sometimes the magic shield works, and other times it fails miserably, which is when they discover the hard rain of parental wrath and sometimes an intervention by the local constabulary.

Most of the team felt bad—really bad—about what they'd done to A.J. Over the next week many of them came knocking on the Coluccis' door to make sincere, heartfelt apologies. Bruce gave A.J. a brand-new baseball, Joe Vitelli brought and gave his collection of marbles, Tony Baratino proffered his collection of Spiderman comic books, and so on down the line.

"They were cool," Tony told Robbie a little while after his act of contrition. "I expected the worst, but A.J. only said 'Thanks, big guy,' and then he shrugged and jerked and woot wooted some more and tol' me that he accepted my 'pology.

"And get this—he told me to fergit about it an' said we could still be friends an' that he knew we didn't mean anything by it an' anytime he was asked, he was ready t'play ball with us again."

Not all of the Krushers felt the same.

The Partonis and Stan Hershowitz were particularly bitter, telling everyone they could that their punishments far outweighed the crime. They were sullen and morose, and even after being commanded by their parents to make a direct apology, refused to do so but swore they had. Instead, they vowed revenge upon the Coluccis, and although they did not have a specific plan in mind at that time, they were of a single mind.

From previous peccadilloes and subsequent punishments they had experienced, each Krusher knew time would eventually be the great healer. Robbie had to promise his parents that he would try to keep away from "those boys," even though they knew and he knew that this would most likely not happen. A few days later he was well enough to sit out on the upstairs porch but still couldn't have visitors and was lying in a lounge chair finishing off Asimov, bundled up like the Pillsbury Doughboy.

The King was out taking a walk when he saw Robbie on the porch. Their gazes met for a few seconds before he continued on his way. Something happened in those fleeting seconds when their gazes silently locked. Robbie's was a gaze of empathetic sadness; Mario's contained a single, penetrating question: *What would you have done, Robbie, if you were there?*

Robbie knew what the answer was supposed to be. But he didn't know if he would have had the courage to do the right thing if he had been on the field that day.

Mario's gaze haunted Robbie for months.

CHAPTER 13

Revenge of the Krushers

"**M**an, I'm telling ya, I'm still pissed to the max!" Larry Partoni paced back and forth in front of the stoop of his house where all the Krushers had gathered to read comic books one month after the incident with A.J. "That King, that big fat dick oughta not have gotten me 'n' Jesse in trouble. Can you believe that there ain't gonna be no Crystal Beach for us this year?"

Larry's brother, Jesse, nodded in agreement, with an angry scowl. Stan Hershowitz chimed in: "Yeah. Lookit my legs. I still got welts 'n' marks, and fer what? Just 'cause we had a little fun with that retard boy. It ain't fair. It ain't fair at all!"

"We're gonna get him, and we're gonna get him really good," said Jesse. "Me 'n' my brother ain't gonna take this, 'specially from someone like The King. I wanna give him a lesson he ain't never gonna fergit. Who's with us, huh? Who's gonna help us, huh? You ain't gonna chicken out on us, are ya?"

Larry added, "Yeah. BAWK BAWK BAWK BAWK"—tucking his hands under his armpits, he flapped them up and down—"You guys chicken, or what? Whose gonna help me 'n' Jesse get The King? BAWK BAWK BAWK BAWK."

George Johnson stared silently at the tops of his sneakers. Robbie focused on his never-ending and never-successful attempt to juggle three rubber balls. Tony Baratino and Johnny Tabone buried their heads back in the comic books they were reading. Bruce concentrated on the bottle of pop he was downing, and the rest of the Krushers, except for Stan, tried their best to ignore the Partonis' recruitment efforts.

But Stan was enthusiastic. "I'm in, fellas. I'm in alla way. I ain't gonna let a fool like The King get the best of me, 'cause if he does, then who's the real fool, huh? Whatever we do has gotta be so big that The King gets a message 'bout foolin' around with us, right?"

Only the Partonis agreed with Stan, nodding vigorously.

It was quiet for moment, then Joe Vitelli spoke up: "I don't know 'bout the rest of youse, but I had enough already. I ain't chicken, but I been thinkin' that lettin' things alone is the way t'go. I don't want no more trouble from my pop—he gave it to me good enough as it was."

Robbie couldn't help feeling, however, that even though the call for action was going to be ignored by just about everybody, there was unspoken concurrence that a cool prank would be appreciated.

"Hold on a minute, *paisans*," Robbie said. "Maybe I don't have a right to say anything 'cause I wasn't there, but did ya ever stop to think that what you did was just plain wrong and maybe you should take what you got like a man and forget about it?"

Tony, Johnny, Bruce, and George nodded in agreement with him.

"Robbie," said Stan, "you shaddup! You ain't got no say in this whatsoever 'cause you weren't there an' you din' get smacked around. You're outta this. Period. End of sentence."

Except for Stan, Jesse, and Larry, the rest of the Krushers buried their heads in their comic books to avoid conversation and confrontation. The three conspirators walked away together, talking animatedly, beginning to plot their revenge. Stan turned around, looked directly at Robbie, raised his fist, and slowly extended his middle finger.

That evening, when the street was dark and silent, Stan, Jesse, and Larry slipped out of the Partonis' house. Jesse was carrying several cartons of eggs, and the boys began to systematically heave them against The King's house, carefully avoiding windows so as not to wake anybody up should a window happen to break. By the time they finished, the entire brick facade of The King's house was covered in a sticky, yolky mess, and eggshells were splattered everywhere.

The whole thing was over in less than three minutes, and after looking around and determining that they were not going to be caught, they slapped each other on the back, laughed, and went home. They couldn't wait to tell the Krushers what they had done and how they had avenged a miscarriage of justice.

When they awoke the next morning, the first thing they did was to inspect their handiwork, hoping they could catch The King, Mattie, and A.J. scrubbing madly away. But to their amazement and confusion, 77 Kreskin was absolutely clean. Not a trace of yolk, not a smidgen of egg white, not the smallest particles of eggshell could be found. They couldn't see any indications that a cleanup effort had been accomplished, as the house looked exactly like it did every day.

What they did see was The King sitting on his throne in the middle of his driveway, porkpie crown perched upon his head in its usual place, looking no worse or better—nor even different—than he always looked. To the conspirators it was like a scene out of *The*

Twilight Zone, as if the incident had never happened and time had somehow warped through another dimension.

That evening, the boys told the Krushers about their adventure.

"I'm tellin' ya," said Jesse, "we egged The King's house good…real good, and there was nobody aroun' t'see us do it. Man, when we left, there was egg drippin' all over the place—but this mornin'…nothin'. I mean absolutely nothin'."

"Yeah, yeah, sure ya did," said Joe. "If ya did what ya said ya did, then The King would be out scrubbin' away this very moment. I don't know 'bout the rest of you, but I don't believe ya did it. You guys see anythin' weird 'bout The King's house? How 'bout you, Robbie? You, Brucie?" They all shook their heads no. "Hey, boys, money talks, bullshit walks."

"No, no! I'm tellin' ya, we did it! We honest t'God plastered that house. I don't know what happened or how it happened, but I swear we did it!"

Instead of laughing with Jesse, Larry, and Stan, the Krushers laughed at them, a damning laughter that accused them of being bald-faced liars.

Angered, the boys resolved to take an even stronger action, one that would turn the scorn into admiration. They walked away, muttering to one another. Stan visibly reddened with embarrassment after Johnny Tabone yelled out after them in a mocking voice, "Nice job, boys!"

Two nights later, the boys again met in the silence of darkness. Both Stan and Larry were carrying step-ladders, and Jesse had three full bars of Ivory soap in his pocket. Silently and methodically, the boys proceeded to soap every first-floor window of the Colucci's flat within the reach of their ladders. They wrote obsceni-ties, they drew obscene pictures, and for good measure, they left several soapy, waxy messages highlighting A.J.'s handicap.

In some cases, they soaped over entire windows, and by the time they were done, sweaty and exhaust-ed, The King's house was a terrible mess. When they looked upon their handiwork, they were perversely pleased. Again unnoticed by anyone, they slipped back home, smug and satisfied.

Their satisfaction was short-lived, however, turn-ing into abject disbelief the following morning when all traces of their handiwork had completely vanished. Windows sparkled, nary a drawing nor an obscenity remained, and again, not a shred of evidence could be found of any cleanup activities whatsoever.

They were astonished, stunned, and embarrassed. Their revenge had been thwarted and their pride de-flated like a week-old birthday balloon.

After the egg incident, the Partoni brothers and Stan Hershowitz fully expected The King to have an-other confrontation with the neighborhood parents, creating another embarrassing scene. The soap fol-low-up would force the matter. They hoped another chastisement by The King would serve as the boys' re-venge upon their parents for doling out punishments that they deemed disproportionate to what they had done to A.J.

But again, instead of seeing The King laboriously working at removing the boys' latest effrontery, they saw him sitting in his chair, eyes dull and vapid, perus-ing the neighborhood, his actions and thoughts masked by his seemingly impenetrable royal caricature.

Later that day, Larry, Jesse, and Stan told the Krushers about what they had done, and once again they were mocked for telling a whopping lie even after Jesse pulled a nub of soap out of his pocket in a street version of show-and-tell. The Krushers' collective de-rision was nothing less than a match lighting a stick of dynamite.

"Ah, screw you guys, big time and double over," said Jesse. "You don't believe us, huh? Well, we're gonna show ya, all of you—plus The King, that *patoot*. Mockin' us out, huh? Makin' us look like assholes, huh? I ain't gonna let that happen. You just wait 'n' see."

Angry and embarrassed at being made out to be fools by the Coluccis, the three boys neither smiled nor laughed, and they weren't silly or goofy as usual. Instead, they were dark, their usual amiability shrouded with indignation and bitter resentment at The King, at their parents, and at their friends. Storming away, they ignored pleas to stay and cool off.

Robbie ran after them. "Hey, Jesse, wait up. Hold up for a minute fer Chrissake. This is going too far, and I don't like what I see."

"Fuck you, Robbie," snarled Larry. "Fuck you and all the rest of you fuckheads. As far as I'm concerned, we're quits, so whatever yer gonna say, say it now, 'cause I really don't give a crap."

Stan looked at Robbie, and for a moment Robbie thought he saw Stan's gaze begin to soften. Robbie pressed the point: "What's done is done, and I got no idea what The King did, but you gave it your best shot, and it just didn't turn out like you thought it was gonna turn out. So what if you lost—let's move on. What do ya say?"

That was, perhaps, the worst thing Robbie could have said to them. Stan's eyes turned steely hard once again, and suddenly Jesse stepped forward and shoved Robbie hard. Robbie flew back against a parked car and with a thud and a *woof* had his wind knocked out of him.

"Like Larry said, Robbie, fuck you, ya pussy. We don't need ya and we don't need yer blessings or the permission of you or any of those other pussies to do what we want t'do. So, Robbie, here's a warning. Stay the fuck outta our way, 'cause if ya don't, we're gonna hurt ya."

Stunned and gasping for breath, Robbie couldn't reply. They turned on their heels and walked away, and as he started to get his wind back, Robbie got angry. Not because he was hurt, but because a bond of friendship that had been in place for a long time had suddenly been snapped as if it were merely an inconsequential dry twig.

Tony rushed over as Robbie was wiping his eyes on the backs of his hands. He assured Tony that he wasn't hurt, and together they walked down the street, making their way toward home, trying to make sense out of what had happened and speculating about what might happen next.

CHAPTER 14

Stepping Up to the Plate

On summer afternoons on his second-story porch, Robbie would often lay in the well-worn chaise lounge, book in hand. Before settling in he would look up and down the entire length of Kreskin Avenue, sitting in silence, watching and listening to the comings and goings of the neighborhood

In that respect, Robbie was just like The King on his lawn chair throne. But instead of a porkpie hat, he wore a baseball cap. Instead of a beer, a glass of iced tea usually sat on the table at his side. But if the family was out of the house and if he thought he could get away with it, he would sneak a cold Utica Club from the fridge before settling down.

The King and Robbie appeared to share a responsibility for being the neighborhood's watch guard, yet they kept their perceptions to themselves and did not trade intelligence. As The King took his daily walks up and down Kreskin Avenue, he would invariably look to see if Robbie was on his porch, and if their glances happened to meet, they would acknowledge each other's presence with an almost imperceptible nod of heads.

About a week after his encounter with Stan and the Partonis, in the stifling heat and humidity of the summer night at close to three in the morning, Robbie silently left his room. Ever so softly so as not to wake his parents or Addie, he opened the screen door and slipped out to the porch, stumbling through the darkness to reach the comforts of his high hide. There, in the dead silence of the night, tucked in deep shadows, he sat in the stillness of the neighborhood, unseen, undisturbed, and waiting.

As usual, the neighborhood was quiet, but suddenly, faint clicks told him that just a few houses away, doors were being opened.

Robbie watched as the Partoni brothers and Stan met in front of Stan's house. Larry was carrying a toolbox, and together they approached an old yet very-well-kept Chevy station wagon parked on the street underneath a lamppost about five houses down.

Robbie slipped out of the lounge chair and silently crept back inside his house, taking what seemed to be an agonizingly long time. Once inside he made a quick check to make sure that everyone in the household was still asleep. Satisfied, he picked up the phone, dialed a number, and after two rings, a voice answered.

"Who's this?"

"Look outside."

Robbie hung up the phone and silently and unobserved made his way back to the porch to witness the events about to unfold.

Larry and Stan had the hood of the Chevy up and were leaning so far over the engine compartment that their legs dangled off the ground. They were pointing flashlights downward, illuminating Jesse, who had crawled under the car on his back, legs sticking out, the open toolbox close by. Robbie could hear their loud, exaggerated whispers.

"Hurry up, fer Chrissake! Someone's gonna see us!"

"I can't find the friggin' brake line. Shine that light over this way, will ya!"

"What's takin' ya so long? I thought you said this was gonna be one, two, three, an' out! If you was any slower, we coulda hired A.J. an' got the job done faster!"

"Oh, shit! I dropped the cutters…wait, wait…I got 'em! Now hurry up with that light! Are ya some kinda moron? I said t'shine the light over here!"

They were so involved with their task, their intense concentration broken only by Stan's nervous giggles, that they were oblivious to the shadowy figure approaching from their blind side. From his angle, at first Robbie could only see a checkered porkpie hat bobbing up and down as Mario ran quickly and silently toward the un-suspecting trio—he was surprisingly agile and stealthy.

As he approached the boys, the light from the lamppost cast him in a gigantic shadow. Robbie couldn't see his face because his back was turned, but he could see that one of The King's fists was clenched and in his other hand he held a yellow, plastic Wiffle Ball bat. Finally, he was standing directly behind Larry and Stan, still undetected.

Mario opened his stance for balance and grabbed the bat with both hands. He raised it high over his head and with lightening quickness delivered a series of vi-cious blows to the backs of Larry's and Stan's legs. He probably got in about half a dozen blows to each of them before they were able to scramble up and out of their exposed and vulnerable position. On their way out, both struck their heads on the underside of the car's hood, adding to their pain and misery. When they finally straightened up, howling in pain and holding and rubbing their heads, they exposed their stomachs to Mario, who capitalized on the opportunity by deliv-ering another series of blows.

Each blow broadcast a solid thwacking sound that Robbie could hear above their howls and beyond the first rumblings of tears that would come moments lat-er. As the boys turned to run away, Mario managed to catch Stan's bottom with a kick that was so well placed it lifted him completely in the air and made him fall on his hands and knees. He scrambled up and vanished into the night, joining Larry in their now-terrified flight to safety.

Jesse was stuck under the car, frozen by fear, while this was going on. All he could hear was the thwacks of the plastic bat as it delivered blow after blow, and the pained shrieks and sobs of his brother and Stan. "HEY! HEY! WHAT'S GOING ON?" he screamed in a girl-ish voice. "STAN? LARRY? YOU TH-TH-THERE? WHAT'S HAPPENING?!"

Mario threw the bat to the side, reached down, and grabbed Jesse by both ankles, then roughly jerked him out from under the car. Before Jesse even had a chance to react, Mario grabbed him with one hand by his shirt collar and in a single move lifted him straight up into the air until Jesse's feet were dangling off the ground. He was whimpering and feebly kicking his legs in a vain attempt to secure his freedom.

"Ya wants t'know what's goin' on, ya little dick-head?" asked Mario in a hard voice, just loud enough for Robbie to hear from the porch. "I'll tell ya what's goin' on. Yer brother and yer little punk friend just had a meeting with me an' my friend Billy the Bat. That's what's goin' on.

"You think yer so friggin' smart, don't ya?" Mario continued. "That first time when ya egged my house, I dintknow who did it. But me an' Mattie saw a couple of punks runnin' away, an' she had a pretty good idea of who ya were, but we just went ahead an' cleaned it up. Mattie sez to me, 'Boys will be boys' and leave it alone, but honest t'Christ if I woulda got my hands on you punks then, I woulda hauled ya off to yer ma an' pa faster 'n' shit through a goose.

"An' I still dint know who it was that soaped up the house, an' I was mightily pissed when I saw it, but it weren't hard t'clean. Coupla passes with a straight edge an' that shit peeled right off. But I kinda had a notion that you and your brother were mixed up in it."

Mario paused a minute to catch his breath.

"But I let it go 'cause I ain't never been a squealer, an' I dint even call the cops. Mattie kinda figgered that we hadn't seen the end of things yet, but I thought that yer next move was gonna be the ol' dog-shit-in-a-flamin'-bag routine.

"Me oh my oh, was I ever wrong. Who woulda ever figgered that you was goin' ta do somethin' like cuttin' my brake lines? An' when I saw what you was gonna do, how you was gonna put my life in danger…or even worse, what if Mattie was gonna be drivin' somewhere with A.J., God forbid, an' you got them hurt or killed?

"Here's what happened, you *piccolo budiulo*, you little asshole—you woke somethin' up in me that's been asleep fer a long, long time. Somethin' ya don't know about. Somethin' ya don't wanna know about. Ever. But ya woke it up."

Robbie could hear Jesse bawling and whimpering to be released.

"So, I got a little souvenir. Somethin' t'remind ya about this little adventure of yours. Somethin' t'think about if ya wanna mess with me or my family again."

Mario lowered Jesse to the ground, still holding onto his shirt collar. He balled and cocked his fist, and Jesse cowered in anticipation of the blow. Instead of hitting him, Mario reached into his pocket and brought out a small squeeze bottle that held a darkish liquid. As hard as Jesse tried, he could not squirm out of Mario's grasp as he began to squeeze the contents of the bottle onto Jesse's hair, face, hands and any other exposed part he could see. Robbie could see Jesse spitting and sputtering and trying to wipe his eyes, but Mario would still not let him go.

"What you got yerself here is some red india ink that Mattie uses fer one o' her hobbies," said Mario. "Ya can't wash it off; yer momma can't scrub it off—it just kinda wears off in a month or so." Mario brought Jesse closer to him; and Robbie strained to hear what he was saying.

"If yer momma or poppa wants t'know what happened to you and yer brother, just send 'em over t'me, and if they wanna make trouble, you let 'em know 'bout that devil inside me that ya managed to wake up that shoulda kept on sleepin'. An' boy, ya better run away from here. Fast. As fast as you can. But ya better know one or two things that's about as true as true can get.

"If anythin' happens t'my house or my car, even if a bird shits on my sidewalk, or a flower happens t'die, I'm gonna come and hurt you, hurt you real bad. But if somethin' happens to Mattie or A.J., even if it happens if yer a thousand miles away, I'm gonna hunt ya down and kill ya, *capice*?"

Terrified, sobbing hysterically, and stained from head to toe, Jesse nodded in agreement. Mario released him, and he ran off into the night.

It took about a month for the ink stain to disappear, but nothing was ever said about it directly to Jesse by any of the Krushers. For the rest of that summer, the Partoni and Hershowitz families were rarely seen around the neighborhood but frequently discussed.

Robbie was the last stop on the line that led to The King becoming aware of what was going down. He had gotten wind of the scheme to cut Mario's brake line from Joe Vitelli, who got it from both Bruce Lucas and George Johnson, who got it directly from the mouth of

Stan, who just couldn't wait to spill the beans to someone about their plans.

At first, Robbie had been undecided about what to do—remain silent and be a party to a possible accident or even death or be a stool pigeon, a rat, a tattletale, who would certainly be ostracized and quite possibly forced into a fistfight. Finally, he decided that what was about to happen was so wrong that if he did not act to prevent it, he would be just as guilty as if he were the one who was going to cut the brakes.

A few days beforehand, when everyone was out of the house, Robbie called The King, told him about the plan, and then quickly hung up before Mario had a chance to reply or ask any questions. So when Robbie called again in the middle of the night, Mario was vigilant and prepared to act.

Robbie didn't necessarily feel righteous or even comfortable with what he had done, but at the same time, he didn't have even one shred of remorse for what Mario had done to Larry, Jesse, and Stan. Much to Robbie's surprise, neither did the rest of the Krushers, but he still feared that everyone knew he was the one who had ratted the guys out. Later on he found out that everybody, right down to Bruce's little brother, knew about the plans—thanks to Stan's big mouth. With everybody a suspect and with no evidence to the contrary, everybody was also the stoolie.

A few days later Robbie was sitting alone on the porch reading when he heard someone clear his throat down below. It was The King out for his daily stroll and inspection of the neighborhood, and upon hearing the noise, Robbie looked up from his book and found Mario looking directly at him. With a gentlemen's nod, silently, he mouthed two words: *Thank you.*

Robbie could see in Mario's eyes that he would never reveal their shared secret to anyone. Mario smiled for a moment, and Robbie smiled back. With a gentlemen's nod, he mouthed a silent *You're welcome.*

Robbie returned to his book and The King continued his walk, but now they had another connection, this one anchored by a mutual secret.

As Robbie watched Mario walk past his house and continue down the block, his porkpie hat bobbing up and down with each step, Mario as King seemed to be fading away, dissipating in a ghost-like wisp.

Now, what Robbie sensed more than saw was the aura of Mario Colucci the man, a substantial and heroic man.

PART IV

Goodbye, David

CHAPTER 15

David Shumstein

Some years go by slowly and lazily, the days drift-ing by without purpose or accomplishment. Other years seem to pass in a flash, full of adventure, excite-ment, and new experiences, and altogether too short.

The year 1967 passed at the speed of light.

It was a year of profound change for a country struggling with the war, civil disobedience, civil rights, riots, and the loosening of morals showcased in events like the debut of the Broadway show *Hair* and the un-fettered Summer of Love in San Francisco.

It was a year that shattered illusions about the idyl-lic middle class.

It was also a year of profound change for Robbie, casting the die for the man he was to become.

It was a year of firsts: Robbie's first real kiss from a girl named Sandra Weiner, his first real job delivering newspapers, his first touch of a woman's bare breast (again, Sandra Weiner), his first cigarette, his first Gibson guitar, his first attempts to read and understand Shakespeare, and his first vow of silence.

On a sunny Saturday afternoon in early June, Robbie and his grandfather Zeydeh had walked together back from the synagogue and had just finished the usual Sabbath lunch, made merrier because David was home from Chicago for a few days. Sitting in Zeydeh's backyard, the grandfather in an old metal rocker and Robbie in the chair with the cushions, Zeydeh was finishing a story about the time that he forced the notoriously evil owner of a shirt factory in the east side of Buffalo to raise wages and institute mandatory breaks for hundreds of immigrants who were making little more than slave wages.

"So, Robbela, this *goniff* vas paying dos vorkers about thirty cents a day, and then charging for water and even docking dem a penny if they vent to the bathroom. When me and Sid Yablonski heard about this, we knew we had to do someting, so"—suddenly, Zeydeh stiffened in his chair, eyes bulging, hands tightly clutching the armrests, turning an almost impossible shade of white—"So, so...OY! OY! AUUUGHHHH!"—Zeydeh clutched at his chest—"OY VEY IZ MER! MINE HEART! MINE HEART IS EXPLODING!"

Robbie jumped to his feet and grabbed Zeydeh's shoulders. "Zeydeh! ZEYDEH? Are you all right? WHAT'S WRONG? WHAT'S THE MATTER?!"

Zeydeh looked at Robbie with wild, frightened eyes, stiff, clutching his chest, and only replied with more expressions of pain.

"HELP ME! HELP ME! SOMEBODY HELP ME!" Robbie screamed. "DAVID! DAVID! Come quick—something's wrong with Zeydeh!"

David came running out of the house, his cousin Ben on his heels. He saw Zeydeh writhing, his face a rictus of pain and fright, and quickly scooped him up into his arms. He ran with him back into the house, bursting into Uncle Sol's flat, through the narrow hallway and into Uncle Sol's bedroom, where he placed Zeydeh on the bed.

"Ben, quick! Call an ambulance!" he shouted to his cousin. "I think Zeydeh is having a heart attack!"

As Ben ran off to comply, Bubbe, Uncle Sol, and Esther rushed into the room where Zeydeh was clutching his chest even harder and yelling, "OY! OY! MINE HEART! MINE HEART!" Panicked, the family surrounded the bed and tried to comfort him. Addie stood off to the side crying. Esther stood at the foot of the bed wringing her hands. Uncle Sol paced nervously back and forth. Bubbe sat on the bed, holding Zeydeh's hands, saying, "Shh. Shh."

Robbie was frightened, more frightened than he had ever been in his life—he had never seen death so near. Even David was running up and down the hallway, smacking a fist into his hand and yelling "Goddammit! Where are those *momzers*?! Why aren't they here yet?"

Mere seconds later, an invasion of firemen, cops, and ambulance drivers burst into the house in full regalia carrying a forest of clipboards, sharpened fire axes, battered oxygen tanks, handheld fire extinguishers, and—ominously—a stretcher. They rushed to Zeydeh's side, asking family members to please get out of the way while they worked. Outside, Rigby Avenue transformed into a haphazard parking lot for rescue vehicles, a hypnotic show of revolving red and white lights of different sizes and shapes entertaining the customary crowd of morbid curiosity seekers replete with their customary speculations about what was going on.

Despite hands that were trying to restrain him, Zeydeh bolted upright, his eyes impossibly wide, a small trail of drool dribbling down his chin. He emitted an incredibly loud OY!, and then proceeded to deliver what to this day may still be a *Guinness Book of World Records*, earthshaking, window-rattling belch from the very depths of his gastrointestinal workings that was so loud, so sustained, so incredibly melodic in its range and timbre, and so smelly that everyone in the room involuntarily jumped back in surprise.

Zeydeh looked about the room at the assembly of family and professionals, most of whom were standing about with an open-jawed look of disbelief.

"OY! Do I feel better!" he smiled and said, "Dot's de ticket…Maybe next time I should skip the pickled herring, *nu?*"

His color came back almost immediately, he wiped his chin on his shirtsleeve, and then proceeded to hop off the bed with vigor that belied both his age and his damaged hip. Zeydeh assured the firemen and medical professionals that he was just fine, and after a cursory examination, they shook their heads, smiled, and began to pack their equipment away.

Before they left, Zeydeh shook their hands and invited all to share a schnapps as a measure of thanks. They politely declined and left, concurring with Zeydeh that perhaps too much pickled herring was not such a good thing for a man his age.

Less than an hour later, the commotion had dissipated and Zeydeh and Robbie were again sitting in the backyard, where Zeydeh was finishing his story. Robbie wasn't paying much attention, though, as he was still shaken by his first near experience with death.

Later that evening, after the streetlamps had come on and the Krushers had concluded that day's Wiffle Ball play, David and Robbie were sitting quietly on their porch. David was smoking a pipe, an affectation he had recently picked up, much to the chagrin of his parents. Kreskin Avenue was silent, save for the night chirping of insects and an occasional car that passed on the street below. Robbie had a thousand questions but no answers about what had happened earlier that day.

"David, can I ask you something?"

"Sure, squirt, go ahead." David blew a cloud of smoke into the silent and unmoving air, and for a moment he was surrounded by a silky halo.

"Were you scared today?"

"Whaddaya think, ya putzhead? Of course I was scared! I thought Zeydeh was going to die."

"David, what happens when you die?"

Robbie could sense David looking at him from the depths of the shadows.

"Weird," said David.

"Wait a minute! You calling me weird? You're the weirdo, and I can give ya about a billion reasons why, starting with that long beard that makes ya look like a young Moses!"

"No," laughed David, "It's because that's the exact same question I'm asking on the final exam for the Philosophy 401 class I taught this semester.

"And here's the right answer in just two words: 'NOBODY KNOWS.'"

"Huh?"

For a few long moments, it was silent, save for the rustle of David chewing the mouthpiece of his pipe. He took a draw, then blew another cloud of smoke, making a cascade of perfectly round smoke rings that drifted away as they watched.

"Here's the deal: no mortal who has died has ever come back to give us the scoop on death, so some of my mentors would say what we know or think or believe is 100 percent real and 100 percent bullshit at the same time.

"But since you asked, here's what I think. First, do you want the entire six years' worth of stuff I studied and learned and questioned and debated? Or the Classics Illustrated comic book version?"

"Umm… let's go comic book if ya don't mind."

"OK. Your loss. Here goes.

"I think that God—whatever God you believe in, wherever he may be—has a stick that measures how well we've lived our life and how good we are. How we measure up isn't dependent upon physical strength or faith or religion or country or politics or even what planet we're from.

"That last one's for you in particular."

"Har de har har," Robbie said mockingly, throwing in a rude gesture for good measure as an encouragement for his older brother to proceed.

"I believe that God favors the pious over the impious but weeps every time a killing is done in his name."

David tamped, relit, and drew in the cherry-scented tobacco, exhaling slowly through pursed lips to send a cloud of white smoke skyward only to be trapped by the green-and-gray canvas awning.

"Can you dig that?"

Robbie wasn't sure and shrugged his shoulders.

"God's stick measures how we, individually, have treated our fellow man by action and thought. The kind and the just receive God's rewards, but others do not. So when you ask me about what happens when you die, I think you stand before God and he uses his stick to take the measure of your life, and if on balance you measure more to the kind and the just, you receive the favors of God's eternal grace.

"But I'll tell you this: even after all that I've read and learned and studied, I'm still confused, nowadays more than ever before."

"But what about Zeydeh?" Robbie asked in a quavering voice. "How's he gonna be measured when he really does die?"

They stayed up talking about Zeydeh, about what had happened (or not happened) that day, about life and death, good and evil, justice and injustice.

Near dawn, David yawned, rubbed his eyes, and suggested that it was time to hit the sack. Robbie ended the conversation by asking his brother to listen to a new song he had written called "The March of Zeydeh" and proceeded to deliver a fantastic, realistic impression of Zeydeh's earth-shattering belch.

They both laughed hysterically even though David tried to be composed and mature.

Then they went to bed.

The following day was rainy and ominously gray. Robbie was on the porch, reading, when David came out clutching an oversized black briefcase that looked like a gigantic doctor's bag, stuffed full of books, folders, magazines, papers, and other unidentifiable detritus.

"I was thinking more about our talk," he said to Robbie. "I want to show you something."

He retrieved a thick folder full of articles, photographs, clippings, and page after page of notes written in David's unique, cramped handwriting. Finally he stopped, removed a picture clipped from a magazine, and handed it to his brother.

In the background of the picture was a crowd of shaved-head Asians wearing what appeared to be long robes. The foreground of the picture was both horrible and compelling. A man was sitting on the ground, legs folded and arms crossed, burning in the middle of a pillar of fire. His robe had burned away, and his skin was charred and blackened, peeling away from his face.

Appalling as this picture was, what chilled Robbie to his very core was the calm, serene look on the man's face as he went to his death. The caption under the picture read, "Quang Duc, a Buddhist monk for fifty-one years, immolates himself to protest Ngo Dinh Diem's policies, Saigon, 11 June 1963."

"Eww. Gross," said a horrified Robbie, seeing death presented in a way that he had never imagined before…the unthinkable pain of the burning monk reconciled with the serenity on his face. As Robbie stared, transfixed by the photograph, David shoved another in front of him.

Equally as disturbing, this picture showed a small man holding a revolver about two inches away from the head of another small man. The man holding the revolver had a snarl on his lips and a grim look of determination. The man about to be killed looked terrified and was trying to shy away from the inevitable bullet. This photo's caption simply read, "Viet Cong infiltrator about to be executed."

"So, Robbie," David said softly as his brother continued to stare, mesmerized by the two pictures, "what do you see in these pictures? Think about this for a minute…both pictures show a man about to die a horrible death, and both deaths are based upon convictions—one of faith, the other of politics.

"When God is measuring these people, are they going to be rewarded or punished? And what about the guy who is just about to pull the trigger? How will God's measuring stick be used when his time is up?"

Robbie listened with great focus over the next hour as David made the war in Vietnam real, giving its context and exposing its harsh realities. He learned that nearly twenty thousand American soldiers had already lost their lives and that the war was increasingly unpopular with many in the country.

As he talked, David continued to peel away the veneer of Robbie's naivete.

He spoke harshly and forcibly about an undeclared war foisted upon an unsuspecting America by politicians interested in political orthodoxy and a military industrial complex interested in profits—more than they were interested in young men. By the time David was done, Robbie's immature WWII-and-John-Wayne perception of the righteousness of America's involvement in Southeast Asia was shattered.

"Dad and I have been arguing a lot about this," David said. "He believes what we're doing is right, and I believe it's wrong—so wrong, in fact, that I've been helping to organize protests and I've been arrested a few times. I don't want to fight with him. That's one of the reasons I haven't been home as much as I would have liked."

Robbie had been aware that for almost a year they had argued strongly on several occasions.

Abe Shumstein could not and would not see his son's position. He told David, with great conviction, that being an American was a privilege, not a right, and that there were certain obligations and responsibilities that went along with that privilege. After all, he reminded David time and time again, he had served his country, and even though he was wounded, that service was in no small measure a fundamental reason for the safety and security their family now enjoyed, which David apparently took for granted.

"Dad believes that serving in the military is a small price to pay for the freedoms we enjoy," he told Robbie, "but I think that it's those freedoms that give me the right to voice my opinion and march in demonstrations and even talk to my little brother about how I feel.

"I will not kill. I will not be measured by God for taking another life."

The father-son arguments did not end in compromise or resolution. As adamant as his father was in maintaining that if called David must serve, David was equally adamant in informing his father that he intended to fight against the war and refuse to participate in it. If it were not for David's love and respect for their father, their arguments would have created an irreconcilable rift that could never be bridged.

David rummaged through his briefcase for a few seconds before pulling out an official-looking letter. "I want to show you one more thing," he said to his brother, "but you gotta promise me that you're not going to say anything, just yet, to the family. I'm going to tell them tomorrow."

Robbie promised and began reading the letter. His eyes swelled with tears.

It was an induction notice ordering David to report for military duty on August 1, 1967. If inducted, there was a very high probability that David would be sent to Vietnam.

CHAPTER 16

A Most Unwelcome Decision

A fierce March wind howled, bringing an angry flurry of snow off Lake Erie, making life miserable once again for the weary, yet winter-wise denizens of the city. Inside the Grover Cleveland Federal Building, the cavernous room painted in two tones of drab green paint was hot and stuffy.

An American flag hung listlessly in one corner and, other than a portrait of Lyndon B. Johnson on one wall, the room was naked and unadorned. In the front of the room, seven white middle-aged and elderly men sat in wooden chairs behind a long table, nameplates identifying them as members of the Erie County Selective Service Draft Board. Notebooks and folders of varying sizes were piled high in front of each, and their expressions were a combination of boredom and anger.

Twenty-four-year-old David Shumstein, bearded and long-haired, sat behind a table about ten feet in front of them. His winter coat was folded neatly on the floor next to a briefcase bulging with books and papers. An open thick notebook occupied most of the table in front of him, its title page proclaiming, "David Shumstein: Application for Conscientious Objector Status 1-O."

A mean-looking gray-haired man sitting in the middle of the long table banged a gavel two or three times, quieting the buzzing drone of disconnected conversations and forcing those gathered into dramatic silence. Except for the clanking and hissing of the steam radiators, the room became still.

"Order! Order! The room will come to order!" thundered the gavel-wielding man. "We will now consider the application of"—he put on his thick wire-rimmed glasses and peered at the first page of the notebook before him—"a Mister David Shumstein, residing at 54 Kreskin Avenue in the City of Buffalo, New York, for status of conscientious objector. Mr. Shumstein, you have ten minutes to make a presentation to this board, after which we will be asking you a few questions. Do you understand?"

David nodded.

"Good—we will not be making our decision today, but when we do reach one, you will be notified by mail. You may begin."

David shuffled a few papers nervously, cleared his throat, and began. His presentation had been carefully prepared, polished time and time again until it was a masterful balance of emotion and reason. To support his points he quoted Russell, Gandhi, Blake, and Kierkegaard. He reached into both the Old and New Testaments and even delved into the Talmud. In a measured voice he ticked off the reasons, one by one, for his moral objections to the war, concluding with selections from Thoreau, Descartes, and John Locke on the nature of man and his relationship to government. By the time he was finished, he was drained and breathless.

From the far end of the table an elegant-looking man wearing a tailored three-piece suit spoke up. "So, Mr. Shumstein, you've done a brilliant job structuring your presentation, and I'm very impressed at the sources you've used to support your position. But something's missing here. I really don't care what Kierkegaard or Gandhi have to say, and I hope that you don't think that you're even in the same league as these brilliant men. Now, let's get to the nub: what do *you* think? Why don't *you* want to serve your country?"

David looked directly at his questioner. "It's simply this. I will not kill another human being for my country or for any reason of state or politics. We—and I don't mean just we in this room—should be striving to achieve a higher moral order, a higher consciousness, so conflicts need not be resolved using violence and certainly not by taking the life of another human. I will not do this under any circumstance."

"Hmm. I see, Mr. Shumstein. Are you saying that you would not kill or use force under any circumstance? What if your family is threatened? Or how about if an enemy of this country invades our shores? What would you do then?"

Before David had a chance to reply, other members of the board launched their assault:

"Are you a Mennonite or a Quaker?"

"Have you ever fired a gun?"

"Are you a Communist or a Communist sympathizer?"

"I see in your application that you were a member of the Students for a Democratic Society. Have you ever participated in student demonstrations?"

These questions were the opening salvo of a barrage that the board obviously fired at every conscientious-objector applicant. David parried each thrust with a thrust of his own, and as his frustration mounted, his disdain for his questioners and their well-rehearsed queries was apparent in his responses. No matter what he tried or said, he felt that he could not break the barrier of their conscience, and it soon became evident that his presence was a mere formality in a decision that had been made well in advance of his presentation.

After thirty minutes had gone by, the chairman looked at his watch and banged his gavel, signaling an end to the hearing. He thanked David for his time and the careful preparation of his case, and even though he told David that a decision from the board would be forthcoming, his eyes gave away the fact that a decision had already been made: David was going to be inducted into the military. David gathered his papers, stuffed them back into his briefcase, put on his coat, wordlessly turned on his heel, and left the room.

Ninety days later he received a Notice of Induction ordering him to report to Fort Dix, New Jersey, by August 1, 1967, to fulfill his duties and obligations to his country. His classification was 1-A-O, signifying he was a conscientious objector registrant available for noncombatant military service only. It was more than likely that David was going to be going to Vietnam as a medic, one of the most dangerous occupations in the entire military.

All the serious discussions in the Shumstein family, from finances to appropriate punishments to report-card reviews, took place around the kitchen table. Mom and Dad would occupy their usual positions, and then, dependent upon topic or appropriateness, one or all the children would join.

Discussing vacation plans was always fun, witnessing Addie squirm under the scrutiny of a report card review was delightful, accepting responsibility for misdeeds and their consequent punishment was uncomfortable, and discussing finances was always a private matter for which children were expected to remain out of earshot and confidence.

On the very next day following his talk with David, Robbie burst upon one of these family conferences after an afternoon of listening to the Partoni brothers and a few of the other Krushers express, once again, how they would satisfy Mrs. Konstakous if given the opportunity. As their collective ruminations that day had been particularly graphic and vivid, Robbie was in an ebullient mood that quickly dissipated when he came into the kitchen.

Robbie's mother, Addie, and Bubbe were crying. Dad scowled. Zeydeh had a pained expression, and David sat dejected in his chair. The letter from the draft board was unfolded and lay alone in the center of the table.

"At the beginning of the year I received a letter from the government that my student deferments expired," explained David matter-of-factly. "They told me that I had been classified 1-A and was being drafted."

"I wrote them back asking to be exempted from the draft because of my moral opposition and asked the draft board to reclassify me as 1-W. That means that as a matter of conscience I objected to the war, and instead of going into the military, I would agree to do community or volunteer work.

"They gave me an opportunity to present a petition and my case to the Erie County draft board in March…remember when I was home for a few days back then?

"Here's their response," he said, pointing to the letter. "I got it a few weeks ago. They said no and refused to give me a 1-W classification. They made it clear that the army expects me to report for duty in August, but I don't know if they'll be sending me to Vietnam."

"What are you talking about?" his mother sobbed. "Vietnam is war, and war is killing and death and misery, and now you're telling us that you think there's a chance they're going to send you to that place? *Oy g'vald*, there's bombing and shooting and cruelness over there! I see it every night on the television! I don't want to sit shiva, and I don't want that you should go!"

"Well, it's not all bad," David told them in his best trying-to-soothe voice. "They said that I could be a conscientious objector, but I still had to go into the army.

The family looked at David, upset and confused and uncertain about what this meant.

"So, they gave me a 1-A-O classification. That means that I still gotta go, but I don't have to carry a rifle or shoot anyone or drop bombs. I don't know where

I'm going once I finish basic training, but wherever it is, I'm not going to pick up a gun.

"Maybe they'll make me a clerk and send me to Greenland, or maybe I'll be an orderly at a military hospital in Florida, but I won't be a combat soldier. As far as Vietnam goes, who knows? Maybe I'll be sent there, maybe not. We'll just have to wait and see."

Zeydeh strained to hold back his emotions. "So, Dovid, is this what you're telling me? That those ignoramuses at the draft board wouldn't listen to you? That instead of letting you help people here, they're making you go into the army? It doesn't make sense! A plague should come on all of them!"

"Zeydeh, I don't have much choice," replied David. "I talked to a lawyer, and he said that if I don't go, the U.S. Army will hunt me down and throw me into jail. If that happens, I'll never be able to finish up my doctorate, much less get a job teaching. But because of my classification I won't go in to kill anyone."

To that point, David's father had remained silent, but now he spoke up. "David, I know that this is a sad thing. Nobody likes it when a family member must go away, especially to war, and it hurts a little more when your son is going off to the military. But like I told you a hundred times before, this is a responsibility that you have because you're an American, and it's the right thing to do to be worthy of those privileges we have as Americans.

"But I have also come to realize that you are a *mensch*, and I respect your objections—I don't believe in them, but I respect them—and if you serve your time as a clerk or as a medic, in or out of Vietnam, it's fine by me, so long as you serve your country.

"Now, we're not going to argue any more about whether what's going on in Vietnam is *dreck*, 'cause what's done is done. But if you should end up having to go, like I did, then go with honor and distinction, and when you come home, I know that you'll be proud of what you have done."

The kitchen was silent for a few moments except for quiet sobs. Zeydeh thumped his cane on the floor a few times and spoke up. "Dovid, you know dot I've never been an ass kisser, and I got plenty of lumps to prove it! But ve got a pretty good deal in this country, und maybe doing this thing is a vay of repaying for what we gots.

"It seems to me dot you stood up for vat you belief and dot's good enough for me. So, you do this ting and come back to us and then get on with life. When it's all over, it's done with, it's as unimportant as dung in a meadow."

"But Zeydeh," Robbie broke in, "what about Vietnam? What's gonna happen if David is sent to Vietnam?"

"*Kine-ahorah*," he replied softly. "Dovid, you shouldn't know from bad!"

Two months later the entire family accompanied David to the Federal Building where thirty other young men and their families had gathered for the bus to Fort Dix in New Jersey. Some of the young men were jubilant and enthusiastic about going off to war, their families proud and happy; some parents clutched their sons, some hugged, some wept. One by one, the family gave David hugs and well wishes, and Mom gave him a special lunch full of his favorite treats for the long bus ride. They had long ago spent their tears.

With a wave from the door, David entered the bus, and they saw him take a window seat. The bus roared to life with a plume of noxious black smoke, and the driver closed the doors with a hiss of compressed air. As the bus started to move, David looked out the window, pressed his fingertips to the glass, and looked at his brother, mouthing a silent "Goodbye, Robbie."

They stood and watched the bus pull away and disappear around the corner, carrying David away from them. Abe Shumstein herded everyone together, back toward the car, on what was one of the saddest days of their lives.

CHAPTER 17

Letters from David

"**R**obbie, Robbie, come back into the house!" his mother yelled from the porch to where he was playing a game of catch in the street with George Johnson. "You got a letter from David. Come see!"

"Catch ya later, Georgie Porgie," Robbie said as he made a final catch, tossed the ball back, and ran inside. On the kitchen table was the letter, which he immediately grabbed and tore open. After making his way to the porch and plopping into his reading chair, Robbie began to read David's familiar handwriting.

David wrote about his strange journey from Buffalo to Fort Dix, New Jersey, sharing an observation that the outward mask of the recruits' bravado made a poor cover for their inward fear of the unknown and unexpected. He told Robbie about meeting another highly educated, older 1-A-O conscientious objector named

Donald MacIntyre on the bus from Buffalo, a man everyone started to call Grampa because he had streaks of premature grey in his hair and a long beard like one of the brothers on the Smith Brothers cough-drop box.

David's description of the madhouse at Fort Dix made Robbie grin as he tried to imagine his brother in the middle of a gigantic processing center with two thousand other recruits, beard gone, head shaven to bald perfection, standing only in his socks and underwear.

"The next day the crack of dawn," David's letter continued,

I'm ordered to report to a nondescript office and a nondescript lieutenant who tells me that because I scored high on the army's IQ test, they're going to send me to Officer Candidates School. But then I told him to look at my file and pointed out that I was inducted as a conscientious objector, and truth be told, wasn't all that interested in being an officer.

He gives me this look like I could have said that I'm a Communist organizer from the planet Trafalgar who came to impregnate all Earth women in the morning and ruin capitalism in the afternoon. Then he huffed and puffed and squished his face all up until it was a mass of wrinkles and stormed out of the room.

David told Robbie about sitting alone for over two hours in the office before a couple of MPs came in and hustled him off to another office where they shoved him into a chair in front of a captain sitting behind an enormous desk. This captain had a folder opened in front of him with David's name on it and on the very top sheet a yellow piece of paper had the word TREASON stamped in huge block letters.

The Captain began screaming at me about being a traitor to the country, how spineless I was, and about how they were going to lock me up and throw the key away. He yelled at me for thirty minutes straight, and honest to God, Robbie, his face got so red and his eyes bulged out so far that I thought that he was going to explode like a bad guy in a Loony Tunes cartoon.

The captain offered David a chance to withdraw his C.O., but David told him that he stood behind his convictions and wouldn't change his mind.

"Well, he wasn't too happy about that," David continued.

About twenty minutes later a chaplain walks in, grabs a chair, and sits next to me. So, I'm thinking, at last, a man of God, a man of reason and peace who I can talk to. But instead of giving me a chance to explain my-self, he goes into a tirade full of curses that was even stronger than the one I got from the captain. I just kind of tuned him out and after a while he left.

By then, David told Robbie, he had been in this room for about seven hours and was tired and hungry. A corporal came in and instead of giving him a simple sandwich and a sip of water, he marched David outside and in front of a deck of bleachers where three hundred recruits started to yell and scream, calling him yellow and a coward and a traitor. Some even drew a finger across their throats, suggesting that they were going to slit his throat.

After a night in a nondescript barracks, I re-ceived orders to report to Fort Hood in Texas, and less than six hours later, after a plane and bus ride, I passed through a gated archway and saw a building with a mural depicting a U.S. soldier bayoneting a black pajama-clad Vietnamese. A great gush of blood was spurt-ing from the entry wound, the ground was drenched in blood, the Vietnameses eyes were completely rolled back into his head, and in large letters, a caption read WE KILL COMMIES AND WE LOVE IT! ITS OUR JOB!

A few week later, David wrote again, telling Robbie about how he was placed in a company composed entirely of conscientious objectors, segregated from the rest of the base, according to one master sergeant, to make sure that their poisonous attitudes didn't infect the rest of the trainees.

And in a stroke of fortune, David told Robbie, he'd been reunited with Don MacIntyre, and they'd become good buddies. He mentioned that everyone now called Don MacIntyre "Grampa."

Robbie's eyes widened when he read in another of David's letters that Don was the youngest son of the family that owned the MacIntyre Tire Company and was disinherited for being a "leftie," no less. "Think about it, Robbie," wrote David, "just about every truck, jeep, car, airplane—you name it—has got MacIntyre tires on it."

Robbie laughed again after he read that Don had taken to kicking the tires on every vehicle he came across because he said that it was just like kicking his father and his brothers in the ass and that someone had to do it.

Throughout that summer, David wrote at least once per week. His letters were often morose or full of invective against the system and situation in which he had been brusquely placed.

"The only thing that's keeping me sane," he confided in writing,

> are the guys in my company. We're all of one belief that the war is evil, and at night when we're lying around in these dingy army barracks, we talk about our convictions and, on a more practical level, what we learned about how to start an IV or field-dress a wound.

In other letters, David shared his feeling that outside the C.O barracks, there were boys who were true patriots willing to give up their lives to stop Communist aggression. There were boys who believed it was their duty as Americans to serve their country. There were boys eagerly following in the footsteps of their family's military tradition. There were boys of great faith who came from good families and who had good hearts.

"I feel that training to be a medic is the right thing to do, because if I can save a life, then maybe God will keep a special eye out for me," he wrote.

> *I try to do everything in my power not to think about tomorrow, or the next day or week, or even what lies ahead when I finish here. But the scuttlebutt is that it's just about guaranteed that when we're finished with advanced medic training, we'll all be going to Vietnam sometime in November. I'm told that in a firefight, the life expectancy of a medic is about fifteen seconds...Yikes!*

In late August, about halfway through medic training, David's letter talked about how some of the guys in the company were thinking about shooting themselves in the foot to get out of the army. Some were even seriously contemplating desertion, including Don, who couldn't bear the thought that every military truck or car or jeep carrying someone off to die or to commit murder had his name on its tires.

"I couldn't shoot myself," David told Robbie, confessing that he didn't even know how to hold a rifle. As far as deserting went, David made up his mind not to do it. It wasn't just the possibility of getting caught and sent to jail that stopped him—it was a matter of conscience, pride, and commitment.

"I hope you'll understand this, Robbie," David wrote in his final letter from Fort Hood just a few weeks before coming home.

What I've discovered over the past months is that if I don't prove to myself that I can deal with this adversity, then I'll be that much less of a person for it.

I'm not talking about machismo—I'm talking about inner worth, and I've decided that my inner worth needs to be guided by my moral compass. Running away just doesn't fit with the direction for my life I've committed to.

One last thing...I'll be home in about a month and a half, and I promise that I will simply amaze you beyond all belief when you see my rippling muscles. Get ready for an arm-wrestling beating that will be talked about and glorified forever in the Arm Wrestling Hall of Fame!

When David came home in mid-October, Robbie simply could not believe his eyes. Gone was the bearded, disheveled, and slouching brother he had last seen a few months before; instead, a clean-shaven, immaculately-pressed-khaki-wearing man with a crew cut was suddenly hugging him. Mom and Dad were beaming smiles to end all smiles, and Addie clung to him as if they were epoxied together.

"Private First Class Shumstein reporting as ordered, sir!" David said to no one in particular, accompanying the announcement with a crisp salute. "I understand that there's a roast chicken and some *kneidelach* that need immediate attention, and it is my solemn and sworn duty to attend to these with all due speed. Sir!"

They all laughed. "One order coming right up, soldier!" Mom giggled. "Will those be firm or soft *kneidelach?*"

"Why firm, of course, ma'am! There's nothing soft about this soldier!" And to prove his point, he got into an arm-wrestling stance, motioned Robbie over, and proceeded to handily defeat him six times in a row. Robbie rubbed his arm while David tousled his hair, and with Dad grinning away, Robbie promised that by the end of his visit, David would leave with a curse on his lips from being defeated by his fifteen-year-old brother.

The next two weeks went by in a blur, and the fact that David would be leaving for Vietnam seemed to be conveniently and temporarily forgotten. Mom and Addie showed off David whenever and wherever they could, and not a day went by that the entire clan didn't gather for dinner so David could regale them with funny stories about basic and advanced medic training.

When their landlady, who lived in the downstairs flat, sliced open her finger quite badly with a carving knife, David was there to coolly and efficiently stop the bleeding. If he had been carrying his medic kit, he could have just as easily put a few stitches in and administered antibiotics instead of packing her off to the hospital. His knowledge and confidence were impressive.

The night before he left, David, his father, and Robbie found themselves alone, the ladies having left to pick up a farewell cake and a last few items David had requested. They sat around their kitchen table, Dad and David sipping on beers while Robbie worked his way through a Coke. Their father sighed and turned to David.

"So, it's off to Vietnam you go, eh, Dovid? I want to let you know how proud I am—how proud we all are—of you."

"Proud of what, Dad?" replied David. "My shiny shoes? My haircut? The fact that I can suture a wound?"

"No. No. I'm proud of the fact that you're serving your country and handling your responsibility. Don't you feel better about it?"

David glared at his father. "No, Dad, I don't feel better about it at all. I'm scared and confused, and now that I've seen how things work from up close, I'm opposed to what we're doing more than ever.

"At the hospital I heard the stories of the men who had been there. I cleaned and tended their wounds. I heard their screams and moans. I put the ones who died into bags and wrote the instructions out for shipping them home like they were a box of oranges you order from Florida.

"Do I feel better about it? Do I think the misery and suffering is justified? No, Dad, I don't."

His voice a little harder, Dad replied: "You don't have to tell me about those things! I was there in war! I did. I saw. I held my best friend in the whole world in my arms when he died in Anzio, most of his head shot away. But we did it because we were asked to do it, just like you're being asked. You do it because your country needs you, and you have an obligation."

"An obligation? What obligation?" sneered David, his voice rising in anger. "I'm not going through with this for my country—I'm doing this for myself. Our country is wrong, just 100 percent plain wrong about this war, and if there's any obligation, it's to exercise my rights of free speech to make my voice known about just how wrong and stupid and evil this situation is.

"Who do I have an obligation to?" David continued. "Lyndon Johnson? Robert McNamara? General Westmoreland? Those fat cats that own the factories that are turning out guns and bullets and bombs and getting rich in the process? No, Dad, I don't have an obligation to them."

"D-David!" the father stammered, "these are our leaders! They deserve our respect!"

"Maybe yours, Dad, but not mine," said David sadly, and with that he got up and walked away from the table.

Outside of a gruff "goodbye," a "take care of yourself," and a handshake at the airport the next day when they dropped David off for his flight to California, Abe Shumstein did not speak to his son again.

That would haunt Robbie's father until his dying days.

CHAPTER 18

Shiva

Coming just seven weeks after his visit home, David's funeral and burial were surreal. Robbie was there, but not there. He listened to the prayers and the eulogies but did not hear them. He saw and felt the anguish of his own loss but could not acknowledge the anguish of others. He clutched at his mother's listless arm, feeling the coarse material of her black dress, but could not find solace. He looked at familiar faces but did not see them. When he helped bearDavid's simple wooden coffin to the grave, he felt the weight but not the burden.

At the graveside, dirt shoveled into the open grave fell in achingly slow motion, clods striking the wood with an exaggerated and amplified thump that seemed to reverberate from headstone to headstone throughout the cemetery. Unwelcome and unwanted, death settled upon the Shumsteins, robbing them of spirit, haunting every waking moment. Death made their lives colorless and tasteless, casting a deep shadow over their thoughts and actions.

Addie and Robbie were at school and their father at work when a government car pulled into the driveway, discharging two grim-faced army officers. Upon introducing themselves, they asked Esther to sit down because they had brought some bad news about David.

Robbie's mother screamed in terror and fainted, falling out of her chair to the floor. Her wail brought their landlady rushing upstairs, where she saw the two officers trying to revive her with smelling salts and a wet washcloth. Knowing immediately that David had died, and horrified and close to being sick herself, she rushed to the phone to call Abe at work, urging him to come home immediately.

Abe came home to learn that while on patrol, David's platoon had come under enemy fire and in the ensuing firefight nearly half of the platoon, including David, had been killed.

David had performed his duties as a medic heroically and with valor, exposing himself numerous times to go the aid of the wounded. As he was loading the very last wounded soldier onto a rescue helicopter, he was shot in the head by a sniper and killed instantly. His commander recommended that the U.S. Army award David a Bronze Star for his bravery.

Over the next week, while waiting for David's body to be returned, Robbie's mother became another person entirely. In her grief Esther had ripped her clothes and pulled out clumps of her hair and would ask visitors if they had seen David because she needed him to run to the store. Or she would look into their eyes and scream, "They killed him! They killed my boy, my Dovid, my angel, my son! Why should I live when he's dead? It should happen to my enemies, not to me!" It was likely she would have lost her sanity if not for the sedatives. She became listless and vacant, her eyes fogged over in a chemically induced haze, seemingly indifferent to all who tried to give her comfort.

Abe Shumstein sat in his favorite chair, barefoot, unshaven, and unkempt, his eyes puffy and red-rimmed. From the moment they had been notified that David had been killed in action, he had spoken less than a handful of words, acknowledging visitors with a thin-lipped smile and a barely audible thank-you.

After David's burial, the family sat *shiva*—a formal seven-day period of mourning. Rabbi Grossberg came to the Shumstein house and led daily prayer groups, which were attended by relatives, Robbie's Jewish friends from school and the neighborhood, and congregants from their synagogue.

Abe would stand to one side, untouchable and unapproachable. He clutched his prayer book tightly to his chest, swaying back and forth, silently mouthing supplications, his eyes closed and tearing, his head raised heavenward. He was lost between ritual, grief, and the penetrating but unanswered questions he was directing to God. He was Robbie's father, but he wasn't himself; his grief cast a dark shadow over his personality and eclipsed the strength they depended on.

The depths of Robbie's father's grief were matched by the depths of his anger—at the army for placing his beloved son in harm's way, at himself for not acceding to David's conscience and joining the fight to help him avoid the military, and most of all at God. He was torn between his love for David and his faith, and an overwhelming and unbearable feeling of guilt, as he believed his stiff-necked attitudes were the very core of what led to David's death. How could this horror nine thousand miles away serve any meaningful purpose? During that week of intense mourning, Abe would rise before the rest of the household and sit on the porch and talk to God.

"Why did you do this? Why did you let this happen to such a good boy, a smart boy, a boy with a future, a boy who believed in you? What made you decide that he had lived long enough? Did you punish him for a transgression? Are you punishing me? Did he die in pain? Did he die knowing of his death?"

Addie was inconsolable. David was her big brother! She was only five when he went away to live in New York, and whenever he returned home, for Addie it was like a birthday/Hanukkah/Fourth-of-July celebration that exploded at the first moments of the tight hug they shared when he crossed the threshold. At twelve, she was old enough to comprehend David's death in physical terms but struggled like the rest of the family to understand its metaphysical and spiritual implications.

"Robbie," she had asked softly after they returned home from the cemetery, jewel-like tears coursing a path from her clear blue eyes down her chin and onto her blouse, "do you think David's in heaven with God?"

"I'm sure he is," Robbie replied, reflecting upon his conversation with David only a few short months before. He drew her to sit beside him on the couch. "David was good and kind and caring, and I'm sure that God accepted him into heaven right away."

"Who killed him, Robbie?" she sobbed. "Who was so mean and evil that they shot him with a gun—in the head?" Her shoulders heaved with each sob, and she seemed to become younger in her grief. "Why did he go to that Vietnam place, and why isn't he coming back to us?

"When he was here a couple of weeks ago," she continued, "he told me that when he came home next time he was going to take me out for the world's biggest ice cream cone and give me a special present from all the way across the world.

"I told him that I wasn't a baby anymore and that instead of ice cream, all I wanted was for him to come home safe.

"But now, there won't be any more ice cream or presents or David joking around ever again!"

Robbie thought carefully for a few moments. "Addie, you gotta believe this.

"There's not going to be much joy or happiness in the house for a while. I know that if David were here right now, he'd tell us that someday there will be and that he'd rather have you remember him and think happy thoughts."

Robbie didn't know what else to say, so he just wrapped his arms around Addie and squeezed tightly, letting her cry until she fell into exhausted sleep against his side. He laid her out on the couch, covered her with a blanket, fetched a well-loved and tattered Pooh Bear from her bedroom and put it beside her as if he could somehow magically shield her from troubled dreams.

During that week of mourning there was a seemingly never-ending flow of relatives, coworkers, neighbors, and friends who dropped by to express their sorrow, bearing gifts of food that quickly overtook every nook and cranny in the house. All the Krushers and their parents dropped by to pay their respects.

Robbie could sense his friends' morbid but understandable curiosity about the gruesome details of David's death and the full particulars behind his medal, but they were most likely rehearsed and forewarned by their parents to refrain from asking the natural questions they felt entitled to ask. Several of them had relatives in the service who had served or were about to serve in Vietnam, but none had experienced Robbie's loss of a brother. Although their inquisitive eyes and imploring faces pleaded for entry into Robbie's hell, Robbie refused to grant passage, as he could not bear the thought of sharing his family's anguish to reconcile their comic-book fantasies of combat with the harshness of reality.

Surprisingly and unexpectedly, the people who provided the greatest amount of comfort to Robbie during that horrible week were Mario and Mattie Colucci. Four days after the funeral, Robbie was sitting alone on the downstairs stoop, bundled against December's bitter cold, staring vacantly at a street bathed in the weak sunshine that was a feature of Buffalo's harsh winters.

He watched as they walked up the driveway to where he was sitting. Mattie reached out and put a hand on his shoulder.

"Robbie, I can't tell ya how lousy I feel an' how sorry I am fer yer loss," Mario said softly. "Mebbe it's hard ta unnerstan' now, but the pain does go away bit by bit. Believe me, I know what I'm talkin' 'bout."

Startled by the intrusion into his private moment, Robbie quickly turned his head to really look at Mario. He was tired of hearing about how sorry people were and nauseated at his role as a receptacle for their sympathy. He wanted to be left alone, to wallow in apathy and emptiness and the comfort of his misery and nothing else.

But there was something in Mario's eyes—in the way he stood and in the way he was looking at Robbie— that deflated Robbie's growing despair. His eyes told Robbie that he did know and that he had insights and that he had a special gift of awareness that went far beyond the perceptions that neighbors had of him.

"Do ya mind if me an' Mattie sit an' talk to ya fer a bit?"

Robbie grabbed a couple of the landlady's lawn chairs from the hall leading to her flat and motioned for them to sit.

"As a matter of fact, I wanna show ya somethin' that I had forgot completely about until a day or two ago, when Mattie showed it t'me. It's somethin' I haven't seen or even thought 'bout fer a long, long time. Mattie, you got it?"

She nodded and reached into her coat pocket.

"Robbie," said Mattie, "about seventeen years ago I picked this up from the floor next to a hospital bed where a severely wounded nineteen-year-old marine was lying and put it into my pocket. This marine was a hero, and what I'm going to show you was given to him personally by General Douglas MacArthur."

From her coat pocket she removed a slim velvet-covered black box, opened it, and handed it to Robbie. Inside, lying on a pure-white silk lining, threaded onto a simple ribbon, was a thick, gold cross. "Do you know what this is?" she asked softly.

Robbie shook his head "No."

"It's called a Navy Cross. The only medal that's higher is the Congressional Medal of Honor, and that small, skinny marine won this award for what he did on top of some frozen hilltop in Korea back in November of 1950."

Robbie looked at her, at the medal, and then back at her again, unable to comprehend what she was talking about, why she had the medal and why she was showing it to him. She leaned over and grasped his hands in hers and looked into his eyes. "That nineteen-year-old boy is here with me today, sitting at my side and in front of you. He threw that medal away—because what he had done and what he had seen sickened him.

"I don't know why I hid it away and saved it all these years," Mattie continued. "Maybe there was a purpose after all, because after we heard about David, I saw this man here beginning to slip back into that boy again. I knew that it was time to confront the demon head-on."

Robbie gasped in shock and surprise. Mario? The King of Kreskin Avenue was a decorated war hero? The *shlemiel* neighbors made fun of, who was the lodestone of their neighborhood's superiority complex—he was a marine cited for gallantry in action...a skinny Mario? Robbie was staggered and his mind reeled as he tried desperately to grasp an overwhelming assault of incongruities and shattered perceptions.

Momentarily, he stopped grieving.

"Wh-What? H-H-How?"

Mario leaned toward Robbie and spoke in a low voice. "I din' have no idea that Mattie had that thing until a couple a days ago. Man, was I surprised when I saw it! Ya din know that she was my nurse, did ya? Robbie, I'm gonna tell ya some things now that I never tol' anyone else 'cept Mattie.

"My mama and papa, my brothers an' sister, not even my closest friends never even knew 'bout these things 'cause I kept them inside a myself. I don't 'xactly know why I'm gonna tell them to you, but I think it might make both of us feel better when I'm done. But what I'm gonna say is private-like between us, an' I don't want anyone else t'know, *capice*?"

Robbie nodded.

"I was hurt bad, real bad, an' I was in a hospital fer over a year just recoverin' from my wounds. They healed up pretty good, but what dint heal was the wounds inside a my head, if ya know what I mean. My friends were dead, and I was betrayed. I dint want that medal an' I took it off and tossed it away when that General MacArthur left.

"Those wounds in my head ain't never healed, Robbie. An' at first I couldn't think 'bout anyting else. If it wasn't fer Mattie, I woulda ended up in the loony bin. The nightmares never go away—they just kinda hang aroun' an' they're always there just below the sur-face—some of the times, not as much now as it use ta be, they come up an' I have a real hard time until my meds kick in an' Mattie helps make them go away. The last time it happened was a few weeks ago when I heard ' bout David, an' the time before that was when those punks were messin' around with my car."

Mario told Robbie about what it was like to be a marine and what he was like before he went to war. He spoke of his patriotism, of what he believed about the concept of honor, about his overwhelming desire to serve his country, and about the pride and enthusiasm he felt at first. And how, later, that pride and enthusi-asm seemed hollow and meaningless.

When he started to talk about those violent days in November some seventeen years past, his eyes started to glaze. Mattie reached over to squeeze his hand, then held it until the moment had gone. Mario brought the bugles and whistles of the charging Chinese to life, the gagging stench of death upon the wind, the stomach-knotting chill of fear.

His talk of his platoon's betrayal was delivered in a monotone. The longer he spoke, the more Robbie came to an epiphany of the whats and whys and hows of Mario becoming The King of Kreskin Avenue. Perhaps the greatest gift Mario gave was that he brought insight and understanding and a measure of closure to Robbie's brother's senseless death—David's vehement objection to taking a life was made tangible and real by the effects war had had upon Mario.

Here was a man who had made sacrifices, who had experienced the deaths of his beloved friends and comrades, and who had killed, again and again and again. Here was a man who was metamorphosis incarnate, changed forever and ever, still tormented and tortured.

"So, Robbie, I do know how yer feelin' and what you an' yer family is goin' through, 'cause I been there an' in a lotta ways I'm still there. I been watchin' that TV and seein' all that stuff 'bout Vietnam an' it makes me wanna puke. We shouldn't oughta be there, an' those boys, like yer brother, shouldn't oughta be dyin' 'cause there ain't no sense to it, no sense to it at all.

"Seein' all those pictures on the TV has been hard on me, Robbie. It makes me angry an' sad an' scared all at the same time. I've been strugglin' t'contain myself.

I don't wanna go back to the nightmares, but David's death made it all crash down on me again.

"I was with him, Robbie. I saw it. I felt it. I heard it. It was 'bout as real as real could be, and then next thing I knew, I was standin' on that hill in Korea all alone again, frozen right down t'my bones. All alone.

"Then Mattie brought out that little black box over there and showed me what was inside, an' she reminded me that throwin' that thing away was the very first step toward getting my mind put back t'gether again. An' suddenly I remembered all those little and big steps Mattie and me took together, one at a time, day after day, sometimes movin' ahead, sometimes movin' backwards like last week. I ain't never gonna be like I was before Korea.

"So Robbie, here's what I come to tell ya. Yer brother's death is gonna change ya forever, an' I pray t'God that it's not gonna change you like what happened t'me. Ya gotta take it step by step, one day at a time, and by 'n' by, yer gonna feel better—different fer sure, but better. An' if there's anything me 'n' Mattie can do t'help you or yer family, you just let us know, not only 'cause I owe ya one, but 'cause I know that Mattie 'n' me can help ya think things out if ' n' when yer confused.

"An' since we're sharin' secrets and such stuff, the next time you come over to work with A.J., I'm gonna tell ya about how I wooed Mattie so youse can use those secrets to woo yer wife!"

Robbie smiled for the first time in weeks. Mattie stroked his face, and Mario patted his shoulder. The lampposts had come on while they were talking, and after they left Robbie was alone in the fall twilight. He was a little less confused, but still bitter and angry at the senselessness of David's death.

CHAPTER 19

Last Letter, Postmark Vietnam

On the seventh day after David's funeral, the Shumstein family finished sitting shiva, and Addie removed the sheets covering all the mirrors in the house. Ben and Uncle Sol loaded their car with the low stools they'd used for the week to return them to the funeral home. The house was cluttered with the echoes of death and mourning, from the trays of untouched cookies and candies to haphazardly placed prayer books and yarmulkes donned to recite Kaddish every day.

During the period of intense mourning and grief, Zeydeh and Uncle Sol had been pillars of strength. They took care of all the funeral arrangements and politely but firmly rejected the army's offer of a color guard. They set the calling hours for the family, organized the daily minyan—the quorum of ten men from the synagogue—arranged for Rabbi Grossberg to talk to each family member alone and to all the family together, and made sure that the trivialities and banalities of everyday living proceeded.

Robbie sat alone in his room that day, staring out his window at the bleak sky and silent leafless trees posted like sentries around the Shumstein house. Still addled by tranquilizers, his mother was lying in bed, weeping softly, her flowered bedcovers wrapped around her like a shroud so that only her face was visible. Addie and her father were in the living room, watching some moronic sitcom on the television, but the actors' silly pranks that usually brought smiles and sometimes outright belly laughs failed to penetrate their misery, and they sat apathetic and unresponsive.

Clutched in Robbie's hand was a tear-stained, slightly crumpled letter that he had just read again for what seemed the thousandth time.

Phu Cat Air Base, Vietnam
November 5, 1967

Robbie:

It seems hard to believe that less than three weeks ago we were sitting around our kitchen table eating corned beef sandwiches. If there was a way to move Sugarman's Deli over here, we'd make a killing!

After my last visit home, I ended up at the Overseas Replacement Center in Oakland, and they loaded all of us up on planes. There was free beer on the flight, and let me tell you, about 80 percent of the passengers were convincingly and thoroughly drunk when we walked off the plane at Long Binh. I feel sorry for the poor S.O.B.'s on VEP (Vomit Elimination Patrol). Stepping off that plane, though, was sobering.

It must have been about 120 degrees and one thousand percent humidity, and in less than a minute I was drenched in sweat. As we marched off the plane, we passed a group of about 100 or so guys getting aboard another plane.

Robbie, they looked like they came from another planet. Here we were in brand-new clothes carrying brand-new gear, and there they were—dirty, sweaty, unshaven and covered head to toe in reddish clay. Man, they looked mean, real mean. They didn't look at us, they looked through us with a hard stare, and even though the oldest of them couldn't have been more than 25, they were like old, worn-out men. A couple of them gave us a one-finger salute, if you know what I mean, and as we started to board this bus that's covered almost entirely in mesh screen they began to chant, "Fresh meat! Fresh meat! Fresh meat!"

We're taken to this building on the base where we're going to get our assignments, and I hear these low, muffled thumps that seem to be pretty close. The sergeant in the front of the room yells, "HIT THE DECK!" and the next thing I know, I'm on the floor with about 200 other guys, and we're all tangled up in our clothes and gear trying to scramble underneath one another. Then the sergeant yells out, "All clear! Get your sorry asses up and off the ground you sad sacks of shit and welcome to 'Nam—you've just gone through your first mortar attack. I guess Charlie just wanted to give you a proper introduction!"

The next day, I'm on my way to Phu Cat Air Base. Man, I don't think I could have dreamed up a more bizarre situation. Here's this place that looks like a little city, except there's barbed wire everywhere, and it's hot and dusty. My orders are to spend a few weeks here at the base working in the hospital, but tomorrow I'm being transferred to a place called Dong Tam where there's another base camp that needs medics. It's about 100 percent sure that I'll be going out on patrols with whatever unit they assign me to.

Once again, when I got to Phu Cat they tried to give me a weapon, but I refused. The lieutenant who's talking to me gets this confused look on his face and orders me to pick up a weapon and again I refuse and tell him that I'm a conscientious objector. Man, I thought his eyeballs were going to pop right out of his head, and he says to me, "What are you, fucking nuts??" and I reply, "Maybe I am, but there's no way I'm ever going to carry that thing." So, he kind of shakes his head sadly and just gives me my orders.

Oh, by the way, guess who never showed up at the Overseas Replacement Center! Don MacIntyre—Grampa! That son of a gun just up and quit like he said he was going to do, and they've officially listed him as AWOL. A couple of MPs and a few real scary looking guys in black suits came to talk to me about him, and they asked all kind of questions about where he was and what happened to him and did I ever talk to him about his plans and so forth. I couldn't tell them anything (and not that I would have told them anything) because Don never told me what he was going to do. I sure hope that he's safe.

The sounds and sights are very strange here, Robbie, and full of contradictions. It's beautiful and ugly at the same time. We're here to "help," but all I see is resentment on the faces of the Vietnamese. There's drugs everywhere, especially heroin, and someone told me that you can get anything you want right outside the gates of the base, from exotic birds to women. In the week or so that I've been here, the base has been rocketed two times, but after each attack, guys scramble out of bunkers like a bunch of worker ants to repair the damage, so that fifteen minutes later it's as if the attack never happened.

Robbie, I don't know what's going to happen to me; it's all in God's hands. But if you will, for a few moments, let me be a bit morose, because I want to talk to you about my death. (I can just hear Bubbe saying "kine-ahoreh" right about now!)

First, a couple of practical things, just in case.

I made you and Addie the beneficiaries of my life insurance policy the army gave to me, and I want both of you to use it for college and for no other purpose, OK? You can do what you want with any of my other stuff except for a box I've got tucked away in the storage room in the basement marked "papers." It contains just about every paper and report and all my journals that I've kept over the years. I want you to have that and keep it because it represents who I was. I'm thinking that if my thoughts are safe, then I'll always live on.

Do the best that you can to comfort the family. I'll want you to remind Dad to get in touch with Dr. Lawrence Guyman at NYU, my advisor and a close friend. He's holding a few "just in case" letters that I've written to everybody in the family, and he'll know what to do.

I have one other request, and it's a pretty big one: I want you to fight against this war with all your might and soul. It's wrong, Robbie; it's immoral and unjust, and it's only going to stop if people like you get together and through your actions and words make people see how senseless it all is and maybe, just maybe, you'll be able to save some lives. I can't tell you what to do or how to do it, but I'm depending upon you to help bring a stop to this madness in whatever way you can.

Sorry for being so maudlin, Robbie, but remember that talk we had about God and death? I feel a certain measure of calmness and serenity *because deep down inside I know that if something should happen to me, I'll have God's reward.*

But hey, more likely than not, I'll be home in about a year with a hundred thousand stories to tell you. Ooops! Almost forgot another thing I want you to do. Hold this letter in your left hand and make a fist with your right hand. Now with your right hand, put your knuckles on top of your head and rub them back and forth REAL HARD!

You see how smart and talented your brother David is, Robbie?

Even 8,700 miles away I still managed to give you a noogie!

Your loving brother
David

The bleakness of December gave way to the snowy dreariness of January. Robbie usually looked forward to fresh snowfall, to the biting crispness of the air and the whiteness of the blanket that made everything look crisp and new, but this year it only looked ugly and felt bone-chilling cold. Even though Robbie's sixteenth birthday was only a few days away, he was morose and unenthusiastic.

The Shumsteins struggled to return to some semblance of normalcy: Abe returned to work, Addie and Robbie went back to school, and Esther dragged herself through the motions of keeping the household together.

Zeydeh and Robbie resumed their Saturday ritual, walking to and from the synagogue, shuffling through the snow, arms tightly entwined like first-time ice-skaters, for mutual support and as a defense against a slip or tumble. There was comfort in the ritual they silently shared, each acknowledging dependence by the tightness of his grip. Their unspoken thoughts filled the air.

One such Saturday, a month after David's funeral, as he and Zeydeh returned to the Rigby Avenue house after shul, Robbie felt his spirits lifting. For a change it was bright and sunny, the cold air was invigorating, and the Krushers were engaged in a titanic snowball fight. Robbie was officially deemed a noncombatant, thanks to his responsibilities as Zeydeh's escort.

Upon entering the house, they stamped the snow off their boots, hung their jackets on hooks in the hallway, and immediately basked in the warmth and the smells of Bubbe's freshly baked challah and homemade chicken soup, which was warming on the stove. Their cheeks were rosy and their hearts were a little lighter from the invigorating walk home, and for the first time in over a month, Robbie was going to ask Zeydeh for another story after lunch. Their spirits, however, were immediately crushed when they entered the flat.

Sitting around the dining room table was the entire family; the women were crying again, Uncle Sol and Robbie's father looked angry and horrified at the same time, and Ben was sitting with his head resting on his arms, his face hidden.

"Vat's the matter?" asked Zeydeh, his face a mask of stone. "Vat's wrong here? Who died? Is it my sister Bernice?"

Without lifting his head, Ben pointed to a torn envelope and a single-page letter on the table. Robbie rushed over to grab it and brought it to Zeydeh so they could look at it together.

Zeydeh's face contorted into a horrified grimace.

Robbie felt an intense, burning anger and nothing else.

The letter was addressed to Benjamin Shumstein, informing him that his pre-induction physical for entry into the armed services was scheduled for January 15, 1968.

Robbie let the letter fall from his hand.

It wafted gently to the ground, where the whispered rustle of its landing echoed the sound of Robbie's first, quiet footstep in his journey to honor the obligation David had placed on his shoulders.

PART V

Donald MacIntyre

CHAPTER 20

A Privileged Black Sheep

Donald Patronus MacIntyre was the youngest of four sons of one of the wealthiest families in America. His great grandfather, Angus MacIntyre, a Scottish immigrant from Glasgow, arrived in America in 1860 as a twenty-year-old, in time to be conscripted for service in the Union Army a few years later.

Angus had five daughters and one son, Fergus, who from the time he was in diapers could often be found on the floor of his father's successful carriage-building business near Akron, Ohio. Angus insisted on four things for Fergus that were to become a benchmark for future generations of male MacIntyres: a college education, a stint in the military, service as a laborer in various capacities on the factory floor, and, by the time he was in his midthirties, a management position in the company.

Fergus was a business genius of the first order, and by the time he was thirty-five in 1905, he occupied a position as his father's right-hand man. He grasped the importance of Henry Ford's invention and set about to convince his father that a profitable business could be built upon tire manufacturing.

By 1910, the MacIntyre Rubber Tire Company had become one of the largest tire manufacturers in the country, employing over one thousand people with annual sales in excess of $5 million.

By the start of the First World War, MacIntyre Tires could be found on the trucks, airplanes, cars, wagons, and carts of the armies of the United States, Great Britain, France, and Italy, and the company opened its first overseas manufacturing plants.Fergus sired a son, Cyril, in 1900, followed by five daughters. Like his father, Cyril spent his youth on the ever-expanding floors of the company's factories. In 1917 and with his father's blessing, Cyril enlisted for service in the army, serving with distinction and honor in France. He returned to Akron in 1919 missing an eye courtesy of a fierce German artillery barrage. The family thought that his eye patch was dashing, but many in their social circle found it macabre.

By the mid-'30s the MacIntyre Rubber Tire Company had annual sales in excess of $50 million, manufacturing locations around the world, vast holdings in rubber plantations in Southeast Asia, and military contracts with over twenty countries. The MacIntyre family amassed wealth of staggering proportions and became a leading family of America's upper crust.

Cyril did, however, break with generations of MacIntyre family tradition by fathering four sons and one daughter. Cyril's first son, Robert, was born in 1925, and with factory-like scientific precision, another child appeared on the scene every four years until 1942, when Cyril's last child, a son he named Donald, was born.

Donald's brothers toed the family line; Robert and John served in the navy and air force, respectively, during the Korean Conflict, and brother Richard entered West Point in the late 1950s. Each also completed a college degree: Robert in business, John in law, Richard as a CPA. Each started his career at the now-renamed MacIntyre Tire Company pushing a broom on a factory floor.

Time was not kind to Fergus. His son and daughters started to notice in the late 1930s that he seemed be "going soft in the head."

The only family member who seemed to be able to reach Fergus and make him smile was Donald. Fergus could spend hours cuddling and cooing with baby Donald, singing him songs and reciting silly rhymes.

As Donald started to walk, they could often be seen together walking hand in hand, the grandfather stooping to accommodate Donald's unsure and unsteady gait, as they rambled around the MacIntyres' massive estate.

Donald did not know his father well, as business demands kept him away from home for extended periods. Even in those rare moments when they were together, his father was cold and distant. His mother was pre-occupied with charities and social events, and his brothers, being so much older, paid him little heed.

For solace and comfort and whatever little human affection he could snatch, Donald turned to his grandfather Fergus, retired from the company and in his seventies.

Fergus filled the emotional void left by Donald's immediate family, and the boy's love for his grandfather grew stronger and stronger, as if fueled by Fergus's advancing dementia. They would spend hours together talking and singing and laughing, drawing pictures, reading books, or even dressing up in silly costumes and playacting.

Near the end of his life, Fergus lost interest in how he looked, was constantly belligerent, and could not even remember the names or faces of his children or wife. Yet he became lucid and aware when Donald was near, his anxiety fading to tenderness, his hostility turning into tranquility. He died when his grandson was eight, and Donald was inconsolable for nearly a year afterward.

In addition to a straightforward dissolution of his assets among the family, Fergus bequeathed Donald a gift that none of the other grandchildren received— an investment trust funded by an initial contribution of $750,000. Set up in secrecy by Fergus's lawyers, Donald's trust was unknown and untouchable by any other family member. The trust contained a provision that Donald was not to know of its existence, nor would he receive control of the funds, until his twenty-fifth birthday. Shrewdly managed by the bankers chosen by his grandfather, by the mid-1960s Donald's inheritance had grown to a staggering size for its time.

Much to the chagrin of his parents, as Donald grew up it became apparent that he was unlike his brothers in virtually every way. Where they were enthusiastic about the business, he was nonchalant at best, sometimes embarrassing his father and older brothers by refusing to do even the simplest of tasks when taken to the factory.

Where his brothers were stiff and ramrod straight in their manners and habits, he was slovenly. Where they had willingly acquiesced to the plans and destiny envisioned by their father, he felt constrained and trapped. He read the masters of literature reverentially and was awed and inspired by the works of Chagall, Dali and Pollock, but his brothers' ideas of great literature ran more to the works of Zane Grey and their tastes in art to the illustrations of Norman Rockwell.

The older brothers were technicians seemingly governed by strict laws and procedures etched in stone; he was a free spirit governed only by a desire to experiment, tugging and pulling at the fabric of his family. One other characteristic separated Don from his brothers—while they were adequate students, he was an outstanding student, easily handling any academic challenge.

At age fourteen, Donald refused to attend the elite private boys' school that his brothers had attended, resisting the pressure of his father's threats to send him off to a military school "to learn some discipline and how to act like a man." Donald simply told his father that he could put him in chains and throw him in the trunk of the car and deliver him bound and gagged onto the doorstep of whatever fine institution his father had selected but he should fully expect that Donald would run away.

Nevertheless, his father enrolled him in the Exeter Military Academy just outside Detroit, then physically dragged him into the school, only to receive a call from the school's commanding officer a few days later that Donald had run away and couldn't be found. Donald returned home a day later, dirty and hungry, having hitchhiked his way back to Akron. Less than twenty-four hours later he was attending classes at the local public high school.

By the time he was seventeen, Donald had become enmeshed in the Beat culture, sneaking away from home once or twice a week and hitchhiking into Cleveland, where in the smoky dives he listened to avant-garde poetry and music, exposed for the first time to Kerouac, Ginsberg, and other Beat authors. His copy of *On the Road* was disintegrating from having been read so many times, and hearing Ginsberg himself read "Howl" in a tiny Beat club in the basement of a warehouse off Euclid Avenue was an awe-inspiring experience for the tire heir.

In contrast to his father's and brothers' impeccably ironed white shirts, narrow ties, tailored suits, and immaculate grooming, Don, by the time he was a freshman in college, refused to wear anything but all-black clothes. The constant presence of sunglasses and his wild hair would have amused Grandfather Fergus in his later years but was a constant source of irritation to his father, to the point that Cyril banished Don from family gatherings.

Don rejected the idea of staying in Ohio for college, choosing instead to attend Columbia University. While he continued to float easily through his classes, his real education came from the politics of social change, where his involvement in the growing civil rights movement set the stage for the final confrontation with his family. As a freshman he became a member of the Student Nonviolent Coordinating Committee and joined the Freedom Riders for a trip into the Deep South, where events broadcast on TV made a stunned nation painfully aware of the brutality of racism in Alabama and Mississippi.

Don's family first learned of his involvement through a phone call Cyril received from the sheriff of Jackson, Mississippi, where Don had been arrested with two hundred other protesters.

Instead of imposing a fine or jail time, the sheriff agreed to a donation of MacIntyre tires for the entire fleet of county vehicles for a period of one year. Before being released, the sheriff lectured him: "Now you look here, young man, and be thankful that your daddy is so generous. Otherwise you'd be servin' jail time right now.

"Who are you to be tellin' us that we ain't been treatin' our Nigras down here quite right, and 'bout how we need t'be changin' our ways 'bout who kin sit where an' who can ride where and with who? Now I gotta tell you, Mister MacIntyre, we sure don't 'preciate no young Commie-inspired whippersnappers comin' to our town an' tellin' us that Nigras are just as good as white folks. No sir!"

The next day, using the company plane, Donald's brother John flew to Jackson and retrieved a dirty yet unbowed Donald. The lectures about Donald's responsibility to the family name began on the plane ride home and continued almost up to the very moment Donald returned to Columbia that fall for his sophomore year.

Most stinging of all was his mother's parting comment: "Really, Donald, dear. We simply can't have you mixed up in this distasteful Negro business. We've always been very good to the coloreds who work for us and that's good enough. You've got to think about your future, you know. You don't want to ruin yourself over this nonsense with those kinds of people!"

Donald did exactly what his mother requested—he thought about his future. He knew that he would never go into the family business and that he wanted to dedicate his life to social change. For the next several years he worked quietly and efficiently in the background, joining other student organizations and even participating in the first serious protest in 1963 against U.S. involvement in Vietnam.

In August of that year, he was one of the many whites who heard Martin Luther King, Jr., tell an assembly of over two hundred thousand people in Washington DC that he had a dream that one day all Americans would enjoy equality and justice.

The quiet, however, did not last forever. After graduating magna cum laude and before he was to begin graduate school on a fully paid philosophy fellowship at the University of Michigan, Don returned home. It was the Freedom Summer of 1964, and Don announced his intention to go to Mississippi and help register black voters. He informed his parents and siblings that he was going to be home for just a few days before attending a week-long orientation session at Western College for Women in Oxford, Ohio. From that session, he would be driving down to Mississippi and expected that he would be there throughout the summer.

After Donald announced his intentions to the family gathered in his father's cherry-paneled den, the room was momentarily silent, save for the ticking of an antique clock perfectly centered on his father's large, impeccably organized desk. Wordlessly, Don's brothers, sister, and mother moved and stood behind Cyril, who, seated at the desk, grimaced in distaste. Don sat in front of the desk in a well-worn leather chair, facing his family, prepared for the showdown that he now knew was inevitable.

"Why, young man, you'll do no such thing!" Cyril bellowed, his one good eye flashing dangerously. "I'll tell you *exactly* and *precisely* what you're going to do! You'll work in shipping this summer and, come

September, you'll enlist in the marines! By God! That's just what you're going to do!"

Don's brother Robert, his face a mask of anger, continued the tirade: "Donald, you're a good-for-nothing bum; that's what you are! We'll not have a dangerous radical in our family, and you'll buckle down and toe the line, or else."

As if signaled by a conductor, the rest of the family joined in chorus, alternately castigating Don for his unwillingness to acquiesce to his destiny and belittling his civil rights advocacy. They continued nonstop for nearly forty minutes while Don remained silent and stony-faced.

He gripped the edges of his chair and stood up, looking at each of his family members with a mixture of confidence and serenity. The next six words he spoke were the last he was ever to say to his mother and father, and he would not speak to his brothers or sisters again for over thirty years.

"No," he said quietly, "I will not do it."

"Then I have no alternative, Donald," his father said stonily. "You are hereby disinherited from the family and must immediately leave this house. Do not return, do not call, do not contact any of us ever again, or at least until you see the error of your ways, come to your senses, and beg my forgiveness."

Donald shook his head sadly and turned to walk out the door. He walked briskly and confidently toward a future of his own making. Nearly one month to the day after the estrangement, he was arrested in Jackson again, but this time there was no rescue from his family.

He took a beating, served ninety days in a fetid jail cell with half a dozen other young protesters, and when he was released happened to notice and then knowingly smirked at the new MacIntyre tires on the police car that escorted him to the country line and unceremoniously dumped him on the side of the road.

Don hitchhiked his way to Ann Arbor where an unsettling piece of news reached him—his student deferment had expired, and he was being called into the service. He quickly managed to revive his deferment and for the next three years was successful in renewing it as he moved from graduate program to graduate program across the country.

Cut off from his family's money, he was constantly broke, depending entirely upon the meager stipends he received as a graduate fellow and an odd job or two here and there. Except for an extensive collection of books, he could pack his entire belongings into one duffel bag, and soon after discovering he could trade books for cash or food or even a place to crash for a night, he found that he was completely and utterly mobile and free.

In 1967, while attending the University of Buffalo, twenty-five-year-old Donald MacIntyre was notified that all deferments for graduate students were terminated. His appeals to be classified as a conscientious objector were denied. In what seemed to be a flash, he was sitting next to some guy named David Shumstein on a bus going to Fort Dix, New Jersey.

For some strange reason, his travelling companions were calling him Grampa.

CHAPTER 21

From Conscientious Objector to Deserter

A conscientious objector like David, Donald found army life miserable, and he was constantly complaining and constantly getting into trouble with his superiors for the condescending way in which he flexed his obviously superior intellectual capabilities. He drew more guard and KP duty than anyone else in the platoon and was always just a touch more slovenly or a tad less respectful to his superiors than was demanded by the army's strict regulations and culture. He did, however, diligently apply himself to learning about his roles and responsibilities as a medic, for if he was to be placed in a situation in which another's life depended upon him, he wanted to be as ready, steady, and knowledgeable as possible.

Don's C.O. status was founded upon an unshakable belief that the country's involvement in Vietnam was morally and spiritually wrong. He was not afraid to fight for what he thought was right, and the stitches that were part of his experience in Jackson bore witness to this fact. As Don moved through basic training and advanced infantry training, his convictions grew in strength.

Seeing teenagers molded into mindless killing machines appalled and nauseated him, and what he perceived to be the callous indifference of the officers on the base was revolting. He held a small measure of hope that there were officers who were caring and compassionate, but from corporal to general, and from the moment he stepped on the bus in Buffalo to when he entered his current predicament, he had not been exposed to any of them.

Witnessing on television the atrocities occurring in Vietnam, reading about them in newspapers, and hearing the firsthand stories of those who had served tours of duty reinforced his convictions. The final assault and insult that led Don to a new life came from a sergeant who, upon returning from a tour of duty in Vietnam, was lecturing the C.O. platoon on survival techniques in the jungle.

The sergeant wore around his neck a small leather bag that swayed to and fro as he paced up and down the classroom. The sway of the bag mesmerized the class until everyone was concentrating on the bag, oblivious to the lecture about the intricacies of camouflage and the best way to capture and devour beetles.

"Seems like you dickheads are more interested in my little friend here than in learning about some things that could just possibly save your life out in the bush," the sergeant twanged as he fondled the leather bag. "Well, let's get it over with so we can get back to learnin' what's important and what's not. Come on up here to the front of the room and gather 'round the table."

The entire class encircled the small table. The sergeant lifted the cord from around his head and carefully undid the drawstring of the bag, then dumped its contents on the table, scattering what appeared to be a more than a dozen brown and withered banana-shaped pieces of clay.

One private picked up one of the pieces and examined it closely. "Hey, Sarge…what is this thing? It looks like it's got little pieces of hair on it?"

The sergeant laughed, reached for the small piece and scooped the scattered ones into the middle of the table where they made a small pile. "Listen up, shit-dogs," he said menacingly, "what we got here is the best lesson in survival that I know how to give you. What we got here is the ears that I cut off all the gooks that I killed who were trying to kill me. Now here's the lesson: you got to get them before they get you.

"Class dismissed."

Several of the class turned and vomited on the floor, another fainted, and Don turned his head away in horror and disgust. That evening in the barracks he told David about the class: "I just can't take it anymore. I'm becoming dehumanized, a part of the machinery, and I'm torn about what to do." Don looked around to see if anyone was eavesdropping before continuing. In a whisper he said, "David, I'm getting out of here, and I want you to go with me. If we stay here any longer, we'll lose our souls."

Don was going to desert, but David was going to serve as a medic and place his fate in the hands of the universe. David asked Don not to reveal any of his plans so David couldn't be forced to divulge them if interrogated, and Don agreed.

A few weeks before Don was to put his plan into action, fate intervened in the form of a letter he received from a law firm in Cleveland. His eyes widened in surprise and he broke into an impossibly large grin as he read the letter:

```
September 10, 1967

The Law Offices of Bookbinder,
Marsh & Duncan, PC
129 E. 8th Street
Cleveland, Ohio
(216) 397-9456

Mr. Donald P. MacIntyre
Fort Hood, Texas

Dear Mr. MacIntyre:

    For some time now we have been try-
ing, without success, to find you, as your
```

family does not seem to know or care about your whereabouts. If this letter has indeed reached you, please call me at your earliest convenience.

It is my pleasure to inform you of the existence of a trust fund set up for your exclusive use by your paternal grandfather, Fergus MacIntyre, in 1943. Originally funded with an initial capitalization of $750,000, your trust has been managed by our firm in conjunction with the investment banking firm of Scanlon Howe Grossberg in New York City.

The very existence of this trust and its terms is known only to me and Morton Howe, a founding partner of the bank. Please be advised that under the trust's key provision, it became yours to do with as you will upon your reaching your twenty-fifth birthday. It is my understanding you reached this milestone on April 15, 1967.

Through aggressive yet careful management of this trust, less our fees over the years, it has now grown to $4,257,893.87. Only three people in the entire world know of its existence now that you have been informed by this letter. As I mentioned above, it is wholly yours with no strings attached. Until we receive further instructions from you, we will not reveal its existence to any third parties but will continue to manage and grow the funds until contacted.

Please contact me as soon as possible so plans can be made as to the fund's disposition. It is hoped that you will

```
consider a continuing relationship with
Bookbinder, Marsh & Duncan.
    May I wish you Happy Birthday and
congratulations?


                            Sincerely,
            Seymour Bookbinder, Esq.
```

Don read the letter again and again and again. Each time his smile became a bit wider and his eyes a bit brighter, until he started to laugh uncontrollably, drawing the unwanted attention of his barracks mates. It took him a few moments to realize that suddenly and surreally he was rich beyond his wildest imagination, and he became giddy and light-headed. He sobered as he reflected upon his grandfather, dead now some seventeen years, and he struggled to recall the man's face but remembered the aura of his affection.

Running out of the barracks clutching the letter, Don scrambled to find the nearest pay phone, where he quickly dialed the number listed in the letter, calling collect, and asked to speak to Seymour Bookbinder—and would the receptionist kindly tell him that it was Donald MacIntyre calling?

Bookbinder answered his phone with a message of congratulations, but before he could make a pitch for retaining Donald's business, Don interrupted: "Mr. Bookbinder? I have some instructions for you. Please listen carefully and have everything set up for me when I come to Cleveland two weeks from now."

Donald Petronius MacIntyre was about to become a citizen of the Commonwealth of Canada.

CHAPTER 22

The Rescue Plan

Donald MacIntyre awoke, raised his arms above his head and stretched languorously, scratched at his coarse but not yet full beard, and then startled, momentarily insecure about where he was. As consciousness slowly returned—more slowly than usual because of an unusually bodacious night of beer and reefer—he felt the warm presence of another body next to his—a girl with long and greasy hair, lying face down, whose name he couldn't remember. With the blankets pulled down to her waist, he stopped for a moment to appreciate the smoothness of her skin and the curve of her back before rising from the bed into the early morning chill.

Although both the bedroom and his apparent conquest of the previous evening were unfamiliar, his daily rush of reality suddenly jolted him into full awareness that he was somewhere in Toronto, Canada. He had deserted from the United States Army almost three months be-fore, and his friend David Shumstein was dead, killed in action outside Dong Tam two months earlier.

In fact, he had just learned about David's death the previous evening through the expatriate grapevine, and before getting stoned and drunk to relieve the pain and guilt he felt, he called the Shumstein family.

"Hello?"

"Umm. Yeah, man. Like, who's this?"

"It's Robbie. Who's this?"

"Cool. Very cool. Robbie, man, my name is Don MacIntyre. I don't know if you know who I am, but I sure do know a lot about you. I went through basic and advanced medic training with your brother down in Texas, and we got pretty close."

"Are you Grampa?"

"Ho! Nobody's called me that name for about four months now…I gotta tell ya, I do not miss it in the least! But yeah, I am—or better yet, I was—Grampa. How did you know that name?"

"Well, David wrote to me about you and talked about you and what you did when he was home. You're the guy whose family owns that tire company, right?"

"That's me, my friend!" Don exclaimed, "I never got a chance to tell David that I was headed to Canada, but here I am, safe and sound, but now that I heard about what happened, I'm fully pissed…and sad.

"Man, first you call me Grampa and then you gotta dredge up some of that other funky stuff about my family, eh? Well, because I don't know you, I'll forgive you this time! But that's not why I called, bro'. I know it's been a while since it happened, but I just heard about David.

"Heavy, man," Don continued after a respectful moment of silence. "I can't even begin to tell you how sorry I am and how lousy I feel. Did you know that I tried for days and days to convince him to come with me, but he wouldn't even consider it? But to each his own, I say. I respected him for his convictions and decisions, and I know that he respected mine."

"Well, thanks, Gram…I mean, Mr. Mac…I mean, Don. Where are you? What are you doing? Is there anything I can do to help you?", asked Robbie, trying to be polite.

"Hey, bro', I appreciate it, and I'm cool for now. No hassles, if ya know what I mean. I'm living up here in Canada, in Welland, not too far from Buffalo—and now I'm a legal immigrant. I don't think I'll be coming home anytime soon, and I'm not gonna miss it too much, but thanks for your offer of help. I called you because I wanted to see if there was anything that I could do for you or your family, dig? Anything, bro', I mean anything at all."

Robbie thought for a moment and spoke softly into the phone. He told Don about the predicament of his cousin and the family's feeling of despair. Just thinking about Ben going into the service so closely on the heels of David's death had sent them into a tailspin.

"We just don't know what to do," he told Don glumly.

"Canada."

"What? What about Canada?"

"Why not move Ben into Canada to start a new life like I did?"

"What...how...when?" sputtered Robbie. "You mean like hop across the Peace Bridge, let him out of the car, and wave goodbye?"

"Nope," replied Don. "I haven't done this be-fore—I got here before things heated up—but I'm thinking that it's probably a little more complicated than that. And take it from me, it takes some money to get set up in a new life.

"But don't worry. I've got plenty of money, and I would be overjoyed to help family Shumstein!"

Robbie thought for a minute and then roughly outlined an idea.

Don was silent, then laughed. "Wild, man! Absolutely freakin' wild! Let me think on this for a lit-tle while, Robbie, and I'll get back to you in a day or so. How does that sound?"

Robbie agreed and hung up the phone. He had a lot to do if his idea was going to work, and he had to do it fast, because just two days before, Ben had gone through his induction physical and passed with flying colors.

Serendipitously, Robbie's journey had just taken a giant leap forward.

CHAPTER 23

Putting the Plan in Motion

The late afternoon winter sun cut through the slats of the blinds, casting shadows upon the flowered wallpaper that gave the small dining room a prison-like gloom instead of the cheer and comfort the pattern was intended to convey. The chill in the room came not from a lack of heat but from the despair of the assembled Shumstein family, facing the need to send another of its sons off to war. Zeydeh, at the head of the well-worn mahogany dining room table, looked over his family, still deep in the throes of grief over David's death.

"Nu, is there any vord from the lawyer about how to get Ben out from the army?"

Uncle Sol, a light patina of sweat visible on his balding pate, spoke wearily: "Papa, we got news but it's not good. The lawyer talked to the draft board and to the army, and since Ben is not an immediate member of David's family, there's nothing to prevent the army from drafting him. His deferment has run out, he passed his physical with flying colors, but if there's any good news at all, it's that Ben could probably go in as an officer rather than just as an ordinary infantryman.

"Now the lawyer had one other thought," Uncle Sol continued. "Ben could apply for status as a conscientious objector and—"

Robbie's mother cut off her brother-in-law in mid-sentence: "And what? What, Sol? So he can become a medic and get shipped off to Vietnam? So he can get killed like Dovid? Is that what you want? Another funeral, another week of shiva, another casket in the ground? Another—"

"Esther, Esther, please!" said Uncle Sol in a rising tone. "Who should possibly want that, God forbid?! All I was going to say was that the lawyer said that if we wrote to the army and told them about what happened, then there was a fifty-fifty chance that Ben wouldn't have to go to Vietnam."

Esther looked at Sol, tears of anger glistening in her eyes. "Fifty-fifty? Fifty-schmifty! That's what I say! What do they do at the army place? Go behind a curtain and toss a coin? Heads you go to Vietnam and die, tails, you go God knows where? Sol, is that what you want?"

The adults began to argue back and forth, their anger rising in proportion to their frustration, their faces contorting in fury, their voices creating a crescendo of invective competing to be heard. Even Bubbe, usually silent, joined in the chorus of cursing, her Yiddish coming so fast and hard that only Zeydeh could understand her, and the more she cursed, the redder in the face he got.

Off in corner, listening, Ben Shumstein had already made up his mind that he was not going in the service. Ben wasn't a deep philosophic thinker like David, but he was smart, a recent graduate of the engineering program at the University of Buffalo. He was honest, quick with jokes and smiles, generous with his time, and a wizard at fixing up cars that were more junk than transportation.

As was said by Jewish families in the neighborhood with eligible daughters of marrying age, Ben was "a good catch."

"I'm not a hippie, a radical, a socialist, an anarchist, or a member of the Communist Party," he told the assembled family, "but I know right from wrong, and what we're doing in Vietnam is wrong. I want no part of it!"

Robbie remembered David and Ben spending hours together sitting on the porch, smoking pipes, drinking cheap wine, deep in animated conversation. David's death was the final straw in Ben's journey from an uninterested bystander to a committed foe of the war. The driver of his commitment and decision was more than just peer pressure, the grim nightly news, or protests on campus.

It was the smell of the grave.

Vilification and profanity flew about the room like verbal phantasms, shapeless and amorphous—clashing, ricocheting, dipping and diving around and between one another, sometimes in English, sometimes in Yiddish, sometimes a mixture. Then, as if depleted of fuel, the arguments abruptly stopped, and for a few moments the only sound was that of panting and breath catching.

Sheepishly they looked at each other, knowing that their collective tirade had solved nothing about Ben's situation, but suddenly Esther started giggling—the first time since before David's death that she had shown even the slightest bit of frivolity. Her giggles infected Ben, then Robbie's father, and soon everyone in the room was laughing uproariously, and like a pressure valve on a steam cooker, their laughter released their anger and brought them back to reason.

"So," Zeydeh said, smiling and twinkle-eyed, "ve're back vere ve started. Vat can ve do? Can ve hide Ben? Can ve refuse to take him to the army place?"

Up to that point Robbie had remained silent, save for being infected with the same riot of laughter. The room had quieted down, each absorbed in their own thoughts, looking for hope, testing ideas, and finding little reward in their mental gymnastics.

Finally, he spoke up. "I have an idea," he said cautiously. "Canada."

The family looked at him blankly. Ben raised his head and gave him an inquisitive look. "Robbie," his father asked directly, "What are you talking about?"

Robbie placed a worn and well-read *Time* magazine on the kitchen counter. The headline on the cover promised readers a story about Canada becoming a haven for draft dodgers and resistors, a story replete with heart-wrenching personal accounts, including one about a family whose son's journey to Alberta, Canada, started with a discussion around the dinner table, similar to the discussion the Shumsteins were now having.

"Are you saying all Ben has to do is to walk across the bridge and all his problems are solved?" asked Uncle Sol. "Is there some kinda good fairy living in Niagara Falls we don't know about?"

"Well," Robbie said, grinning, "you might say that if you believe good fairies are likely scruffy and live near Welland instead of the Falls. Let me tell you about a phone call I got a few days ago…"

And so Robbie told his family about Don MacIntyre and his friendship with David and about the path that Don had chosen for his life. Robbie told them about a kind of loophole that Don had figured out with some smart lawyers. Once Ben got into Canada, Don would sponsor him and give him a job in his fledgling import-export business. Then Ben could qualify as a landed Canadian immigrant, become a permanent legal resident, and get on a path toward Canadian citizenship.

This way Ben could avoid the draft.

Suddenly the atmosphere in the room changed like a hot summer day suddenly refreshed by an unexpected sweet, cool breeze. Resignation was replaced by a glimmer of hope, despair by cautious optimism, and for the first time in weeks, Ben became animated and excited, as if the cage he was in had bars of papier-mâché that could be easily broken.

Instead of curses, the tiny kitchen exploded into a cacophony of wonder and hope and joy, everyone competing for a share of voice that was blunted by a whirlwind of jumbled suggestions and animated expressions of jubilation.

Robbie tried to make himself heard above the riot of noise. "Hold it! Hold it! HOLD IT!"

He finally managed to quiet them, but they were still nervous and fidgety, mentally making plans for Ben's escape, each wanting to learn the how and where and why of proceeding.

"There's a couple of very important things for you to know," Robbie continued. "First, I learned there's no turning back. Once Ben goes to Canada and declares a new status, he can't come back to the United States. Ever. If he does and if he's caught, the army will throw him into jail for the rest of his life. Ben, can you live with that? Do you understand that you can't come back?"

"Jeez, Robbie," asked Ben, "does that mean that I can't see any of the family ever again?" The family's initial enthusiasm was rapidly slipping back toward despair.

"No. That means you can't come here," Robbie replied, "but there's nothing to stop us from coming to visit you anytime we want."

Smiles reappeared.

"Ben, do you think you can live with that?"

Ben looked around the room—everybody was nodding. In turn, he looked at Robbie and nodded, too.

"Good! Now, let me tell you about the other problem," said Robbie. "We have to get Ben into Canada and—"

"Robbie, that's easy!" Uncle Sol interrupted. "We'll get into the car, and in twenty minutes we'll be across the border. Ben, get your things together! C'mon, everyone, get dressed, let's go!"

They all started to get up.

"NO!" Robbie said. "SIT DOWN! You've got to let me finish. It's not as easy as hopping into the car and taking off.

"Don told me that if the government finds out that you helped Ben in any way you'll become an accomplice, and you'll get thrown into jail! Once Ben doesn't show up when he's supposed to, where do you think their very next stop will be? I'll tell you where…right here. And then when they ask you if you know where Ben is and how he got there, you're going to have to lie, and if you get caught, then we have accomplished absolutely nothing.

"Ben has got to be smuggled into Canada, and you can't know anything, anything at all, about how and when and where it was done. Then when the government men come around, you can tell them honestly and truthfully that you don't know how he did it. The only ones who can know are Ben and me. They'll never suspect that a sixteen-year-old is involved, and I'll never even be questioned."

"But Robbie," his mother implored, "you're only sixteen. What do you know from all this stuff?"

"I've seen and heard and read and talked about Vietnam and David's death. You don't have to be grown up to see that it's wrong and useless," he replied. "You can't escape—it's everywhere. His death left a hole inside me and I can feel David telling me—he even told me in a letter!—that I gotta help and do something— anything—to make it right and give his death some meaning.

"Don's put a lot of the pieces into place," Robbie went on, "and there's only one or two more to go. Ben, you will be safe, I promise you. But you and everyone in the family have got to trust me. When I tell you it's time to go, I'll mean it's time to go that very moment with just the clothes you've got on your back, nothing else.

"You can't tell anybody, and don't do anything different than you would ordinarily do—just act and be completely normal. You probably won't even have a chance to say goodbye, so over the next week or so make sure you get in all your goodbyes to the family."

At first the family was silent, stunned by what they had to accept, yet they realized that Robbie and Don's plan was the best hope for saving Ben from David's fate. As they began to quietly discuss the implications of the plan, Robbie asked Ben if he could have the induction notice for a few days. He grabbed it and shoved it into his pocket before slipping way.

But before the plan could work, he had a phone call to make and someone to visit.

CHAPTER 24

Goodbye, Ben

In January it gets dark swiftly in Buffalo, and by six p.m. the lampposts would come on, feebly penetrating the gloom through the snow that often fell in howls and gusts. On Kreskin Avenue and other streets throughout the city, snowplows would make one mandatory attempt at clearing the street, providing only temporary relief to drivers seeking passage. That relief was often accompanied by the misery of neighbors who had to trudge out, shovel in hand, to clear mounds of entrapping snow piled on to the bottom of their driveways by the powerful plows.

Straining, and grunting as they hand cut a passage through the ugly winter waste that held their garaged cars prisoner, they shared a common belief that the higher the mound at the end of their driveway, the greater the devilish glee the snowplow drivers derived.

Those less fortunate, who had to park on the street, would find that their cars had become amorphous lumps, white and clean on top and skirted with dirty gray everywhere else. They often accompanied their efforts to free their imprisoned beasts with curses and promises of retribution, and if they were in a particularly spiteful mood, shovelful by shovelful, what they removed from around their cars would end up on the recently cleared driveways of the garaged fortunates.

It was on one of those ugly January evenings that Robbie left his house to put the next part of his plan into place. Even though he didn't have to go far, he was still bundled against the cold, identity hidden beneath a shapeless winter coat and the all-too-necessary scarf and hat demanded by both the weather and his mother.

Robbie went a few houses down the block, kicking his way through piles of clumpy snow. At his destination he removed his hat and scarf, knocked on the door, and was greeted by an enormous presence with an overwhelming smile.

"Hey! HOOPHOOPHOOP. It's Robbie!" shouted A.J. enthusiastically. "Whatcha doin' here, Robbie? It ain't time for homework, is it? Fer gosh sakes HOOPHOOP! HEY MA! HEY MA! Guess who's here—HOOP CRAPCRAP—It's Robbie! Take off yer boots—HOOP—an' come on in!" A.J. grabbed Robbie's hand and pumped it up and down enthusiastically.

"Hey, A.J., how ya doin'?" Robbie answered, returning joy with a broad smile of his own. "Is your dad home? I need to talk to him for a few seconds."

As A.J. ran to the back of the house hollering for Mario, Robbie took off his coat and looked about the spotless tiny living room. Above a faux fireplace hung a new picture of Jesus, executed in an abstract style. He wandered to stand before it and was quite taken aback by its complexity and difference from all the other photo-like renderings of Jesus that his goyish friends had hanging in their houses. While Robbie was absorbed by the picture, Mario walked into the room.

"Different, ain't it?" Mario said, startling Robbie, "Mattie bought it when she was over in Europe after the war, and we had it in our bedroom for a while, but I just moved it here. Takes a little bit o' gettin' used to, but it's kinda growed on me after alla these years. So, Robbie, siddown. What brings ya over on a fine night like this?"

Suddenly, Robbie got very nervous and started playing with his hands. Mattie came into the room, wiping her hands on a well-worn dish towel. She greeted him with a smile and asked if he wanted a cookie and some milk, and upon his mumbling thanks, she disappeared back into the kitchen. Mario collapsed into an overstuffed chair and extended his legs, exposing socks that had big holes in the toes. Robbie sat timidly on the edge of the couch.

Mattie came into the room carrying a pitcher of milk and a batch of homemade chocolate chip cookies, fresh from the oven, steam still rising from their warmth. She sat on the arm of Mario's chair.

Although Robbie had rehearsed about a thousand times before this discussion, he was more than a little apprehensive about the questions he was about to ask and the favor he was about to request.

"Umm, Mario?" Robbie began, "are you still trucking stuff into Canada?"

"Yep. Sometimes twice a day, sometimes even more."

"What type of stuff do you carry?"

Mario looked at Robbie curiously, unaware of where the conversation was going. "Well," Mario replied, "all kinda stuff, an' I don' even know what it is till I get ta the dispatcher, an' he tells me where ta go and what ta pick up an' so forth an' so on. Some days its parts and some days it could be 'frigerators. It don't matter much t'me what it is, s'long as I get paid! Why do ya ask?"

Robbie put down the cookie he had been nibbling on and looked directly into Mario's face. Speaking softly, barely above a whisper, Robbie said, "Because I got a job for you—something I want you to take to Canada. Something you never took before. A person. A man. My cousin Ben. He's got to get out of the country quietly and without anyone knowing, and he needs help to do it."

Mattie's eyes widened and she dropped the towel; Mario bolted upright in his chair. "Lemme git this straight, Robbie…you want me t'smuggle yer cousin inta Canada? Fer God's sake, why? Why dontcha just get inta yer car an' take him there yerself?"

Robbie reached into his pocket, brought out a piece of paper, and with head hanging down handed it to Mario. Mattie moved closer to see what it was, and after reading the first few lines, let out an involuntary gasp and put a knuckle to her mouth. Mario, after finishing, clenched one hand into a fist. The other hand fell to the side of his chair, where he dropped Ben's induction notice.

"My God—oh my God," whispered Mattie, "I can't believe the government wants to go after Ben after all your family has been through. Can't your family do something to get him out?"

"I am doing something," Robbie replied. "That's why I'm here. I need your help. Ben needs your help. Our family needs your help."

He told them about Don MacIntyre and explained the plan they had mostly worked out. Mario would get an order from the MacIntyre Import Export Company in Welland, Ontario, for the delivery of some goods. One part of those goods was to be Ben.

Robbie told them why it had to be someone unconnected to the family and explained how no one except for two or three people would even know about when and where it was going to happen.

He told them that the family had discussed the matter at great length and had agreed that sending Ben to Canada was the best course of action. Nobody, not even Ben, knew that Robbie was talking to Mario, and Robbie promised that no one would ever know about his involvement.

Mattie and Mario looked at each other for what seemed like an eternity. Their gazes carried unspoken messages and images: of a young boy on a frozen hilltop, of deceit and betrayal, of a despondent man recovering from terrible physical and mental wounds, of losing his humanity, of a caricature of royalty, of the horrible images of war splashed nightly across their television screen, and of a funeral for a young man who did not deserve to die.

Mattie shook her head, but Robbie couldn't tell if it was in approval or disapproval. Mario spoke: "Robbie, yer askin' a lot of me. Ya want me t'break the law an' carry a draft dodger inta Canada, an' if I get caught then they'll take away my truck an' I gets trown inta jail, an' my whole family suffers."

His words caused Robbie's burgeoning hope to deflate like a pin-pricked balloon, for there was no alternative plan—it was this or Ben was off to the army or jail. He reached up to wipe away the tear that was forming in the corner of his eye and pulled another letter from his pocket. "Before you say yes or no," he said softly, "there's something else I'd like you to read—it's the last letter I got from David."

Reading over Mario's shoulder, Mattie's eyes brimmed with tears, and she tightened her grip on his shoulder. Mario was grimacing, and the further he read, the tighter he squeezed the arm of his chair. When they were done, Mario carefully folded David's letter, handed it back to Robbie, and looked into Mattie's eyes. Mattie looked back at him, and they sat silently for a few moments.

"Well, Robbie," Mario said with a smile as Mattie patted his shoulder, "it ain't as if I never carried a ting or two that wasn't supposed ta be carried either inta or outa Canada. I'll do it, but it's gotta be done just right."

Robbie felt as if his chest was going to explode. Did he hear right? Was he going to do it? Mario smiled that gap-toothed smile, his eyes twinkling, and he laughed and confirmed his decision. For the next couple of hours, they discussed how and when it would happen until, with Mattie's assistance, a foolproof plan was developed.

The next day, Robbie called Don.

Two days later, they carried it out.

Even though the city bus was heated, Ben and Robbie shivered beneath the layers of winter clothing that had done little to ward off the numbing predawn cold. At 5:30 a.m. the frozen streets were virtually deserted except for the occasional snowplow, and in addition to Ben, the bus driver, and Robbie, only one other soul, bundled androgynously, was being transported to their destination. It was quiet save for the bass rumblings of the bus as it moved through the deserted, darkened streets.

Ben was still unaware where they were going and who they were going to meet. Less than thirty minutes earlier Robbie had slipped into Uncle Sol's flat, waked Ben, and bade him to get dressed. As agreed, Ben carried nothing and left his house without wishing his family farewell. As they trudged to the bus stop, their boots making crunching sounds on the freshly fallen snow brought during the night, Ben was groggy and silent. Now, in the bus, he was alert and anxious, his eyes nervously darting to and fro, full of questions and concerns.

Robbie peered into the darkness, trying to pick out recognizable landmarks, until at last they approached their stop. He stood and pulled Ben up by the arm, then he tugged on the cord to signal the driver that the next bus stop would put an end to the journey. The bus hissed to a stop and disgorged them back into the bitter cold, then with a blast of greasy black smoke, continued down Main Street.

They had another couple of blocks to walk, and Robbie engaged Ben in some meaningless small talk to relieve his apprehension about what was coming next. They reached the open gates of the Niagara

Dispatch Terminal and stumbled into a frenzy of activity as both small trucks and large 18-wheelers were either backing up or driving away from acres of loading bays.

Great belches of smoke filled the air as the drivers shifted gears. Robbie had to grab a mesmerized Ben by the arm and yank him out of the way of one behemoth bearing directly down at them. With an ear-shattering, piercing blast of his horn and a dirty look that told them quite succinctly that they didn't belong there, the driver roared past and out of the gate.

When they finally reached Bay 32, they saw a dirty truck proclaiming its ownership in fading letters: M. COLUCCI, INTERNATIONAL TRUCKING. There stood Mario, wearing his battered porkpie hat.

Surprised, Ben stopped dead in his tracks. "What's The King doing here?" he asked in an exaggerated whisper. "What's this all about, Robbie, and how is The King involved in all of this? I'm not sure I like what's going on…"

"Shh!" Robbie implored Ben. "He'll hear you, so shut up, will ya?! This is the guy who's gonna save your life. He's gonna be the one to take you into Canada, and we've worked out a pretty simple plan, so listen to him real good—it's not only your life at stake; it's his as well. Now hang on—here he comes, and whatever you do, don't you dare call him The King, OK?"

As Mario walked over to greet them, Ben nodded agreement. Although Mario solemnly shook the gloved hand of each of the Shumsteins, he had a funny little grin on his face, and there was a twinkle in his eyes. "How do, boys," he said, breath coming out in cloud-like bursts. "Ready fer our little adventure?"

They both nodded.

"OK, then! Ben, here's how it's gonna be," instructed Mario. "My back is killin' me, so yer gonna be my helper t'day, loadin' the truck here an' unloadin' it up at this MacIntyre place. When we cross inta Canada, you let me do the talkin', an' all you gotta do is tell 'em where ya was born, *capice*? Now, whatever ya decides ta do 'bout goin' back with me is upta you, if ya catch my drift, so to speak, *capice*?"

Mario grinned, Robbie grinned, and then Ben broke into a wide smile. The plan was so simple, fool-proof, and it even didn't involve a lie, because Mario was going to make sure that Ben did indeed load and unload the truck. Mario pointed to a stack of boxes and a hand truck and told Ben what to do.

Before he left as a temporary teamster, Ben hugged Robbie and gave him a kiss on the cheek, which made Robbie blush. "Thanks, Robbie," Ben said, still smiling. "I'll never forget this."

He turned and started loading, leaving Robbie alone with Mario.

"Robbie," said Mario in a serious tone, "ya ain't got nothin' ta worry 'bout. I got everyting under control. Now get outta here an' get t'school just like we planned. When ya get home, you look for the sign we talked about. I promise ya it'll be there."

Robbie turned and walked away, retracing his steps to the bus stop, alone with his anxieties. As he waited for the bus, a line of trucks roared past, splashing sprays of slush and ice in their wake. The last truck to pass gave a long and plaintive blast from its horn, a blast that hung in the air with the now-graying light of dawn. He could still make out the name on the side and was able to catch a glimpse of a checkered porkpie hat flashing by.

Robbie watched as the truck faded from view, wondering whether the next hour would bring relief or disaster, and if it were not for the driver yelling at him to get on board after the bus pulled up, he would have remained completely lost in thought. As it was, that day in school was unbearably long, and more than one teacher directed him to get his head out of the clouds.

Finally the school day ended, and in his haste to get home, Robbie ran up the block, nearly bowling over Rose Partoni as she methodically shoveled her sidewalk clean. Breathlessly, Robbie stopped in front of 77 Kreskin. There in the window hung a single crystal ornament. He smacked his fist into his hand and laughed.

Both Ben and Mario were safe.

PART VI
Peace Bridge

CHAPTER 25

Solving Steckman's Problem

At 5 p.m. on Fridays, the time that it took to cross the border from Detroit to Windsor was always almost unbearable, but the regulars were used to it and spent the time in their cars, resigned, listening to the radio or idly daydreaming before it was their turn at the inspection booth. This particular Friday night in late February, 1968, seemed to be taking an unusually long time, and the commuters grew increasingly impatient, wondering whether there was an accident on the bridge or if those jerks at the Canadian Border Patrol had understaffed the booths once again.

The two long-haired boys in the beat-up Volkswagen van festooned with stickers and a symphony of painted psychedelic images weren't aware that the crossing was taking an inordinately long time. They had been on the road for over eighteen hours, and truth be told, they were still a little wasted from the pot they had smoked an hour or so before. With Jim Morrison blasting from the 8-track, they couldn't care less about the traffic, because finally they were less than a half mile away from avoiding the jungles of Vietnam.

They got it together enough to turn the 8-track's volume down upon reaching the Canadian inspection booth. With two truths and one lie in response to the inspector's queries—their country of birth and birthplace, and a statement that they planned to be in Canada only for the weekend—they anticipated a quick release. They were only moments away from their new lives. After all, the pamphlet they got at the anti-war rally on campus virtually guaranteed that crossing the border into Canada was safe and one of the easiest ways to avoid the draft.

When they were directed to pull over and park their van in front of an ugly nondescript building, their indifferent self-assuredness turned into paranoia as they worried that perhaps the inspector had smelled pot or saw some paraphernalia that, in their stoned state, they had failed to hide. When a group of serious uniformed men holding weapons approached and then surrounded their vehicle, they had a suspicion that being stoned and having a dope pipe in the van was not one of the brightest ideas they had ever had.

The young Americans were taken into the building and interviewed while the van was searched, but to their amazement and relief, they were not arrested. All was not rosy, however, as they were informed that they were being refused entry into Canada and were to return to the States. Once back in the van, they smiled and congratulated one another, and again became smug and self-assured, believing that their path away from Vietnam and toward Canadian citizenship would only be a few days and another crossing site away.

Upon their arrival back into the States, though, the American inspectors directed them to yet another dirty gray building, where they were greeted by a phalanx of FBI agents and military police. Parked off to one side of the building was a drab, olive green school bus with wire mesh on the windows; it was half-full of dejected young men, some staring vacantly from within their enclosure, others with their heads hanging down.

When they saw that the writing on the bus said, "U.S. Army," they came to the sudden realization that it would be a very long time indeed before their next sojourn into Canada.

If they had arrived at the border a week earlier, instead of sitting in a prison bus, they most likely would have been winging their way to Vancouver or Toronto or Montreal or one of a dozen other havens where thousands of their peers were now residing under the protection of Canadian employment and sponsorship. In fact, just the previous week it had been relatively easy to get into Canada—all you needed was to look presentable, have a few bucks in your pocket, and declare at the border that you were seeking landed immigrant status.

Over fifty thousand young Americans had already taken this route to avoid being sent to Vietnam, but the door was abruptly slammed shut by the Nixon Administration.

Now, daily at border-crossing points from Washington State to Maine, any vehicle carrying a male American citizen between eighteen and twenty-five was automatically pulled over and sent to a special inspection station. There, Canadian customs officials checked identifications against a list compiled by American authorities of men who had deserted or who had failed to show up for pre-induction or induction activities. If a young man's name appeared on their list, he was refused entry into the country and sent back across the border.

What was particularly troubling, however, was that the Canadians were now required to telephone the American authorities waiting on the American side of the border to report that the Canadians had refused entry to someone. Under this new policy and approach, the next four years would see more than seventeen hundred young men sent away to rot in military prisons and another fourteen hundred rounded up and immediately taken for induction and a trip to the nearest basic training camp.

Within just a few days of the new policy going into effect, John Steckman and his staff at the Friends for Nonviolent Opposition to the War knew they had a problem—a major problem. For the past three years they had traveled across the country counseling young men who hoped to avoid the draft, funding their sparse operations through the sale of various pamphlets with titles like "Ten Things Every Conscientious Objector Must Know" or "Stretching Your Student Deferment" or "Medical Deferments and You." They had spoken at churches and synagogues, at college campuses, at small gatherings in the homes of Friends, and even in booths in locales ranging from farmers markets to Rotary Club conventions.

The problem they now faced was that one of their bestselling pamphlets, "The Canadian Alternative," had suddenly become obsolete.

It wasn't the fact that they had lost a source of revenue that troubled Steckman; it was the fact that the Canadian government, pressured by the United States, was cracking down on immigration with a particular emphasis on young men between eighteen and twenty-five—solely to catch draft dodgers and deserters. Steckman, other proponents of civil liberties, and the rising tide of Vietnam War objectors were outraged by the new arrangement but helpless to effect any change.

There was a loophole, however: if you were already in Canada and could prove that you held a job, you could apply and would be given landed immigrant status. So the trick was to get someone into Canada and line him up with work—but how?

Steckman thought long and hard, searching for a solution, and suddenly he thought about his old friend from Columbia University days, Don MacIntyre, the tire heir. He had heard through the grapevine that Don was newly rich and living in Canada but did not know where, and even if he found him, Steckman was unsure if MacIntyre would even be willing or able to help.

John picked up the phone and began dialing friends from his Columbia days and contacts he knew who were living in Canada, from Saskatoon to Nova Scotia. He finally got a lead that Don was living in Welland, Ontario, and running a small import-export business. With more than just a little trepidation, he dialed the business number but was instantly gratified when he heard Don answer the phone.

"MacIntyre Import-Export. You've reached the main man, the head cheese, the Big Kahuna himself. What can I do you for?"

"Well, Big Kahuna, if you can tell me who this is, then I'll reward you with riches and fame beyond your wildest dreams. Here's a clue: a while back you flopped at my pad for about a month, and by the way, you still owe me fifty bucks' rent."

"Steckman? John Steckman, is that you?! Well, color me a fascist neo-Republican, you old dog! How did you find me? You must need that fifty bucks awful bad!"

"Donald, ma boy, I told you I was in a magnanimous mood, so I forgive you that fifty bucks! How the hell have you been? I heard that you had gotten yourself into a jam with ol' Unca Sam, and I'm glad to find that you're alive and well and obviously out of his clutches. I just bet you got a story to tell."

"Steckman, I gotta story to beat all stories. Let me fill you in on what's been happening since you let me flop at your pad."

And so Don did, telling him about losing his deferment shortly after they last saw one another. He continued with a bitter outburst about his short stint in the army, but his tone brightened immeasurably when he recounted the incredible stroke of good fortune that had brought him to his present state of well-being. "And how about you, Steckman—what's up with you these days?"

"Well, Don, I got a story to tell you also, but it's not turning into the happy ending that I'd like it to be,"

Steckman said wearily. "As a matter of fact, that's the reason why I tracked you down…I'm looking for some help, and if you can't help me, maybe you can turn me on to someone who can."

As Don listened to Steckman tell his tale, he became angrier and angrier, interrupting occasionally to ask a question or clarify a point. By the end of their conversation, Donald know his life was going to change once again—he was going to save lives after all, but on a battlefield quite different from the one he had managed to escape just a few short months before.

"Give me a couple of days to think about a few things," said Don. "Maybe I can come up with an idea or two that'll fly."

Don hung up the phone and smiled faintly, feeling both amused and incredulous about the mysterious workings of fate. It appeared that the gods had decreed a new mission and purpose for him.

CHAPTER 26

Don's Audience
with The King

The insistent jangling of the phone broke Robbie's concentration from the book he was reading on the front porch. It was still on the cold side, but Abe and Robbie had worked together to bring the porch furniture back outside and to unfurl the awning from its winter of hibernation.

He was suddenly and rudely jolted from *The Mouse That Roared* back to Kreskin Avenue. "Robbie! Robbie!" his mother yelled, "it's for you. Come and get the phone!"

He grumpily extracted himself from the chaise lounge, unhappy that he had to leave the raiding party from the Duchy of Grand Fenwick just when Tully Bascomb was about to capture the quadium bomb.

"Hello," Robbie said testily, "who's this and whadd-aya want?"

"Howdy do there, little bro'," said the voice on the other end of the line. It took Robbie a few moments to realize that it was Don MacIntyre. "I haven't talked to you in a few months, so I wanted to give you a big hello—from me and from our mutual friend who's doing pretty good up here in the frozen wastelands."

They chatted for a few moments, making small talk, careful to disguise what they were saying for any listeners. After the weather and sports report, Don got down to business.

"Robbie, I've got something cookin' where this time I need your help...and the help of Mario. What I'd like to do is meet with both of you over in Fort Erie sometime next week—I'll tell you what it's all about there and then. Can you make it happen?"

It took a little bit of convincing, but Mario agreed to the meeting. Robbie even earned a few bucks by helping Mario load and unload his truck on his runs for the day. At the small restaurant where they met Don in Fort Erie, they made a particularly odd-looking trio: a teen-aged Jewish boy; a bearded, long-haired businessman/hippie; and a short, fat, somewhat greasy-looking man in an old porkpie hat.

Don and Mario looked at each other warily, as if they were prizefighters about to enter the ring. Everyone ordered food, and Don and Robbie made some small talk while Mario remained silent and removed. Don told a funny story about his and David's first attempts at starting an IV, and Robbie laughed at the image he created of the volunteers that were probably still cursing them to that day. Even Mario smiled at the story, giving Don an opportunity to discuss the business at hand.

He started by telling them about the changes in policy and procedure that were resulting in boys of conscience being trapped at the border. He punctuated his story with the tales of several extreme cases of violent arrests and detentions that made Mario wince. Don filled them in about the phone call he got from his Quaker friend and explained the loophole that appeared to be the only possible avenue of escape. The only problem, Don continued, was that these boys needed to find a way into Canada.

Now fully alert, Mario sat up straight in his seat, pushed his meal aside, and leaned toward Don sitting across the table. "Hold on! Wait a second here!" Mario said intensely, "Is this what this meetin' is all about? Are you askin' me t'start smugglin' draft dodgers 'n' deserters inta Canada? Lookit here, Robbie"—he glared at the boy—"you got some balls bringin' me here 'bout this thing. Gettin' Ben over was one thing—this is somethin' else, an' I ain't interested!"

He started to push away from the table, but Don grabbed his arm and asked him to sit and hear him out.

"Mr. Colucci—Mario—please take my word on this. I asked Robbie to do a favor for me and he had no idea why I wanted to meet with you. All I asked him for was to get you here—he's not involved in any other way. This is between you and me and a lot of young men who are going to die for no good reason whatsoever."

Don talked to Mario and Robbie about what life was like for Ben and how, together, they had helped about a dozen young men find a new purpose and start a promising new story. He told them about how he had recruited other Canadian businessmen to provide jobs, resources, and assistance to help their new employees become citizens of Canada.

Don passionately made his stories come to life with examples of safe harbors, like the one a young family from Tucson found in Quebec. The young man's father and uncle had both died on the beaches at Anzio trying to bring the world back to morality, sanity, and justice, but the thought of killing or being killed in a morally unjustifiable war was too much to bear.

Don told Mario about the officer who deserted after a tour in Vietnam. His experiences over seventy-seven days of the battle of Khe Sanh had driven him almost to the point of suicide before he escaped to a new job and a new life in Vancouver.

Finally, Don told Mario that the conversation they were having was the same conversation that American expatriates were having—after a cautious, slow, and meticulous vetting process—with sympathetic truck drivers in every city and town where there was a border crossing into Canada.

"You know and I know," Don said, "and for that matter, millions of other people know that this war is not right. What are we there for? Is our country in danger? Is our American way of life being threatened or destroyed? Just who are we fighting for?

"At what point is the line drawn between duty, honor, and what's just and moral?" he pressed. "I want you to think about that."

Don was animated, his eyes flashing angrily as he continued. Mario was listening in rapt attention.

"Mario, I know you've heard about the Tet Offensive, and I know you've seen and heard about the stories coming out of Khe Sanh, right?"

Mario nodded.

"We lost about five hundred good, decent boys up at that godforsaken base and killed about ten thousand Vietnamese. But let me show you some things that you might not have seen on your TV."

Don pulled a stack of photographs from his briefcase and placed them before Mario and Robbie. Each was grislier than the one that proceeded it, and as Robbie flipped through the stack and then handed each picture to Mario, he felt himself beginning to get sick. Mario's eyes began to glaze over, too, and he grabbed the pictures that Robbie had been looking at and the ones that remained in front of him and thrust them back at Don.

"No one oughta be seein' this stuff," Mario said softly, "'specially not Robbie here. You tell me whatcha want, an' I'll think about it, OK? I gotta talk to Mattie an' I ain't makin' no promises, *capice*? I'll let Robbie know 'bout my decision an' he'll get back ta ya."

Mario pushed away from the table, grabbed Robbie by his shirt collar, and left the restaurant without even saying goodbye.

CHAPTER 27

Discussion in the Kitchen

A casual observer witnessing two people sitting in silence might assume that a conversation had concluded in indifference or disagreement. That observer's analysis might be correct if the silence were punctuated by an exhausted sigh, the distraction of lighting a cigarette, a nervous affectation like hair twisting or mustache twirling, or most significant of all, wandering gazes.

On the other hand, for lovers the voids between words often carry the most meaningful and poignant messages. For lovers who are also husband and wife, quiet and unhurried silence is a special type of intimacy.

The silence that enveloped the small kitchen table in the Colucci house that evening was of the latter sort. Dishes had been washed, dried, and put away. A.J. was in the living room, where to the modest displeasure of his parents, he was absorbed in the antics of the

Monkees. The tinkling of the spoons stirring was the only sound as Mario and Mattie sat wordlessly, yet they spoke volumes that cut through the wisps of steam rising lazily from their cups. Mattie looked at Mario, her hand resting lightly on his, subconsciously stroking, and although he was intently peering into his coffee, they were more absorbed by each other's thoughts than by their own.

That evening before dinner, Mario had told Mattie about the events of that afternoon, and now both were struggling to reach a decision. Mario looked up from his cup into Mattie's eyes, then down again, and then finally back at her, before he spoke.

"Jeez, Mattie. I dunno 'bout this thing that guy MacIntyre is askin' me t'do. I'm all kinda mixed up about it. Some of me is tellin' me t'do it, but some of me is tellin' me that it's not the right thing t'do."

"Mario," Mattie said softly, now holding and stroking his hand with both of hers, "this is a very big decision—the kind of decision that changes lives. Any of these big decisions is going to have good points and bad points, and it's the kind of decision that's going to have risks. But there's not only risks involved here—there's rewards, also. Don't you think that you have to look at the rewards just as hard as you have to look at the risks?"

Mario nodded. Mattie left the table and quickly returned with two clean pieces of white paper and a pen.

She put a big "NO!" at the top on one, then she waited for Mario to speak.

"Well, here's some of the bad stuff," Mario started, using his fingers to tick off each one. "First, this thing is illegal, probably treasonous, an' I'd be breakin' the law in about a hunnert diff'rent ways. Secon', if I get caught, then it's off t'jail I go an' that's gonna put you an' A.J. in some kinda bad place. Third, I don't know how ta set somethin' like this up, an' an awful lotta people are gonna need t'keep it a secret."

Mario sat silently, watching Mattie translate his thoughts onto the paper with the big "NO!" When she finished, she looked up at him, pen poised, and Mario scratched at his bald spot as if he could stimulate his thoughts into words.

Then he continued: "Here's another thing I don' like about this. I love this country an' I was willin' t'give up my life for it when I was a kid. I probably still would if I thought it would be the right thing t'do—not like this Vietnam piece-a-crap we got ourselves in.

"I still b'lieve with all my heart in the American way, an' I remember what it was like when I was a kid, pretending I was one of those marines in the Pacific when we beat those Japs. I was proud of what we did back then. It was the right thing t'do—we was fightin' evil— an' I wanted t'be a part of it. We got a strong heartbeat in this country—that's what we're all about—it's about doin' good an' protectin' ourselves an' bein' willin' t'put it all onna line if we hafta.

"I can't help thinkin' that doin' this thing is like bein' a traitor to the country," he continued. "It's makin' me crazy 'cause we're doin' a bad thing over in Vietnam, but it's still my country that's doin' it. Do I hafta b'lieve that my country is always right no matter what? Do two wrongs make a right?

"Jeez, Mattie," he said, scratching his head, "these are some pretty big things for an ol' truck driver t'think about."

"Well Mario, these are big things," Mattie replied, "but think about this—let's say that it could be set up so it was secret and in a way that you felt good about. Let's say this way could minimize the risks of being caught. How would you feel about it then?"

"OK, I guess, but there ain't no such thing as a foolproof plan."

"Didn't we come up with one for Ben?"

"Well, sure, but we're talkin' 'bout a lot more 'n' just a boy or two. It worked real good that one time, but it ain't gonna work time after time. It's gotta be somethin' different."

"All right," Mattie said, "let's just say for a minute that we do come up with something different. Let's say it's going to work, and let's say I'll work with you to make it work. What about the plusses?" Mattie reached for another piece of paper, put a big "YES!" at the top, and looked up for Mario's next words.

They sat silently for a few minutes, listening to A.J.'s laughter from the other room, as Mario struggled to put voice to his thoughts.

"Lemme tell ya, Mattie," he said in a strained voice, "those pictures I saw this afternoon made me wanna puke. They weren't any diff'rent from what I saw in Korea...grenades is still grenades 'n' mortars are still mortars 'n' bullets are still bullets. Maybe they was dressed diff'rent then we was, 'n' maybe the 'quipment was diff'rent, but lemme tell ya what was exactly the same—the looks on the faces of those kids. Not just the dead ones—at least not those dead ones that still had faces 'n' heads. It was the look on the faces of the live ones. Their eyes was lookin' right inta mine. They was burnin' holes inta me.

"But there was one of those pictures I can't get outta my head, Mattie. I could tell by the picture that some kinda attack was just beaten back. There was a lotta smoke everywhere, an' these big holes inna groun' where mortars had hit, an' in a foxhole that's surrounded by sandbags, are these two kids. One of the kids is dead, an' there's blood everywhere. The other kid is standin' up, an' his face is all dirty an' sweaty, an' his helmet is off, an' he's all covered in blood, but you could tell that it wasn't his blood. The kid's rifle is layin' on the ground, an' he's holdin' something with both hands stretched out toward the camera.

"So I looks a little closer, an' what he's got in his arms is a severed arm, an' ya could see the bones 'n' muscles ''n' stuff comin' outta one end. An' then I looks a little closer, an' the guy layin' on the groun' ain't got but one arm left.

"Then all of a sudden I could smell it, Mattie. I got filled up with the smell, like I wasn't at that restaurant. I was there right in that picture. I could smell the blood 'n' the shit 'n' the piss 'n' the sweat 'n' the puke. I think I even coughed because of the smell of the cordite 'n' the smoke. I was there, Mattie, I was right there like I was a ghost or somethin' that nobody could see.

"But that's not the worst of it," he said, shaking his head. "It was the look on the face of the guy holdin' the arm of his buddy. He was lookin' right at the camera, an' his eyes was open really wide an' he was screamin'. All ya could see was these two white eyes inna middle of this dirty face an' this big open mouth. An' I could hear him screamin', Mattie, an' I heard him screamin' all day long, an' even now it's still ringin' in my ears.

"So, write this down on your paper. If I decides t'help, then some good boys ain't gonna have t'face what me an' that boy in the picture had t'face. An' second, maybe that screamin' that's inside of my head will go away. Maybe. So here's what this all comes down to—bein' a traitor with the risk of goin' t'jail and killin' our family against savin' some lives and maybe makin' the screamin' that's back in my head go away."

Mattie was just watching him speak, not writing anything down.

"I dunno, Mattie," he continued. "This ain't easy, an' I gotta be honest with ya—there was a couple a times t'day that I wished we didn' ever go over to the Shumsteins' house an' talk ta Robbie like we did. I never thought in all my dreams that it was gonna lead to us havin' this talk.

"I just thank God that yer here helpin' me go through dis thing, but I ain't gonna aks ya what you would do. All I wanna know is that whatever I decide, yer gonna be by my side."

For a few minutes, both sat in silence while Mattie wept softly. But in that silence, there was still communication. It was a torturous decision. It would put them at great risk. Mario could be called a traitor. But yes, a plan could be developed to minimize those risks. Yes, the lives of some number of young men would be saved.

Mario knew that regardless of which way the decision was to go, Mattie would be at his side.

CHAPTER 28

Seven Hundred
Acts of Treason

Sitting in a diner in a seedy Philadelphia neighbor-hood, Jimmy Gilcrest was alone and scared. He carried only a simple knapsack with a few changes of clothing and a phone number written on a scrap of paper, a number he had dialed about an hour earlier. He had left Cincinnati less than a day before, following the explicit instructions not to tell anyone he was leaving and to travel as lightly as possible. Now he was waiting for some guy named John to show up, and all that he had been told was that John might be able to help him get away from the military police who were hot on his trail.

No matter how hard Jimmy had tried to convince his friends, parents, and the local draft board that he was morally opposed to the war and wouldn't serve if drafted, they just didn't listen. They advised him to "act like a man" and "do your duty" and accused him of cowardice and being a Commie sympathizer.

He was virtually shanghaied to the induction center by his father, but from the very moment he refused to raise his hand and take the loyalty oath, the army knew they had another troublemaker to break. When he refused to obey even the simplest of orders, they threatened him with arrest for treason, and when given the opportunity to leave the base upon the occasion of his first liberty, he deserted and never looked back.

Now, without a plan and running out of options, Jimmy had been on the lam for over a month, always just a step ahead of his pursuers. Finally, a friend at Colorado State University who had been hiding him suggested he get in touch with the Friends for Nonviolent Opposition to the War. That connection had finally put him on his present course, and with little more than seven bucks in his pocket and an abundance of blind faith, he was sitting in a dingy coffee shop awaiting whatever fate was to befall.

The tall stranger who approached and finally sat down next to him immediately put him at ease with a warm handshake and friendly smile. The stranger told him that his name was John, and that he knew all about his circumstances and that he could help if Jimmy was willing to trust him implicitly. The young man nodded in approval and was escorted to a nondescript, windowless white van and put in the back, where he saw that two other young men, similarly dressed and carrying only a simple piece of luggage each, were sitting on hard benches affixed to the van's sides.

Some eight hours later, although weary, they got an adrenaline boost and their hearts started to race when they pulled into an enclosed parking lot and finally into a cavernous building on the south side of Buffalo that was owned by MacIntyre Properties, Inc.

They were greeted by a tall woman with a pinched face wearing her hair in a severe bun. She fed them and made them feel at ease. The building was large enough to accommodate an entire fleet of trucks and a warehousing operation, but outside of stacks and stacks of boxes, there was only one truck, identified only as M. COLUCCI, INTERNATIONAL TRUCKING.

After resting for a while, they were met by a short, fat man wearing a funny hat who made them hop into the ordinary-looking truck. He stepped on a small button on the truck floor that looked like nothing more than a knot in the wood, but suddenly the inside far wall of the truck swung away, revealing a small padded compartment with a few blankets on the floor, a space just large enough to accommodate the three of them.

The woman gave them a few simple instructions, escorted them into the compartment, and once they were settled in, the short man once again stepped on the button. Within seconds the inside of the truck appeared to be nothing more than empty and ordinary. Sitting in the dark and too scared to even talk, they could hear only the sounds of boxes being moved into the truck, a large bang when the rear doors were locked and sealed, and finally the deep throb of the engine as it roared to life and began to shift gears as the truck lurched forward.

Less than fifteen minutes later, the truck reached the border, where the driver, wearing a familiar checkered porkpie hat, engaged in light conversation with the same border guards that he had seen every day, sometimes two or three times a day, for over fifteen years. With a "See ya later," they waved him through without inspection—as they did ninety hundred and ninety-nine out of a thousand times—and the truck once again lurched forward toward its destination, some twenty minutes ahead. Even if the guards had asked him to open his truck, all they would have seen was boxes stacked from floor to ceiling, marked for delivery to the MacIntyre Import/Export Company.

Once they reached their destination—a building similar in appearance and privacy to the one Mario had left less than a half hour before—the truck was unpacked, the compartment revealed, and—blinking in the glare of the bright lights of the huge warehouse the three young men stumbled out and were greeted by a smiling, bearded man who shook their hands enthusiastically and welcomed them to the Commonwealth of Canada.

All the boys were then immediately given jobs in the ever-expanding and successful MacIntyre Import/Export Company, and a few weeks later were taken to the Canadian immigration authorities where, upon proving they had some money and a job and a sponsor, were given landed immigrant status.

From there, these new immigrants were free to go anywhere in Canada they wished.

And so it went for over three years, sometimes once a week, sometimes once every two weeks, and sometimes during "the busy season" of summer as Mattie called it, four or five times a week. Never once was a suspicious eye cast toward Mario, and each trip that began with apprehension and tension ended in success.

The young men came from different backgrounds and from all over the country. Some were the sons of farmers from the grain belt, others were the sons of doctors from California or pharmacists from Florida or truck drivers from Michigan or factory laborers from Maryland. They were white, black, yellow, red, and brown; Jew, Gentile, Buddhist, and Muslim. Some were married, most were not; some had a college education, but most were just high school graduates. While some were just running away from an obligation, most shared a common bond of opposition and reaction to the injustice and senselessness of their government's actions in a land almost ten thousand miles from their home.

By the time the draft ended in 1973, about two hundred thousand US citizens had refused induction. Thirty thousand made their way into Canada, and in 1974, Jerry Ford offered "work for amnesty" for those who wanted to return to the United States. Three years later, a peace-loving peanut farmer from Georgia offered a full unconditional presidential pardon to any draft resister or dodger who wanted one.

Mario Colucci and his wife Mattie rescued over seven hundred people.

Among those rescued was one short, fat, and somewhat greasy little middle-aged man, who on the outside looked and acted the same to his neighbors, but who was at peace and ease inside, for his demons had been vanquished.

As time passed and as memories dimmed, the neighborhood witnessed the changes in Mario. With arching eyebrows and tiny wrinkles on his forehead framing them, his eyes now sparkled and danced when he smiled. They spoke of knowledge, but not intellect; comprehension but not keen-wittedness; and sagacity without judgment.

Even after leaving Buffalo to attend Penn State, Robbie was still involved, helping the Friends for Nonviolent

Opposition to the War on campus, anonymously helping troubled and confused young men make their connection to a new life, and occasionally offering a ride from Penn State to a nondescript truck terminal on the west side of Buffalo.

He also continued to grow the relationship with the Coluccis, and with maturity he grew more introspective. They had a bond, a clique of sorts, with only three insiders and a few outsiders. It wasn't a bond of family love, and it had nothing to do with Kreskin Avenue ties.

It was a bond of trust that grew to include respect, colored over time with a patina of dependable familiarity.

Once a year or so for over forty years, the recognizable smell of freshly baked chocolate chip cookies wafting through a slightly cracked open window meant that Robbie was on his way over to 77 Kreskin.

And they never ran out of conversation.

Over the years, Robbie talked about his journey from teenage conspirator to vociferous and oft-arrested war protestor and part-time criminal, to the heartaches of middle age, and all the stops, stumbles, and successes on his life's journey and the path that had gentled him over the years.

Mario and Mattie were thrilled by the births of Robbie's children, excited and curious about his decision to quit the law, comforting when he told them of his failed first marriage, and encouraged to see him bright and enthusiastic when he talked about his new wife and new business as editor and owner of a small but growing book-publishing company.

Mario shared stories about growing up on the west side, some of which Mattie had not heard before and earned her husband a well-arched eyebrow. Mario reflected upon and talked to his wife and young friend about the horrors of combat he had experienced and how, with Mattie's help, he overcame his post-traumatic stress disorder in the 1980s.

In letters, testimonies, phone calls, emails and other forms of communication, Mattie continued to battle the US Department of Veteran Affairs and disbelieving mental health professionals to overcome their perceptions and treatment of "combat fatigue." Less than ten years after Mario's last delivery to Canada, the American Psychological Association put post-traumatic stress disorder—PTSD—into The Diagnostic and Statistical Manual of Mental Health Disorders.

In 1989 the VA's National Center for PTSD was created, and since then, Mattie told Robbie, the center has become leaders in creating treatments like Cognitive Processing Therapy and Prolonged Exposure Therapy. Her role in helping vets and others suffering from post-traumatic stress would largely go unrecognized, but she never sought limelight or accolades.

Through the years, Robbie came to understand Mattie's strength and character, and his respect for her fierce protective instincts and the steadiness of her guiding hand grew steadily over time. He learned about Mattie's time as a combat nurse, her struggles to protect Mario and A.J. from barbarities and cruelties, and of the conversations between husband and wife about the critical life decision they had made.

They shared with Robbie their anxieties and fears of getting caught, the depths of their soul searching in their moral tug of war, and anecdotes of both funny and scary moments as they'd tucked war resisters behind a false compartment of the truck before their twenty-minute ride into a new country and a new life.

In truth, it was a new life for all of them.

PART VII

Goodbye, Mario

.

Full House

The solemn tones of the pipe organ echoed through the cavernous church and then, with a final, reverberating mournful note, faded to nothingness. Save for the restless shuffling of the congregants and an occasional cough or two, silence momentarily reigned. Standing in the pulpit, the priest looked over the packed church, surprised to see that every seat was taken, and yet over three hundred people were standing.

"And I say to you, amen. Now, at the request of the family, Mr. Robert Shumstein will deliver the eulogy."

The priest welcomed Robbie to the front with an outstretched arm. Robbie thanked him, nervously shuffled his notes, adjusted his glasses, and finally looked up and over the throng who had gathered to pay their final respects to Mario Colucci, The King of Kreskin Avenue.

For a few moments he didn't say anything but instead looked at the assembly of faces both familiar and not.

Mario's son, A.J., now grown out of his Tourette's, sat next to his mother, holding her hand. Still imposing in height and girth, he nevertheless cut a figure of respect, as was his due as Field Supervisor for the Town of Tonawanda Department of Public Works.

Donald MacIntyre, Robbie's mentor and co-conspirator, now balding and approaching seventy-five, sat a few rows behind Mattie. Still a Canadian citizen, he had built his business into Canada's third largest importer/exporter. His partner and president of the company, Robbie's cousin Ben, the very first beneficiary of their criminal act, sat with his family in the same pew.

Robbie's mother was there also, his sister Addie sitting by her side, both appearing as confused and amazed as the rest of their Kreskin Avenue acquaintances. They looked at Robbie quizzically, completely unaware of the story Robbie was about to tell for the very first time.

As the de facto unofficial keeper of neighborhood gossip, Esther had been miffed by his silence over the years but had stopped pressing a long time ago. She had used her grapevine to reach old and new Kreskin Avenue neighbors with news of Mario's passing and funeral arrangements. But there were many more people here than had ever lived on Kreskin Avenue.

Mario's old and newer neighbors were sprinkled throughout the church, the funeral the first time in quite some time that old neighbors had seen one another again.

Robbie saw Faticones and Tabones and Baratinos and Johnsons; he saw Kleins and Weinsteins and Gershmans—all the parents now aged and stooped.

Tracked down by his mother, a few of Robbie's old Krusher friends had managed to make it to the service. Even though he still thought of them as squeaky-voiced, pimple-faced boys, he was happy to discover that time had not treated them any more kindly than it had treated him. Just behind A.J. and Mattie sat Mario's few surviving siblings and his old friends Tommy and Luigi. They, too, were stupefied by the turnout for Mario's funeral, expecting to see only a handful of mourners instead of the thousand or so people crammed into the church.

While he gripped the sides of the pulpit, Robbie thought about his visits with the Coluccis and reflected upon the fact that while he had no idea of the names of the hundreds and hundreds of other people assembled in the church, he knew exactly why they were there.

Before proceeding, Robbie drew an object out from a brown paper grocery bag he had carried up with him—a slim, velvet-covered black box—and held it up for the assembled congregants to see. Inside was the Navy Cross he had last seen over forty years before. Still not speaking, Robbie left the pulpit and slowly walked up and down the long, narrow aisle displaying the box and its contents to everyone, taking a particularly long time to show it to Mario's neighbors and family.

By the time he finished his walk, the people assembled were murmuring loudly, a few recognizing what Robbie had shown, others making educated guesses, but most did not have even the foggiest of notions what they had just seen.

Robbie placed the box holding Mario's medal, opened, on top of his casket and made his way back to the pulpit. There, he again reached into his paper bag and drew out two other objects that he held up for everyone to see: the Bronze Star that Robbie's brother David had won upon his death in Vietnam in 1967, and a battered, checkered porkpie hat, sweat-stained and dirty and ripe from over seventy years of daily use.

Standing silent and motionless, Robbie waited several long moments, until the entire church was completely silent.

"Good morning," he began softly. "Thank you for coming today, especially those of you who traveled a great distance to be here." Robbie looked at Don MacIntyre and mouthed a silent thank you for the effort he had made.

"Many, many years ago, a few months before my brother David was killed in Vietnam, he and I had a long talk about God and death. I was young, maybe too young to understand the implications of our talk, but the gist of it was this: at death, God can be either a rewarder or a punisher, and he makes his decision based upon our actions and deeds while we're corporeal. David believed that God has a stick that measures how we've treated our fellow man, and if on balance we measure more to the kind and the just, we receive God's eternal rewards.

"When God measured Mario Colucci a few days ago, his task and his decision must have been easy, for by any measure Mario most assuredly deserves his eternal reward. But most of you here don't know why, so I brought a few things to show you so that you, too, can take the measure of the man resting at peace before us. Let's talk about that little black box and the medal in it"—he gestured to the coffin—"Less than a dozen people in the whole world know about it and there's only three of us here—me, Mario's wife, Mattie, and his son A.J.—who have touched or held it.

"It's called a Navy Cross. In the way of the military, it's the second highest honor a marine can receive for acts of bravery or heroism, second only to the Congressional Medal of Honor. Over sixty years ago, a skinny, wiry, patriotic young marine private named Mario Colucci won that medal for—and let me read this—'execution of his duties performed in the presence of great danger and at great personal risk that set Private Colucci apart from his fellow marines.'

"On a lonely hilltop in Korea, on a night in December when temperatures plunged twenty and thirty degrees below zero, and with all his company dead or dying, Mario single-handedly held off an entire Chinese army brigade from achieving what could have been a tragic and devastating breakthrough. Well over a hundred of his friends and fellow marines were lying dead around him, and he was individually responsible for turning back a substantial enemy attack."

"Some of you know that Mario was severely wounded—in fact he came very close to dying. But what none of you know is the darkness and depth of Mario's psychological wounds. If it were not for the love and kindness and patience of his wife, Mattie, Mario would have lost his sanity."

Robbie stopped for a moment and removed his glasses. Speaking softly, he directed his gaze and next comments to Mario's brothers, sister, and friends who were sitting stunned by these revelations.

"Don't you think," he asked in a hushed tone, "that if you had been Mario, you, too, would be different from the boy who left his home on Busti Avenue to go to war?

"Mario Colucci was a hero who paid a price that went far beyond his physical wounds—he paid with his heart, his humanity, and with his soul, and if we could ask him if it was worth it, we might not like the answer.

"Now let me talk about the next part of Mario's life"—and with that Robbie picked up and displayed the well-worn porkpie hat—"This nasty, funky, smelly, evil-looking thing…I think I deserve extra credit just for touching it!"

The crowd started to titter, and even Mattie and A.J. were smiling.

"This, my friends, is a symbol of royalty. It's the crown of The King of Kreskin Avenue."

The gasps of the Kreskin Avenue cronies were loud enough to reach the farthest corners of the church, as if Robbie had revealed a heretofore-unknown and embarrassing secret, and each did their best to avoid his direct gaze. He put the hat down on the pulpit and continued, speaking directly to them.

"You weren't wholly responsible for turning Mario Colucci into The King of Kreskin Avenue—a large part of that dishonor belongs to the US military and the Korean War. But if you'd only have known what Mario was like before Korea, your perspectives would have been much different. He was about as lively a boy as one could expect. He was funny and kind and cherished by his mother and father and sisters and brothers. He was a patriot who believed in God and honor and country.

"But when he didn't take part in Kreskin Avenue's neighborhood gossip sessions, or when we saw him sitting dull and expressionless in his chair, or when all of us made fun of the way he looked, we just couldn't help filling the vacuum of our perceptions with caricature.

"None of us knew about the demons Mario struggled with daily—the demons that did indeed change him from Mario into The King of Kreskin Avenue.

"None of us knew that his battered porkpie hat really was the crown of The King of Kreskin Avenue."

While Robbie paused to take a sip of water, the neighbors were murmuring among themselves. Several were teary-eyed, including Robbie's mother. He again waited for silence before continuing, then picked up his brother's medal.

"This Bronze Star belongs to someone else, another hero of another time—my brother, David. He was a medic and was killed in Vietnam saving lives, but his true heroism came in the form of conscience. He was morally opposed to the Vietnam War and went in as a conscientious objector, which back in those days was immensely difficult. David was labeled everything from a 'coward' to a 'traitor.'

"Nevertheless, he did his duty, believing that the universe would keep a special eye out for him because he was going to be saving lives and that—ultimately—his worth was measured by the way he reconciled his moral precepts with the actions and situations he was being forced to deal with. His death was a time of immense grief for my family, and we miss him to this very day.

"For me—and I believe with all my heart, for Mario—David's death was the catalyst that changed him from The King back into Mario. It also was the beginning of Mario becoming a hero again—a hero to the hundreds and hundreds of people here in this church today and even more that aren't here. Let me introduce a few of them to you.

"Is Bill Handerman here? Bill? Would you stand up please?" The crowed turned their heads toward a skinny, middle-aged man who stood near the back of the church. "Bill is a farmer who came to us all the way from Iowa with his wife and kids. Is Joe Falucci here? …Stand up, Joe. Joe is the owner of an insurance agency in Atlanta, Georgia, and he's the president of his Rotary Club. How about Bob Stegleman? There he is over there by the pillar. Bob is a professor of law at Case Western Reserve University.

"And now I invite every man who is here today because of what Mario Colucci did for him…to rise."

In row after row, one by one, they rose until nearly three hundred in the church were standing. They were of all different colors and races and religions and sociologies. They were tall and short, fat and skinny, hairy and hairless. They had come from all over the country; their

315

only common bond was the man resting peacefully in the simple oak coffin at the front of the church.

Robbie let the murmurs quiet and then continued.

"All the men that you see standing here today are here because they were young men of conscience, like sixty thousand other young men, men who refused to serve in Vietnam.

"Over four years in the late '60s and early '70s, Mario Colucci smuggled them into Canada in a false compartment of his truck…"

The church exploded in a burst of heated babble and applause. Bewildered and befuddled at the now-revealed secret, Mario's relations, friends, and Kreskin Avenue neighbors exchanged glances, cries, and conversation for almost five minutes.

Robbie cleared his throat to quiet them before continuing:

"He smuggled them in, starting with my cousin Ben, and he continued doing that until the draft ended. Over 700 young men entered Canada that way, and it's not an exaggeration to say today that Mario's actions saved lives and affected the lives of tens of thousands of parents, wives, children, and grandchildren, and the lives of all of the people that THEY in turn touched over the last fifty years.

"What Mario did was illegal—a cornerstone of treason at worst and a foundation of sedition at best.

Was it the right thing to do? Look around and you'll get the answer to that question.

"Across the US and Canada, and other places throughout the world, there are families and friendships and businesses, good done in the world—joined by one single, definitive common denominator—the bravery of Mario Colucci. In my book, that makes him every bit the hero he was on that nameless hilltop in Korea."

Robbie stopped to let his message resonate, leaving those assembled to ponder the questions he had posed and to question their assumptions about The King of Kreskin Avenue.

"Mario showed all of us that a hero is defined by selfless actions, driven by conscience, toward justice and a higher order of morality.

"If God does indeed have a stick that measures how we've treated our fellow man, then I believe with all my heart and soul that Mario's measure is letting him receive God's eternal rewards. I know that I take great comfort in that belief, and I hope that now you do too."

With that, Robbie left the pulpit and hugged both A.J. and Mattie before finding his seat.

EPILOGUE

L ater that evening, long after the last of the mourners and bereaved had departed, Robbie knocked on
Mattie's door.

"Hello, Robbie," she said, her eyes dry but red-
rimmed. "Won't you come in and sit? I believe I have
some fresh-made cookies, if you're interested."

It was a cool evening, unexpected this late in spring.
Kreskin Avenue was greening up, and standing on Mattie's
stoop, Robbie saw now-quaint streetlights aglow, casting
shadows through maple trees where they had once cast
shadows through magnificent elms now long forgotten.

The neighborhood had changed. Once the step-
pingstone for poorer and lower middle-class families
stretching for the next rung on the American Dream
ladder, it was now trendy. Kreskin Avenue's bones were
still there, and quite visible, but the mad rush of thirty-
and forty-year-old owners bursting with the need and
finances to express their individuality had resulted in a
display of facades bewildering in their diversity where
once the homes were cookie-cutter look-alikes.

Of the Kreskin Avenue of Robbie's youth, only Mattie and Esther Shumstein remained in the neighborhood. Ironically, the facades of their houses, now unchanged for eighty years, were the trendiest on the street.

Go figure.

Robbie and Mattie talked for nearly two hours and one empty cookie plate later. Given Mattie's frailties, they were both aware of the strong likelihood that this conversation was to be their last. It was nearly midnight when Robbie left, clutching the brown paper grocery bag, fitting luggage for the battered porkpie hat he was going to carry home.

Mattie gave Robbie a tight hug, and before she shut the door whispered, "Of course you can, Robbie. I have a feeling that you'll do it right."

Robbie knew the perfect location in his office to place the hat, next to what was most assuredly the very last Lion's Tail in existence—he had purchased it some years back for an exorbitant price from a very old man from a very old Chinese family.

They were going to be inspiration for the story he was going home to write.

The End

ACKNOWLEDGMENTS

October 2019

The seeds of *The King of Kreskin Avenue* were planted well over ten years ago, when I introduced a young Mario Colucci to the world in a short story called "The Lion's Tail."

When it received an Honorable Mention in a worldwide short story contest, I was thrilled, but not so much that I was ready to head off on a new career path. It sat for a decade, untouched and unloved, on a CD thrown into a drawer.

But as I got closer and closer to retirement, I began thinking about Mario again, what his life might have been like before the Lion's Tail, and more importantly, what happened to him afterward. Those thoughts, plus finding the CD after a house-wide search, plus the looming date of my retirement, got this baby boomer off his butt and motivated to action.

Oh yeah, "The Lion's Tale" became chapter 3 of this book with only a modest amount of editing.

I certainly could not have brought The King to life without the assistance of quite a few people, starting with my wife, Janice, and two children, Sarah Vitberg and Shannon Delmarle. They were a fountain of insightful questions and good ideas that helped shape characters and point out inconsistencies in the story.

My good friends Julie and Greg Wood were of tremendous help with their combination of honest critiques and no-holds-barred encouragement. A lot of their ideas and recommendations survived and ended up in this first edition.

Then, there were my beta readers, each with a different angle and each with a fresh perspective on how I could make the story better and more readable. It turns out that all of them were right. These included Nancy and Leon Gossin, Joanne Hill, my niece Linda Budinski, Jane and Tom Walpole, and Michael Francis.

I want to thank Danna Mathias who designed the cover art and interior formatting, and who tolerated my newbie "questions". I also want to send my proofreader, Alison Imbriaco, a tip o'the porkpie hat for helping shape the manuscript with her great insights and an eye for detail and proper grammar.

My greatest thanks go out to my editor, Cindy Rinaman Marsch. She not only used her phenomenal skills to make the story more readable, but also pointed out problems and inconsistencies that only a skilled writer and dedicated editor can find. Cindy educated me on technical writing issues, took me to task for incomprehensible sentence structure, praised me when I turned a phrase in just the right manner, and made me rethink and rewrite critical parts of the story and characters.

In return, I taught her some new Yiddish slang and a few choice curse words.

A. K. Vitberg
Fairport, NY

 A.K. Vitberg was born and raised in Buffalo, NY, and now resides with his wife, Janice, near his two adult children, on a two-acre wooded lot in New York State's Finger Lakes Region. After an award-winning career in marketing and advertising, he wrote his debut novel, *The King of Kreskin Avenue*, reflecting on his coming of age in the turmoil of the 1960s and its similarities to the turmoil of today.

When not making up stories for his grandchildren or telling his never-ending supply of world-class Dad Jokes to his adult children, you can find him, Collings guitar in hand, flat-picking fiddle tunes in local venues or jamming with friends at bluegrass and roots festivals all over the Northeast.